T0343954

This
BOOK
was

DISPENSED

to

_____

by the

MERMONKEY

of

EERIE-on-SEA

The Eerie-on-Sea Mysteries:

MERMEDUSA

THOMAS TAYLOR

WITH ILLUSTRATIONS BY THE AUTHOR

WALKER
BOOKS

First published 2023 by Walker Books Ltd
87 Vauxhall Walk, London SE11 5HJ

2 4 6 8 10 9 7 5 3

Text and interior illustrations © 2023 Thomas Taylor
Cover illustrations © 2023 George Ermos

The right of Thomas Taylor to be identified as author of this work has been asserted in accordance with the Copyright, Designs and Patents Act 1988

This book has been typeset in Stempel Schneidler

Printed and bound in Great Britain by
CPI Group (UK) Ltd, Croydon CR0 4YY

British Library Cataloguing in Publication Data:
a catalogue record for this book is available from the British Library

ISBN 978-1-5295-0213-8

www.walker.co.uk

For Oliver, Patrick, Max, Benjy, Oscar, Leo, Eva, Kaisa, Arthur,
Rémy, Georgiana, Bobby, Stella, Mathi and Rowan. (Phew!)
T.T.

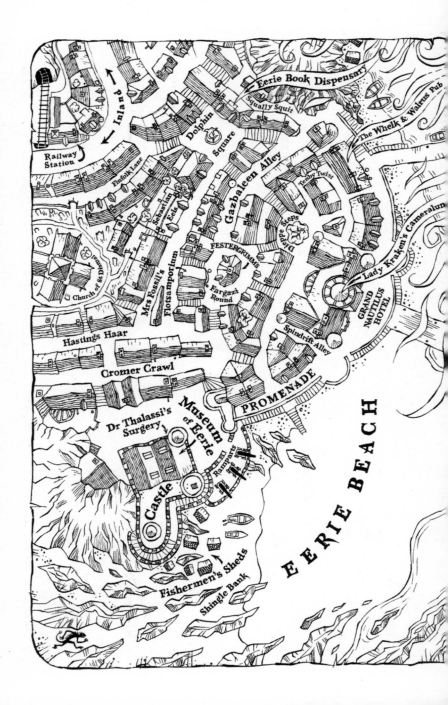

 # CONTENTS

MIDWINTER

TIME.

It's just one thing after another, isn't it?

One moment you're excited about everything to come, the next it feels like those new beginnings were nothing but the first steps towards the end.

"Herbie."

It's the ticking that gets me – the endless ticking of a clock as it counts away all the things you haven't done yet …

"Herbie?"

… and reminds you that you are always late, even for the things you *do* do.

"Herbie! *Wake up!*"

The voice of my friend Violet Parma slaps me back to the here and now. It's evening, and we're in my lost-property cellar, in the cosy glow of the wood-burning stove, surrounded by a century's worth of forgotten items, mislaid whatsits and assorted doodaddery of every description.

Icy snow scratches at the basement window as the dismal weather of late December gusts around the town of Eerie-on-Sea. Violet is in my armchair, up to her chin in blankets and the purrs of Erwin the cat, while I, Herbert Lemon – Lost-and-Founder at the Grand Nautilus Hotel – am wobbling on the bottom step, staring at something in my hand.

Because it's only gone and happened again, hasn't it?

"Sorry!" I gasp. "Did you … did you feel that?"

"Feel what?" Violet regards me curiously. "Your bell rang, you went up and answered it, and now you're back down here, clutching the wall and looking green. What's there to feel?"

I shake my head clear. It's obvious that Violet sensed no eerie vibrations, no dizzy-in-the-head-fizzy-in-the-fingers sensations like the ones I've been getting lately – a weird wooziness that makes my brain go all funny and my thoughts go all runny. But then, getting queasy about things *is* a bit of a speciality of mine, especially when we're overdue for a new adventure.

"It's nothing." I straighten my cap. "Forget it."

"It's not nothing," says Violet as I join her by the armchair. "Something's just been handed in to your Lost-and-Foundery, Herbie, and made you go all weird. And I'd like to know *what*."

Then, before I can stop her, she darts up and snatches the object from my hand.

And what is this thing that set the bell on my desk ringing and my thoughts tick-tocking on the theme of vanished time? Well, see for yourself.

It's a watch.

A battered, broken wristwatch that was obviously lost many years ago.

"Ooh," says Violet, turning it over in her hand. "A wind-up one, too." And she roughly twists the little winder knob between her forefinger and thumb, before burying the watch in her wild hair, about where her ear must be.

"Nope," she declares, disappointed. "Not a tick."

She holds the watch up to show me its shattered face.

"Dead!" she declares dramatically. "Frozen forever at the moment of some terrible crime..."

"Give me that!" I grab the watch back. "I haven't had a chance to check it yet, that's all. It was found by a cleaner down the back of a radiator in the hotel restaurant. Probably been there for years. Just needs a bit of looking after, that's all."

"A terrible crime," Violet continues, as if I haven't spoken, "that happened at midnight!"

"Midnight?"

I look back at the cracked face of the watch. Its two hands point straight up at the number twelve, as if its very last act was to try to surrender.

"Could be mid*day*," I suggest. "Why do you always go for the most alarming option?"

Violet grins and scratches Erwin behind the ear.

"Either way, Herbie, no one will want that watch now. It looks like someone trod on it. Best to just chuck it out."

"Chuck it out!" I splutter, hardly able to believe my ears. "You mean, *throw it away*?"

"Of course," Vi replies. "It's useless. Don't tell me you're going to keep it."

I hold up the watch and turn it in the light. As well as the cracked glass and the dust of decades, the leather strap is baked stiff by radiator heat, and the steel casing is criss-crossed with scratches. I admit, the prospects of fixing this watch are not great. But then I glance over to the small shelf below where I hang my Lost-and-Founder's cap. There, gleaming in the warm firelight and packed full of mechanical wonders, is the pearlescent shell of my trusty clockwork hermit crab, Clermit.

"I can't believe, Vi," I reply, "that even after you have been here a whole year, you still don't get how my Lost-and-Foundery works. It's my *job* to look after this watch, no matter how battered and busted. And get it back to its rightful owner, too, if I can."

With this, I take the winder in my own forefinger and thumb, and give it a steady twist, like a pro. Then I hold it to my own ear.

But if I had hoped to somehow prove a point to Violet, I'm disappointed.

The watch remains silent and still.

And dead.

"Just bin it, Herbie," Violet insists, before adding, "And I haven't been here *quite* a year, have I? Not yet. I arrived on Midwinter's Night, remember? That's still two days away."

Remember?

How could I forget?

And what a not-quite-a-year it has been!

A rush of memories from our adventures barges uninvited through my mind: our near-death experience with the legendary malamander; monstrous mayhem with the storm fish Gargantis; the terror of our dealings with a being known as the Shadowghast; and then – just a few weeks ago – all those gruesome goings-on at Festergrimm's Eerie Waxworks.

My life has hardly been boring since Violet showed up in it.

But I don't say all this, of course. I may be a newer, braver Herbie these days, but I still don't want to encourage talk of adventures, not with the longest night of the year so very close and Christmas just around the corner. Instead, I take up the slimmest screwdriver I can find on my repair desk and pop the back off the broken watch.

Inside, in contrast with the ruined exterior, the watch's clockwork mechanism gleams pristinely. Holding it to the lamplight, I stare into the brass wheels and cogs wondering where to even begin.

"But," comes Violet's voice again, "exciting though my time here has been, what *was* the point of it all?"

I look up to find that it's Violet's turn to stare into space now, her excited mood suddenly gone, her eyes bright inside her hair.

"Prp?" says Erwin.

"A year!" Violet exclaims. "A year since I came here to find my parents, Herbie, and found instead ... you! And Eerie-on-Sea, and a whole new life of adventure and magic. And yet, wonderful though it has been, I'm no nearer to solving the mystery of my parents' disappearance than I was that first night. So, maybe, in the end, this amazing year has all been for nothing, after all."

"It's not nothing!" I say, just as Violet did a moment ago. "I mean, you came to find your parents, Vi, and – and found yourself instead. Like a character in a book or something."

"That's a bit corny, Herbie."

"Yeah, well –" I turn back to the watch – "it's still true."

And then I see it: a tiny, sparkling grain of sand, lodged between two cogs. I take my screwdriver, and – as delicately as I can – I push the grain of sand out of the watch mechanism.

Instantly, I'm rewarded with the sound of a tick, and the sight of tiny brass cogs moving again after how ever long it has been.

"There." I close the watch and hand it to Vi. "Now, if you'll set the correct time, please, I'll write out a lost-and-found label and— Hey!"

I shout this last bit because Violet suddenly jumps out of her chair, scattering Erwin all over the room.

"Herbie!" she cries. "The time! Have you forgotten what we're doing tonight? We're going to be late!"

In a moment she has set the watch, buckled it onto her wrist, and is pulling on her coat.

I do a shudder.

I can't help it!

I haven't forgotten what we're doing tonight, but I was hoping Violet had.

"Don't look like that." Violet grins as she winds her scarf around her neck. "We promised. And judging by the weather outside, it's the perfect night for it."

"That's what worries me!"

I reach for my own coat, trying not to look at the darkness beyond the window. We're just two days out from the night when legend says that a terrifying creature called the malamander emerges from its lair to hunt on the beach of Eerie-on-Sea. It's madness to go near the sea on a night like this, and Vi and I – after everything that happened last midwinter – have more reason to stay away than most. And yet, here we are, getting ready to do just that.

"*Come on*, Herbie," says Vi, opening the cellar window and letting a billow of hard, snowy air tumble into my cosy home. "We mustn't be late." Then she adds, with a wink, "We have a monster to catch."

ANOMALOUS
PHENOMENA

OF COURSE, WE AREN'T really going to catch any such thing. That's just Violet winding *me* up. But what we are here to do is – well, it's almost as bonkers.

Below the town, at the end of the old harbour wall, a knot of people has gathered in the snowy air, huddled in the glow of the harbour lamp. We see a lanky figure in a huge sou'wester coat and skipper's cap, waving his arms excitedly as he addresses the others. This is none other than our friend Blaze Westerley, of the fishing boat *Jornty Spark*, who you might have met already if you've been to Eerie-on-Sea before. With him are three people I glimpsed earlier today as they checked into the hotel.

"It's exciting," says Vi as we hurry through the cold night to join them. "Apparently, they've come all the way from America!"

"*Exciting* is one word for it," I mumble into my scarf. "I can think of others."

As we approach, I get a better look at the three strangers. One is a tall and angular woman, who is wrapped in a long black coat with a high collar. She looks like she has come expecting to be photographed. Then there's a short man wearing huge headphones and – amazingly at this time of night – aviator sunglasses. His figure is made all the more round with the equipment he has strapped over his shoulders, and he holds out a boom with a fluffy microphone on the end. The third of these mysterious guests from over the sea is an imposing, broad-shouldered man with a large grizzly beard. He wears a tweed hunting jacket with many pockets, a wide-brimmed hat pinned up on one side and a tiny pair of spectacles on his nose.

"And that," we hear Blaze saying as we join the strange group, "is the terrible legend of the fargazi. And why, to this day, we fisherfolk of Eerie-on-Sea say the only way to survive a fargazer, is—"

"To tell the truth," finishes the tall woman in black. "Yes, we know. We've done our research."

"Oh." Blaze looks suddenly deflated. "You have?"

"Of course. The fargazi can see through your soul, or so the tale goes. You cannot lie to them. But are you claiming to have actually witnessed one of these creatures? Witnessed a fargazer with your own eyes?"

She indicates to the man carrying all the equipment to

hold his fluffy mic even closer, to catch the boy's reply. This man, I see now, also wears a baseball cap with a picture of Bigfoot on it.

"Aye," Blaze says, eyeing the mic suspiciously.

But then he spoils it by adding, "Well, not *seen,* exactly. I mean, not seen *myself.* My uncle Squint met one once though. When he was a lad. Terrible, it was. He still has the nightmare. From time to time."

"I see," says the woman, gesturing with obvious disappointment for the microphone to be lowered.

"But that's just the *start* of the Eerie-on-Sea Monster Tour," says Blaze quickly. "There are many more legends. Folk hereabouts also tell of the mighty storm fish Gargantis, who nearly destroyed the town. And Gargantis I *have* seen. With my very own eyes. Together with my friends here."

And he nods towards us.

The little group turns, and the furry microphone is shoved our way. I watch the three strangers take in my wonky Lost-and-Founder's cap, and Violet's untamed hair and too-big coat.

"I'm Violet," says Violet. "And this is Herbie."

"Angela," says the woman briskly. "Angela Song. And this is Herman Newtiss," she adds, indicating the bigger man. "Professor Newtiss of Springheel University, Arizona. We're the hosts of the *Anomalous Phenomena* podcast. I expect you've heard of us."

Well, I haven't. And I don't think Violet has either. I don't even know how to spell *Anonymous Philominous*, do I? But this looks like all the introduction we're going to get, because the strangers have already turned their attention back to Blaze. I can't help noticing, however, that the big man in the hat – Professor Newtiss or whatever his name is – stares at us for a moment longer than seems absolutely necessary.

"And where is this so-called Gargantis now?" asks Angela Song. "Do you have tracks? Video? Even a blurry photo?"

Blaze looks completely thrown by the question. All he can do is point vaguely out over the icy sea.

"It's a nice story, kid," says Angela, "but we need more than local colour. At *Anomalous Phenomena,* we 'go past mere anecdote to the truth that lies beyond'. It says so on our website. Our followers like proof."

Vi and I glance at each other, then at Blaze.

"Nice story?" He looks stunned. *"Proof?!"*

"Maybe we should turn," says Angela, "to the reason we're really here: the legend of the malamander…"

And the fluffy mic is thrust back into Blaze's face.

As for Blaze, it looks like he's been pushed too far already. With a final glare at the microphone, he puts his fingers in his mouth and whistles out into the night.

Vi and I look around, agog, wondering what on earth is going to happen now.

And then we see it.

From back along the sea wall, where Blaze's fishing boat is bobbing beside the others, comes a sudden spark of light. It leaps up into the night air, this spark, and then heads towards us, with the wavy, indirect motion of a bumblebee in flight.

But glowing!

"A sprightning!" Violet gasps, her face alive with recognition.

The tiny, brilliant light reaches Blaze, and then buzzes around him, small, but crackling fiercely, its electrical power lighting the tumbling snow around us.

There are more gasps, this time from the three strangers, as the bright little thing settles on Blaze's outstretched finger.

"What in the world…!" Angela begins. Then she gestures frantically to Fluffy Mic Guy. "Are you getting this?"

Fluffy Mike (let's call him that for now) leans in with the furry microphone in one hand and a large, old-fashioned video recorder in the other.

"This is Ember," says Blaze, clearly delighted to have stamped his authority on the group at last. "A sprightning, as Violet says. She likes to follow my boat, and is, well, a sort of mascot for my uncle and me. Aye, she's part of our crew."

"Listeners!" says Angela breathlessly, into the microphone. "I am standing here in the presence of, well, what I can only describe as some kind of – of *fairy*. Or, more likely, some new species of firefly entirely unknown to science…"

But before she can say more, Blaze opens a pocket in his waterproof coat. The sprightning zips over and plops eagerly inside, her warm light vanishing.

"Ember," says Blaze again, patting his pocket gently. "Her

name's Ember. Now, let's return to the town for the next part of the tour."

And he sets off, leading the way back along the harbour wall, regaling his audience as they go with the strange tale of Saint Dismal and his Gargantic Light.

"Do you still think this was a good idea?" I whisper to Violet as we follow. "A guided tour at night, at almost midwinter, in search of Eerie legends?"

"Can't see why not," Violet replies. Then she adds, with a wink, "Besides, the legends of Eerie-on-Sea are just stories, Herbie. Remember?"

"Except we've just seen a sprightning!" I say.

Not, it's true, the sprightning queen I once had the honour of harbouring beneath my cap – this will be one of her tiny guardians that protect the lair of Gargantis. But still, I feel a pang of jealousy towards Blaze with his fierce little electrical friend.

"Anyway," I add as I notice that Fluffy Mike has just lowered a pair of what can only be night-vision goggles over his eyes, "something tells me these people won't be satisfied with just stories."

"When are we going down to the beach?" demands the man called Herman Newtiss then, speaking for the first time.

"I explained," Blaze replies as the group comes to a halt at the harbour wall. "The beach is too dangerous at this time of year."

"Nonsense!" Professor Newtiss laughs, dropping one

enormous hand onto Blaze's shoulder. "Dangerous? I once spent a whole month in the desert, on the trail of the Mongolian death worm. It's our most downloaded episode. I am not scared of a few rock pools, young man. And besides, we have to get down onto the beach if we're to have a malamander sighting of our own."

It was Blaze Westerley's idea to create the Eerie-on-Sea Monster Tour. He started it back in the spring, as something to do when the fishing season goes slack, and it went down well with the summer tourists of *Cheerie*-on-Sea. I suppose it's easy to *ooh* and *aah* at talk of strange creatures and spooky spectres when the sun is shining and your biggest worry is whether or not your ice cream will dribble down your arm. And Eerie-on-Sea has more legends than an August candyfloss has wasps. But, of course, the story everyone loves most of all is the famous legend of the malamander.

Looking back, I suppose it was only a matter of time before someone asked Blaze to hold the monster tour at midwinter itself. Especially when those doing the asking are the makers of *Paragliding Thingummybobs* (or whatever it's called) – apparently a podcast about all things strange and eerie. But it feels odd to have visitors like this, who have come from so far away to our out-of-the-way little town. It's as if Eerie-on-Sea, which is normally so good at going unnoticed, has suddenly lost its misty veil and become exposed to the outside world. But no doubt Blaze thought it would be safe, as long as he avoided Midwinter Night itself. Right now, though, he looks vaguely panicked.

"Don't you want to hear about the legend of the Shadowghast?" he asks, trying to usher his audience away from the beach and into the light of the nearest street. "Or about the long-lost treasure of Purple Pimm? Or—?"

"Another time," Professor Newtiss cuts in. "We need to be where the action happens – the foreshore, near the shipwreck. It's only a matter of time before someone gets firm evidence that the creature exists, and I want it to be us."

"Or proof that it *doesn't*," says Angela Song challengingly, and I realize that this entire conversation is being recorded for their show. "The legend of the malamander is based on nothing more than strange weather phenomena and misunderstandings, Professor. That's what we've come here to prove."

"And yet," says Professor Newtiss, turning out towards the ocean and striking a dramatic pose, because, yup, this is all being videoed too, "for centuries people have reported hearing a monstrous howl from across the bay. Those people must be hearing *something*, Angela. Tonight, one way or another, we're going to get that something on tape."

Blaze's shoulders sag.

"All right!" he says. "Aye! We'll go down onto the beach. Just for a moment. But we mustn't go far – the shore is treacherous at low tide. You must only step where I step, and keep close. And I can't promise we'll actually *see* anything..."

But the podcasters have already set off towards the harbour steps, keeping up a running disagreement about whether or not monsters are real, while Fluffy Mike the sound man follows silently with his kit.

"Wait!" Blaze calls after them. "I said only step where I step!"

"Are you OK?" Violet asks him.

"I wish I'd never agreed to this," our friend replies, running his hands through his shock of red hair before clapping his skipper's cap back on. "And I didn't realize they would be recording it all!"

"You're really going to let them onto the beach?" I ask, wishing more than ever that I hadn't promised to come along too.

"I don't see how I can stop them," says Blaze. Then he adds thoughtfully, "How many can I lose, do you think? Before I get into trouble?"

"Speaking as Lost-and-Founder," I reply, "I don't think you should lose any."

"Best keep them under the pier," Violet says. "Let them poke about in the pools and shingle there. It's the most stable part of the beach, or so Mrs Fossil tells us, and the best lit. Once they've taken pictures of each other's shadows, and recorded the wind, we'll help you get them back to safety."

"We can take them to Seegol's afterwards," I add, hit by sudden inspiration, "for a *monster* portion of fish and chips. That's the only sighting I need."

"Good plan!" says Blaze, looking like he's tempted to skip straight to the chips right now. But then, "Oh, flippers! They're already going down!"

And he jogs off to catch up as, sure enough, the monster hunters begin their impatient descent down the slimy green beach steps without him.

I look at Vi, and she looks back at me. Knowing what we know about the legend of the malamander, the quicker we get these people to the safety of the chip shop the better.

THE SHAPE OF A THING

IT'S EVEN COLDER ON THE BEACH than up in the town. As we step onto the shingle a bitter wind picks up, almost as if the sea is warning us to keep away. It's a warning I'd like to listen to, but the monster hunters are already approaching the water's edge, Angela Song leading the way with her powerful torch. Poor Blaze is left trying to keep everyone to the strip of rock beneath the pier, while we have little choice but to follow.

The pier itself – towering over us like a giant iron centipede on giant iron legs – gives off a tentative electric glow from the garlands of storm-battered lights swinging along its sides. Halfway down, above the inviting warmth of Seegol's Diner, are the flickering neon letters that spell out EERIE-on-SEA in candy-coloured letters.

"Ever spotted it yourselves?" comes a voice, making me jump. We turn to find the towering form of Herman Newtiss suddenly right behind us. And I realize now that while Angela has an American accent, and Fluffy Mike doesn't seem to talk at all (which is ironic for a sound man), Professor Newtiss speaks with a very plummy British accent. He regards us with amusement before clarifying. "The malamander, I mean? Creeping around the town, chewing on the locals?"

I shrug. It seems better than telling the truth.

"It doesn't creep around the town," Violet explains. "It's a wild creature of the sea. It just needs to be left alone, that's all. At least," she adds quickly, "that's what it says in the stories."

"Ah, I see I have found an expert!" Professor Newtiss strokes his beard in amusement. "You will have seen the beast many times, I expect."

"It's hard to know what you've seen," Violet replies, choosing her words carefully now, "when an Eerie mist closes in."

"No sea mist tonight though," the man points out with a wink. "So, no monster, I suppose, eh?"

"You don't believe in it?" Violet asks. "But I thought, from what you said earlier...?"

"A mythical sea creature –" Professor Newtiss raises an eyebrow – "that lays a magical wishing egg on Midwinter Night? Do *you* believe in that?"

Vi and I say nothing. How can we answer this? Not only do we believe in the malamander; we've seen it! We've come face to fang with the monster itself, and – against all the odds – survived to tell the tale. Not that we ever do, of course. Tell the tale, that is. Besides, all I can think right now is how anyone who has avoided being devoured by a creature like that has to be a special kind of stupid to go looking for it again.

"But, to answer your question –" the professor speaks over my thoughts – "I have long suspected there is at least one real monster in Eerie-on-Sea."

"Oh?" I reply.

"Of course, Angela doesn't believe in *any* sort of monster," the man adds evasively. "According to her, there is always a rational explanation for everything. Angela's malamander is nothing but superstition and the effects of bad weather. And yet, despite her scepticism, look at her now!"

And he points to his podcasting co-host, who is striding down the beach, shining a light into the dark, while Fluffy Mike and Blaze struggle to keep up.

"I'm beginning to get a bad feeling about this," I say, with only a hint of wobble in my voice.

"Me too." Professor Newtiss grins. "We're being left behind!" And with this he scrunches off down the shingle to catch up.

By the time Vi and I have reached the others, they've stopped in the glow at the very end of the pier. Beyond, the blackness of a midwinter night is absolute. Only the roar of the invisible sea and the flash of a distant lighthouse tell us there's anything out there at all. Angela Song is peering ahead, but the beam of her flashlight shows nothing now.

"This is as far as we can go!" Blaze cries, holding his skipper's cap on against the wind. "It's dangerous to be even here. We must turn back."

"Where is the wreck?" Professor Newtiss demands. "The wreck of the battleship *Leviathan*? The creature's lair?"

Blaze points out into the darkness, across the expanse of shifting sand and rocks that none of us can see.

"That way! But – it's too far. Maybe, in the morning…" He starts to walk back, beckoning us to follow, but the monster hunters remain where they are, huddled together.

And that's when – right on cue – we hear it: a distant moan, rising to a shrieking howl on the wind as if some abominable creature is calling mournfully into the night. I find myself gripping Violet's arm as I suddenly realize how very exposed we are, at the edge of the last light, surrounded almost entirely by the unseen. Oh, what are we *doing* here?

For a moment there is a stunned silence. Then Professor Newtiss, still performing for the recording, speaks.

"The monster's roar! The malamander! Calling for its long-lost mate, just as the legend says."

"Did you get that?" Angela turns excitedly to Mike. "Tell me you got that!"

The sound man hunches over his equipment to squint at a small screen on the recording device. He waggles his hand as if to say he isn't sure.

"Let's listen again," says Angela, and I realize that we are watching an episode of *Antisceptic Whatever-It-Is* being made, right in front of our eyes.

"An eerie sound," Angela continues, "carried on the night air. Possibly caused by wind whistling around the old shipwreck—"

"Possibly," interrupts Professor Newtiss. "But then again, possibly not. Either way, we'll soon know for sure. And if our monstrous friend really is at home, Angela, it would be rude not to pay him a visit."

So saying, he starts to edge forward into the darkness, testing the beach ahead with his boot.

"No!" Blaze shouts. "The tour is over. Come back!"

"Have no fear." Professor Newtiss sets his hairy jaw heroically. "We know what we're doing. It'll be like our Loch Ness episode all over again."

One by one, the three monster hunters are swallowed up by the night.

Blaze turns to us in alarm. "What should I do?"

Well, I don't know, do I? This whole situation is nuttier than a slice of Iced Bonkers. For once even Violet seems at a loss as the distant, baleful moaning reaches us again. And this time, I swear, it's a little closer.

"Dismal's beard!" Blaze gasps.

But then there comes a sudden, much more human cry, close at hand.

"Eek! Help!"

Blaze flicks his own torch towards the sound, and we see

Professor Newtiss a little way down the beach, one of his legs sunk halfway to the knee.

"Help me!" he cries again, his voice high-pitched and panicky. "I'm sinking!"

No sooner have we noticed the professor's plight than we hear a *SPLOSH* and see that Fluffy Mike has sunk right to his belly button in another sinkhole.

"It's the quicksand!" Blaze calls. "Nobody move!"

Angela, freezing on the spot, is still close enough to the professor to reach out to him. He grabs her arm and – with a whimper of relief – pulls his leg free.

So much for being the big brave hunter of monsters and death worms!

"Quick!" Angela turns back to Mike, who is out of reach of anyone and going down fast. "Throw us the equipment! You need to lighten the load."

The sound man starts frantically tossing his stuff onto the closest rock, as he sinks further still. The professor, who is nearest, jumps to the rock. But instead of reaching out a helping hand, the prof simply picks up the video camera and starts recording the sound man's desperate situation.

"Pull him out!" cries Violet. And when the professor still doesn't move, she darts forward herself.

"Wait!" Blaze grabs her by the coat. "You'll get stuck too."

"We can't just leave him there!"

Then, before anyone can say anything else, and with no warning at all, the wind suddenly dies. An icy calm settles over the beach and the moon appears, and we see the first hints of a greenish mist creep up from the sea.

"A strange atmosphere has fallen over the world," says Professor Newtiss dramatically as he pans the camera around, "a palpable sense of the uncanny."

By now only Mike's head and shoulders are visible in the pool of quicksand. And yet, ever the professional, he's still managing to keep his microphone boom bobbing over the professor, to catch his words. But then his head starts to go under…

Ignoring the danger, Violet jumps from rock to rock and grabs hold of the fluffy end of Fluffy Mike's microphone. In no time Blaze joins her, with yours truly and Angela just behind. We start to pull, though the quicksand pulls back, like a predator refusing to let go of its prey. Finally, though, and painfully slowly, Mike starts to rise.

"Help us!" Violet cries to the professor.

"It almost feels," Professor Newtiss says instead, not helping at all but keeping the camera rolling, "as if the stage is set for the appearance of…"

Then he stops, and looks sharply down the beach, as if something has caught his eye.

Angela lets go of the microphone boom and swings her torch beam into the rising mist.

"What?" she demands. "Professor! Did you see something?"

But as we look it seems that we all see something, briefly

visible in the fog: a tall, pale shape, upright, down by the water's edge.

Watching us.

Then it vanishes in the rising mist, as the night fills once again with roar. And this time there is no wind to explain the strange and terrible sound.

"Was that...?" Angela's torch beam is suddenly trembling. "But – but it *can't* be! Can it?"

"A shape," Professor Newtiss declares for the recording. "The shape of – a *thing*."

"Bladderwracks!" I gulp.

We peer frantically into the moonlit mist, which is rising fast. All I can think is that if there is a monster out there, then we could hardly have laid on a tastier beach buffet if we'd wanted to, not with one of us stuck in quicksand, and the rest unsure where to step. And that includes one bite-sized Lost-and-Founder as an appetizer!

And that's when I realize we've stopped pulling!

With a glug of despair, the quicksand finally closes over Fluffy Mike's head – night-vision goggles, headphones, cap and all – and he's gone. We scrabble desperately at the microphone boom, but before we can heave again, before we can do *anything*, the pale and creeping thing that has brought Blaze's monster tour to such a dramatic end lurches towards us out of the dark.

FLUFFY MIKE DROP

THE TWO REMAINING PODCASTERS, Vi, Blaze and I all fall back in shock as the pale shape rears up at us. As if confirming my second-worst fear, one streaming-wet arm is plunged into the pool where Fluffy Mike is now submerged. Mike, a look of utmost terror on his silty face, is hauled from the quicksand and dumped onto a nearby rock. I'm just preparing to watch the gory spectacle of the monster taking the first bite of its victim – and wondering if maybe fainting would be a good option right now – when the pale creature staggers back to its feet. It heaves with ragged breath and, in the rising mist, turns its faceless head towards us.

And lowers its hood.

In the torchlight, the figure resolves not into the scaled and spiny form of the legendary malamander, but instead into a man in a long waterproof coat. A man we know well.

"Eels!" Violet cries.

Sure enough, standing before us is the tall form of our

arch-enemy, with what appears to be a tool bag slung over one shoulder.

"Eels?" Angela Song is already recovering from her shock. "The writer? *Sebastian* Eels?"

The professor zooms in with the video camera, his beard splitting open with a huge grin of delight.

"Only the very foolish or the very brave –" Sebastian Eels darts a poisonous look at the camera – "dare the beach on a night like this. I know which I am."

"Could we...?" Angela grabs the microphone and tries to wipe the silt off it. "Could we get an interview with you, Mr Eels? For our podcast?"

"Even now," the man replies, nodding to where Fluffy Mike is coughing up sand, "you don't understand the danger you are in. Get off the beach! Get away, while you still can!"

And with these words, Sebastian Eels strides up towards the town, vanishing in a swirl of green mist.

A stunned silence follows, filled only by the muffled roar of the surf from out in the bay. Angela is the first to speak.

"Did you—?" she says, turning to the professor.

"Oh, yes, I got that!" chuckles Professor Newtiss, lowering the camera. "And it will be podcast gold!"

Then Blaze Westerley does the first sensible thing anyone has done since we came down onto the beach. He walks up to Angela, grabs her torch and points it to where the last glow of the pier is already being swallowed by the mist.

"You heard the man," he says, his voice high with shock and exasperation. "We need to go!"

It's only once we've climbed back up the old stone steps to the town, to look fearfully along the deserted promenade, that anyone speaks again. And that speaker is me, eager to mention the fish-and-chips plan, in case, in the excitement, everyone has forgotten.

Blaze shakes his head. "Count me out. I'm going back to the *Spark*."

"Wait!" says Angela. Somehow, despite the excitement, she still seems spotless in her black coat. "There's so much more I want to ask. Especially after what's just happened. If it's a matter of payment…"

"It isn't," Blaze snaps, setting his skipper's cap straight. "If you must know more about Eerie-on-Sea, buy a guidebook. The monster tour is over. For good!"

And he hurries away, little Ember buzzing bright and angry about his head, back to his uncle and his fishing-boat home.

"Was that really Sebastian Eels?" Angela Song asks, turning to me and Vi. "Author of *The Cold, Dark Bottom of the Sea*? Expert on Eerie-on-Sea folklore? *That* Sebastian Eels?"

"Indeed it was," replies Professor Newtiss. "How fascinating that we should have met him already. Especially as he's been ignoring my requests for an interview for months.

I doubt many people know more about the malamander than Sebastian Eels."

And he gives Vi and me another meaningful look.

"Why do you want to interview Eels?" Violet asks.

"Let's get those chips," Professor Newtiss suggests, ignoring the question. "My treat. What do you say?"

"I'm not hungry," says Angela, "and some of us need to get cleaned up," she adds, eyeing poor, soggy Mike as he struggles to get his battered equipment balanced over his shoulders. "We'll go back to the hotel and review the recordings. Something tells me this episode of *Anomalous Phenomena* is going to cause a sensation, even if all we do is prove there's no such thing as malamanders once and for all."

And she heads off into the town, making audio notes into a small recorder as she goes, while the shivering sound man trails squelchingly behind.

~○~

A few minutes later, we find ourselves in the steamy warmth of Seegol's Diner, sitting at a corner table, ordering a slap-up meal of crispy, golden delight with extra yumminess on the side.

"And for you, sir?" says Mr Seegol, with a bow to our strange but generous new companion.

"Seegol's does a good Midwinter Pie," I suggest when I see the professor hesitate over the fishy menu. "If you'd rather."

"That sounds just the thing." The man nods gratefully. He looks enormous squashed into his chair, red-faced in the hot restaurant, still wearing his tweed hunting jacket. "I'll take two."

Once Seegol has bustled off to his island kitchen with our gimongous order, Violet bursts out with a question she's clearly been dying to ask.

"What are you a professor *of*?" she blurts out, somehow managing to make it sound like, "Are you *really* a professor?"

Herman Newtiss fixes her with a beady eye. Then he takes off his small spectacles and slips them into a top pocket as if he doesn't really need them at all.

"'Ologies," he says, with a chuckle. "The monstrous kind."

Then, when he sees us looking blank, he adds, counting off his fingers, "Parapsychology, urban mythology, crypto-zoology ... and any other weird 'ology you care to mention. Name me a crack-pot theory about monsters, ghosts or the supernatural, and I've probably given a lecture on it. They love all that over in Springheel, Arizona."

"You're a professor," I ask, struck by inspiration, "of *weirdology*?"

"I like that," replies Herman Newtiss, tugging his beard thoughtfully. "Weirdology! Yes, we could get that printed on a mug, for our online shop—"

"OK, but –" Violet waves her hands to interrupt – "does this mean you do believe in the malamander? Or does it mean you don't?"

"Now *that*," the man smiles as the food starts to arrive, "is a very good question."

With this non-answer, the professor lifts the pastry lid off his steaming pie and sniffs – in apparent ecstasy – the delicious cloud of savoury steam that puffs out. Then, before my horrified eyes, he picks up a perfectly good chip and dunks it in the gravy!

"Of course, I knew I could count on you two to be inquisitive," Professor Newtiss says, chomping the chip and picking up another. "That's why I got young Westerley to ask you along for the tour."

"You wanted us there?" asks Violet. "But how do you even know about us?"

The professor dips another chip into his pie, this time scooping up a chunk of filling and manoeuvring it into the hole in his beard in a way that isn't pretty.

"I told you before," he replies between mouthfuls, "there is one real monster in Eerie-on-Sea. And, according to my research, there are only two people in the world who know more about him than I do."

"Eels," Violet says, "and – my dad? He certainly knows a lot about the malamander, and—"

But the professor cuts her off, waggling another chip.

"I'm not talking about the malamander, Violet. *Sebastian Eels* is the monster of Eerie-on-Sea! *Eels!* And the pair of experts I've crossed an ocean to consult," he adds, looking us both square in the eye, "is you two."

WEIRDOLOGY

THE SECOND PIE IS NEARLY EMPTY, and the chips running low, before the professor finally pushes his plates away and speaks again.

"To answer your earlier question," he says, "and being completely honest, Violet, no, I do not believe in the malamander. I don't believe in magic, or monsters, or any of it. But you don't need to believe in something to teach it. Not when the students on my courses, the people who buy my books and the fourteen million subscribers to Angela's little podcast, are so eager to do all the believing for me."

"Fourteen *million*?" I am amazed.

"Nearer fifteen, actually," the professor replies, sounding like he can hardly believe it himself. "There's money to be made from people believing in things that aren't real, Herbie. Lots of money. But you only get that money if you give the people what they want. So, while Angela takes a sceptical and scientific approach to the stranger things in our world,

I dial up the spookiness and beasties and pretend to believe it all. And our listeners love it."

"What *do* you believe in, then?" demands Violet, looking unimpressed.

"Gravy," replies Professor Newtiss after a moment's thought. Then he grabs the very last chip, swirls it around the saggy pie crust and pops it in his mouth. "And lots of it."

"I don't understand what any of this has to do with us," I say then, wishing Seegol would come and take the plates away. I want to go home now, but what the professor says next keeps me pinned to my chair.

"Things are about to change in Eerie-on-Sea, Herbie. And I'm going to be the one who changes them. True, plenty of people have heard about the legends of this place over the years and written obscure pamphlets and the odd book about it, but, amazingly, the wider world has no idea Eerie-on-Sea exists.

"Well, I'm going to fix that. This place is a gold mine! Our episode on the malamander is just the start. By the time *Anomalous Phenomena* has finished, everyone will have heard of Eerie-on-Sea, and all its secrets, and I ... I mean, *we* – Angela, and the team – will be set for life. Why, Herbie, we'll probably even do an episode about the boy who washed up in a crate of lemons with no memory of his past."

"You even know about *that*?"

I'm stunned. I'm going to be broadcast to millions?

"Of course I do." The professor looks pleased at my

reaction. "And soon the whole world will, too. Especially if they subscribe to our premium membership."

"What if we don't want the whole world to know?" Violet cries, looking panicky. "What if Eerie-on-Sea doesn't want to be a podcast?"

Professor Newtiss shrugs.

"It's too late for that, Violet," he replies. "We're already here. And you can't keep the modern world out forever. But there is still one mystery I can't get a handle on. And that's the puzzle of Sebastian Eels himself. This is where you two come in."

"Unless we don't," I reply. "Come in, I mean. Why should we help you? This is our home, not a gold mine."

The professor shrugs again. Then he reaches into his jacket pocket and pulls out a fat notebook stuffed with slips of paper and extra bits, all barely held together by a tired old elastic band. He slaps it down onto the table with a thud. On the cover, written in biro, are the words *EERIE-ON-SEA*.

"To be honest, Herbie," the professor says, "I've been researching this place for so long that we could make paranormal podcast history even without your help. But ever since my first run-in with Eels, I can't quite get to the bottom of what he's up to. It's like the town itself refuses to let me into that particular secret. I bet you two could find out, though. And if you can, well…"

Here he pats the bulging notebook as if it's a Bond villain's cat.

"Maybe, in exchange, I can offer you some information that I *have* found out. About, for example, your origins, Herbert Lemon. Or, let's say, the mysterious disappearance of a man called Peter Parma twelve years ago."

"My dad!" Violet gasps. Before she can stop herself, her hand shoots over to the notebook. But the professor is too quick for her.

"Not so fast." He shakes his head, holding the book out of reach. "What I tell you, Violet, will depend on what you can tell me. And besides," he adds, squeezing the book back into his pocket, "surely you want to see Sebastian Eels exposed, eh? You aren't trying to protect him, are you?"

"Of course not!" Violet cries. "He's a villain."

"Oh, he certainly is that. I've been looking into his crimes since I first met him, many years ago."

The professor of weirdology sees he has our full attention now, and settles comfortably into his chair.

"This was way back when I was still a fresh-faced folklorist at a respectable university. Not much gravy on my chips then, if you get my meaning. Spent my days teaching spotty kids, and my evenings researching the legends of the sea. Sebastian Eels was already well known, so I was flattered when he asked to visit me to discuss the malamander. Asked to see my research. Well, I didn't see any harm in showing him. But then, that night, after he'd gone, came the break-in."

"You were robbed," says Violet, as if she isn't at all surprised. The professor nods.

"Someone stole all my research papers on the very subject Eels had come to see me about. Well, it doesn't take a Sherlock Holmes to work out whodunnit, dussit? And I was amazed that someone like Eels would have risked his reputation to steal from me like that. But, it seems, he just didn't care. I did, though. This is when I redirected my research abilities towards a different subject: Sebastian Eels himself. And what I found was shocking.

"The 'great' writer is behind a string of crimes against my fellow folklorists, collectors of the strange and connoisseurs of eclectic *objets d'art*," growls the professor. "Ever heard of something called Ocean Potion? Well, Eels tore the recipe for it out of a priceless medieval book. Priceless! Ever heard of the Shadowghast lantern? No? Well, I'm not surprised, but Eels stole that, too. The man has a string of museum break-ins and art thefts to his name. But it's not just the burglaries. Oh, no! Your local author is even guilty of –" the professor leans forward and grips the table edges with his enormous hands – "murder!" he mouths, at the top of his whisper.

"Murder?" I squeak, nearly losing my cap.

"Allegedly," concedes Herman Newtiss. "Nothing was ever proven, of course. I tried to interest the police, but they're even worse than Angela when it comes to wanting hard evidence. *I* know he's guilty, though. Eels may be slippery, but he can't wriggle away from me. And all the things he took – the papers, the artefacts, the books – have one thing in common: a connection with something he calls the Deepest

Secret of Eerie-on-Sea. He's been gathering this material for years, and doesn't care who he has to rob – or rub out – to get it."

Violet and I exchange looks. We've known about the Deepest Secret for a long time, without ever knowing what it actually is. It's odd to hear this stranger talking about it openly, in the comforting warmth of Seegol's Diner. All Vi and I know for sure is that this secret, whatever it may be, is hidden somewhere deep in the labyrinth of tunnels beneath Eerie-on-Sea, known as the Netherways. And that Sebastian Eels has the only map.

"So…" I say eventually, because we can't exchange looks forever. "What do you need from us?"

"An answer," the professor replies promptly, "to this."

He pulls out the notebook again and tugs a piece of paper from it. Then, before Vi and I can say anything more, Herman Newtiss, professor of weirdology at Springheel University, Arizona, slides the slip of paper over to us.

KRAKEN GOLD

IF THERE IS ONE THING you'll know about me, if you're a regular visitor to Eerie-on-Sea, that is, and have been paying attention, it's that I don't know who I really am. Some – the casual tourists we get in summer, for example – might think that a handsome young Lost-and-Founder like me, with the fine name of Herbert Lemon, should be pretty clear about his identity, and be proud of it, too.

But the truth is this: that name and title were given to me when I washed up on Eerie Beach, many years ago, without the faintest memory of who I was and where I came from.

Of course, since Violet came to town she has stirred up a few clues. She wouldn't be Violet Parma if she hadn't, would she? I'm tempted to tell the professor that he's not the only one with a gift for researching things. But the best clue Violet unearthed – that I might be the survivor of a shipwrecked ocean liner called the SS *Fabulous* – turned out to be a dead end as the only record of a ship of that name is from a hundred years ago.

So I'll leave you to imagine how I feel at the sight of this mysterious piece of paper being slid across the table towards us. A bit twitchy isn't the half of it!

"What is that?" asks Violet in a whisper.

"This," says Professor Newtiss, his finger still pinning the paper down, "is the ultimate clue. If you can find out what this means, I will tell you all I know of missing parents and mysterious shipwrecks. Deal?"

Vi and I exchange glances. We've been doing that a lot lately, I know, but despite my best hopes for a quiet Christmas, it looks like a new adventure has crept up on us already.

"Deal," we say at the same time.

"Excellent!" The professor treats us to a beardy grin. "Now, I must get back to the hotel to check that Angela isn't uploading raw footage online without my say-so. But I will be in touch again soon, eager to hear what you've found out."

And with this Professor Newtiss stands clumsily, nearly tipping the table over. He slips his tiny brass spectacles back onto his nose, jams his monster-hunter hat on his head, and strides out of Seegol's Diner, taking a cloud of chip-shop steam with him.

Mr Seegol clears away the empty plates and then Vi and I are alone.

With the folded slip of paper.

"I think," I say as I notice people eyeing us curiously, "that we should take this back to my place. Don't you?"

Violet nods and slides the paper into her coat pocket. We say our goodbyes to Seegol and walk out into the night.

Back in my lost-property basement, the fire has burned low. Erwin is still curled up in the armchair where we left him, but Violet doesn't join him there. Instead, we push clutter aside on my repair desk and shine the lamp down on the still-folded paper.

"What do you think will be on it?" I ask.

Violet gives me that look she keeps for when I ask one of my less-than-helpful questions.

Then she unfolds the paper.

It's a page torn from a diary, covering a few days in August. The year printed at the top is quite recent. Most of the page is blank, but on one of the dates something has been scrawled by hand. And I'd know that spidery handwriting anywhere.

"Eels!" Violet says excitedly, recognizing it too. "This is a page from Sebastian Eels' diary."

And she reads the words out loud:

"When I was only twelve years old,
I sold my soul for Kraken gold."

"OK!" I say, trying to sound excited too. "That sounds – um, what does that sound like?"

"Well!" Vi replies, blinking. "I suppose … actually, I don't really know."

I sag a bit. So much for this being some big clue!

"Wait, Herbie. The professor clearly thinks this is important. So, let's imagine for a moment that it isn't just some bit of random writing on a scrap of paper, but a true thing that Sebastian Eels wrote for – some reason. OK?"

"OK," I reply. "So, now what?"

"Maybe…" Violet screws up her nose, which she always does when she's really concentrating. "Maybe something important happened to Eels, on this date, when he was about our age. Something so big that he remembers it every year."

"Do you think he was ever our age, Vi?" I ask. "I reckon he just crawled out from under a rock, fully formed."

"Herbie, please take this seriously. I know it's hard to believe, but Sebastian had a childhood too, once."

"Fine," I say. "But even supposing that's true, which I suppose it has to be, look at the year, Vi! This diary is recent, but Sebastian Eels must go back to at least pagan times!"

There is a sudden cough.

Violet and I look around to see that Erwin has sat up in the chair. As we watch, he gives another hacking gasp.

"What is it, puss?" asks Vi. "Hair gone down the wrong way?"

Erwin gives us both a look of distress, lets out a final wheeze and then hangs his head.

"Do you think he was trying to say something?" I ask.

"That seemed exactly the sort of moment Erwin would normally have thrown in one of his cryptic sayings."

Violet gently gathers the cat up in her arms.

"He hasn't been looking at all well lately," she says.

I give the cat a scratch behind the ear. He does look a bit off-colour. If that's possible for a white cat.

"Anyway, maybe this is what the professor wants us to do," Violet continues. "He can research Sebastian Eels the famous author all he likes, but what he really wants to know about is Sebastian Eels the boy. About something that happened, years ago, when Eels was only twelve years old. Something that haunts him to this day. Something to do with..."

"Kraken gold." I finish the sentence for Violet. "He sold his soul for it, apparently. But how do we find out about that?"

"The clue's in the name, Herbie," Violet replies. "First thing in the morning, we're going to see Lady Kraken."

THE EERIE HUM

VI AND I HAVEN'T TALKED MUCH about Sebastian Eels lately, so seeing him again tonight and having his crimes laid out before us is an unwelcome reminder of unfinished business. Since our last tangle with the infamous author – our Festergrimm adventure, when he seized the one and only map of the mysterious Netherways – we have waited and waited for something bad to happen. But, so far, nothing has. At least, nothing you wouldn't expect to happen anyway in a strange little seaside town in the dead of winter. Even so, as the days tick by, my sense of queasy uneasiness has only grown. Surely Eels will make a move soon to take the Deepest Secret of Eerie-on-Sea, whatever it is, for himself.

"Unless," says Vi, because I think I said some of this out loud, "he's discovered it already."

"If that's the case –" I lean against the hot-water pipe on the wall of my Lost-and-Foundery and slide down it to a sitting position on the floor – "Professor Newtiss is already too late."

The pipe's not as comfy as the beanbag, true, but the warmth is tingly and reassuring after the freezing beach, and I settle back against it.

"Honestly, Vi, just when I'm daring to think the sneaky Eel might be contained, a pesky Newt appears and stirs everything up!"

The tingly feeling suddenly seems a bit tinglier than normal. This is hardly worth mentioning, I suppose – I'm a tingly, twitchy sort of guy, as you know – but as I sit there, enjoying the hot pipe, the tingle on the back of my skull gets so strong that it starts making my cap slide forwards over my eyes.

"C-c-can you f-f-feel that?" I ask, my teeth juddering with the vibration.

"Oh, not this again." Vi rolls her eyes.

"No, really!" I cry, jumping to my feet. "It's happening again! Put your hand on the pipe!"

So Violet does.

"Maybe it's just the water heating up," she says.

"It's not only in the pipe," I reply. "Now put your hand on the *wall*."

Soon we both have our hands flat against the wall, and there is no mistake. From somewhere deep down in the stonework, there is a strange vibration.

"This is what you've felt before?" Violet asks.

I nod. "But this time it's stronger."

And it's true. By now the sensation is rattling in the centre of my head, as if I can *hear* the vibration as a ringing in my skull.

"O-wow-ow!"

"Erwin!" Violet cries.

The cat, in Violet's arms now, is writhing in agony, desperately scrabbling at his ears. And I can already feel my own mind slipping away, my focus beginning to slide, as something appears in my vision. Something with – eyes? And hair like a halo of tendrils…

"Herbie!" Violet shouts, still clinging to Erwin. "Herbie, let go of the wall. Let go!"

I hear these words. And I *know* letting go is a good idea. But I seem powerless to obey. Then, just at the point when I think I might pass out, the weird vibration stops as suddenly as it started. I let go of the wall and grab hold of Vi. The three of us stand there for what seems like an age, trying to get our thoughts straight.

"That was totally weird," Violet whispers eventually. "A – a hum? An eerie … *hum*?"

"I told you!" I say. "I've been hearing, no, *feeling* that for days now. A kind of non-sound you can feel deep down in your bones, where no kind of sound should be. But that was the strongest yet."

Erwin, clearly terrified by what has just happened, struggles out of Violet's arms. He makes a beeline (cat-wise) for the cellar window.

But then he skids to a halt.

The cat's fur spikes out; his whiskers spring erect. I've never seen his ice-blue eyes look so big and round as he stares urgently at the glass pane. And from beyond it comes a sound – a chilling, in-your-ear-hole *actual* sound this time, and not some eerie hum. It's the sound you'd expect to hear if someone wearing heavy chainmail boots was stalking across the cobblestones outside – chainmail boots studded with metal spikes. It's a scary, unaccountable sound that I'd rather not be hearing at all, but it's nothing compared to what happens next. The stomping grows louder and louder as the whatever-it-is approaches my Lost-and-Foundery, and we hear the worse sound of all.

The deep-throated, bestial growl of something large and angry, right outside my window!

Erwin dives back to the armchair in terror.

And I freeze where I stand, clutching my cap.

So, it's Violet who makes the first move. Edging across the basement, she fumbles for a torch in the lost-torches basket, then tiptoes towards the window.

"Vi!" I gasp in alarm, my voice barely audible.

But Violet, ignoring me, raises the torch towards the cellar window.

And flicks it on.

As the light hits the glass, the effect is instant: a shrieking roar rattles the window, followed by the loud crash of the hotel bins. Then we hear the chainmail clank again, exactly as if something huge and scaly – which had been looking in at the window only a moment before – has leaped away from the sudden light.

"Oh!" Violet gasps as she drops the torch, shooting her hand to her mouth in shock.

"What?" I demand, finally unfreezing myself and rushing to her side. "What was out there?"

"I…" she mumbles, pointing a trembly finger towards the window. "I saw…"

"What?" I insist, wanting and *not* wanting to know all at the same time. "Violet!"

"An eye!" Violet turns to look at me, her own eyes wide in disbelief beneath her uncontrollable hair. "A huge, pale eye right up against the glass, staring in!"

Now, this is *not* the kind of answer a Herbie likes to hear. Not when the Herbie in question is in the place he feels safest of all, and the owner of that monstrous eye was only a pane of very-breakable glass away.

I look fearfully at the window, wishing more than ever that I had curtains. There's nothing there now but the black of the night outside.

"S-s-surely …" Violet stammers, "surely it *can't* be…"

"I'm on board with that!" I reply. "Put me down for as much 'it can't be' as you've got."

"No," Vi replies, jumping towards the window to press her own face against the glass. "Surely – surely I haven't just seen …"

"Don't say it!" I whisper, clutching my buttons.

But Violet says it anyway.

"… the malamander!"

VENOMOUS
TOOTH-NEEDLES

"I THOUGHT YOU SAID the malamander never comes into the town!" I cry. "I thought you said it was a wild creature of the sea that just wants to be left alone!"

"I did!" Violet looks stunned. "It is! But I'm not *really* an expert, am I?"

Aren't you? I want to shout. But Violet is already moving fast.

"We need to get out there, Herbie," she's saying, collecting her old self back together. "We have to get after it."

"Er –" I blink – "why do *we* have to get after it? Can't we leave this one to someone else?"

But Violet has already opened the window. The cold of the night rolls into my home once again, but this time as a tumble of sea mist. Then we hear the distant crash of breaking wood, and a very human scream.

"Come *on*!"

Violet pulls herself through the window in one cat-like movement, leaving me scrambling to find my coat and cap, and whatever courage I can, to follow after.

By now the streets are filled with rising fog that sparkles into frost as it touches the icy walls of the houses. Far above, I can still see the tower of the hotel – the last of the moonlight glinting from its cameraluna window as a cloying darkness engulfs the town.

Then we hear the scream again.

"This way!" Violet jumps over the overturned bins and vanishes into the mist.

"Oh, bladderwracks!" I mumble, running after her.

When we reach the old tree at the bottom of Dieppe Steps, dimly visible in the muffled streetlight, we see the lights of a nearby fishing cottage. Its door is broken open – smashed in like matchwood. Folk are peering fearfully from neighbouring doorways as from beyond the broken door comes a strange, high-pitched whine, mixed with the sound of sobbing.

We rush into the house. "Are you hurt?" asks Vi of an elderly couple clinging to each other on their kitchen floor. An old-fashioned kettle sings on the stove behind them.

"M-m-m…!" the old man tries to say, his face full of terror.

Above him, slashed right across the wall, is a five-fingered gouge in the plaster, as if something monstrous had swiped at the elderly couple with mighty claws and tried to take off their heads.

"Which way did it go?" Violet asks, lifting the screaming kettle from the hob.

The fisherfolk couple points fearfully out into the night. Without saying another word, Violet runs back out of the house and up the old stone steps, taking them two at a time, leaving me to follow.

When we reach the top, we skid to a halt at the edge of Fargazi Round (which is, as I'm sure you know, actually a square). The place is quiet and sparkling with midwinter. In the centre, the tumbledown bulk of Festergrimm's Eerie Waxworks awaits restoration, covered in scaffolding. Nearby is a huge hole in the road – a hole, which, er, Violet and I might have been involved in making during our last adventure.

"We've lost it, Vi," I whisper. "Let's go back."

"Shh!" my friend replies, her finger to her lips. "Listen!"

Then she ducks into a doorway, pointing urgently towards the gaping hole. It's more than big enough to hide a monster, and sure enough, we can hear falling earth and rocks, exactly as if something very large might be down there. We press ourselves into the stone doorway, hoping the shadows will be deep enough to conceal us.

And that's when, in this moment of icy tension, we feel it again: the vibration – the mysterious eerie hum! The weird resonance we sensed earlier in my Lost-and-Foundery has returned. It trembles beneath our hands and backs as we huddle against the door, and once again I *feel* rather than hear the sound in my skull.

"What's doing that?" says Violet in a barely audible whisper.

But even if I knew the answer, I wouldn't have time to give it.

There is an explosion of earth and cobblestones as something huge springs out of the hole in the road. We barely have the chance to see a shape – all jagged lines and flipper edges – leap briefly across the misty square before skittering down the nearest stone steps.

"It's heading back to the hotel!" Vi cries. "Quick!"

So now we're clattering down the steps ourselves, flying headlong in pursuit of something most right-thinking people would run *from*.

More and more people have emerged from their homes, holding up lanterns and lights, peering in terror into the mist.

"What was that?" some say.

"Did you see it?" say others.

"Over there!" someone cries, and we turn just in time to see a crazy swirl in the mist, but not what caused it.

And then we come to the back of the hotel.

"Which way did it go?" Vi demands, looking frantically around her.

"I hope," I say, gasping for breath, "that it didn't go down into my basement!"

"Down..." Violet begins, then she stops. "Or maybe..." she adds, catching my eye.

Slowly, Violet and I lift our heads to look up.

Above us, the cracked and flaking wall of the hotel rises into the mist. At first we see nothing more – the mist is proving to be a real "sea souper" as the fisherfolk of Eerie call it – and it's hard to see much beyond the first-floor windows. But then, just as I'm about to look away, I see it.

A shape, darker than the surrounding mist.

A shape that is clinging to the wall as if by long claws gripped in the cracks.

I squint, trying to make some sense of what I'm seeing. The mist thins briefly and two pale orbs stare down at me through the gap, like a pair of enormous eyes. But no, not *like* eyes at all – the orbs blink, and all my doubts about what we're chasing vanish in an instant: they *are* eyes!

And below those eyes gapes a mouth filled with venomous tooth-needles.

"Oh…" is all I can say as the bottom seems to fall out of my stomach, almost taking my knees with it.

It *is* the malamander.

Able to drop down in a moment to devour us!

Violet leans into me, and I can feel her trembling. But then, amazingly, she finds the courage to speak.

"Hello," she manages, in a whisper of terror to the thing on the wall, "old friend."

The eyes tip as the creature puts its head to one side. It snaps its mouth shut and there comes a clicking, mewling sound.

"But what are you *doing* here?" Violet asks it.

I can already sense the strange hum building again. It

reverberates around us, causing windows to rattle. The creature, as if in reply, lets out a sudden and soul-wrenching roar of fury and despair.

Then it turns, skittering up the wall, leaving nothing but swirling mist, and the hint of a webbed tail flicking behind it.

Towards the hotel roof!

"Herbie, *quick*!"

Violet tears round to the front of the hotel and through the revolving doors.

Inside the lobby, the lights are dim and the reception desk closed. Which is hardly surprising at midnight. But as I finally get through the whirling doors myself, I find that Violet isn't ringing for attention. No, she has slid to a halt in front of the gleaming hotel elevator and is jabbing at the buttons.

"What are we doing?" I gasp as I reach her side.

"We have to go up, Herbie!" she replies, pulling me into the lift with her as the doors open, and then jabbing again to close them. "We have to stop it!"

"Stop it?" I can't believe what I'm hearing.

"Yes!" Vi cries. "Stop it from reaching Meriam. Lady Kraken, I mean. Or anyone!"

Then Violet arranges her fingers and presses all six of the lift's numbered buttons at the same time. There is a *click* behind the dimpled control panel as an extra, *secret* button is revealed, marked with the number 6 and the words *Jules Verne Suite*.

Violet hits this.

"You've memorized the elevator codes, then?" I say, as the lift begins to ascend. "The secret elevator codes that even *I'm* not supposed to know?"

"Of course," says Vi, tapping her feet impatiently. "This is the quickest way to get there."

We watch the display in the lift counting up: 1... 2... 3...

"Oh, come on!" cries Vi. "Can't this thing go any faster?"

But before I can reply that of course it can't, the lift reaches the fourth floor and stops unexpectedly.

The doors open with a *ping*.

Suddenly we are face to face with Mr Mollusc, the hotel manager!

And with him, in the corridor – as if caught in mid-conversation – is Professor Newtiss.

"What the...!" the Mollusc starts to say.

The professor looks no less surprised to see us.

"Can't stop!" I say to the two men. "No room. *Going up!*"

And I punch the button that shuts the lift doors before they can get inside. We continue our climb.

"I'll pay for that tomorrow," I say, "but what was *he* doing there?"

"The manager?" Vi asks.

"No! The professor. What's he talking to Mollusc about?"

But before Violet can reply, we arrive at our destination. The elevator opens into the dark and plushly carpeted corridor of the sixth floor, which leads to Lady Kraken's private quarters. Normally I would take a moment to admire the vast chandeliers that float above us like icebergs viewed from the cold, dark bottom of the sea. Then I'd cower a bit before the long line of Kraken family portraits that stare down disapprovingly at Lost-and-Founders as they approach. But tonight, it seems, there's no time for any of this: Violet is already halfway down the corridor at a flat run.

I catch up as she's pulling the bell cord, making the ship's bell *DING* that tells Lady K someone has dared come to her door.

"Wait, Vi!" I say. "What if she's in bed? It's really late."

Violet rings the bell again anyway, tugging the cord more sharply.

DING!

"Listen!" I say, holding up my hand for silence. "Do you hear that?"

Violet goes quiet.

"I can't hear a thing," she whispers.

"Exactly," I reply.

And it's true. Not a sound comes from Lady Kraken's rooms, nor from the corridor behind us, nor the attic above – not even the crunching sounds you'd expect if a spiny monster from legend was gobbling up the elderly proprietor of the Grand Nautilus Hotel, electric wheelchair and all.

"Maybe we're too late!" Violet cries, ringing the bell frantically now, then trying the door.

Which is, of course, locked.

"Herbie!" Vi turns to me, pointing to my cap.

"No way!"

"Yes way!" cries Violet. "We have to check she's OK."

I reach up to my cap, lift it and slide Clermit into my hand.

Am I really going to do this? Am I really going to break into my reclusive employer's private chambers?

But, since my hand is already gripping Clermit's winder key and turning it in three sharp turns …

Tic-tic-tic-TIK. Tic-tic-tic-TIK. Tic-tic-tic-TIK.

… it seems I am!

Clermit, in a clockwork whirr, sits up in my hand on three brass legs. He extends an extra limb from inside his shell and snips a scissor claw at me in greeting.

"We need to open this door," I tell him. "Please."

With another snip of salute, Clermit scuttles down my body – I really must tell him I'm ticklish – and in no time has climbed the door. He inserts a brass appendage into the keyhole and then turns the lock with a smart *clunk*. He is still scuttling back up my left leg as Violet flings open the door to Lady Kraken's apartment.

And gasps in horror at what we see within.

MOONLIGHT EYES

LADY KRAKEN IS SEATED in her wicker wheelchair, beside the large round table in the centre of her sitting room, just as she so often is when I am summoned to her presence. But everything else about the scene is dramatically different.

First, and most striking, is the cone of moonlight that is beaming down onto the table from an open hatchway in the ceiling. Lady Kraken's cameraluna – the eerie device she uses to spy on the goings-on in our town – is active! The moonlight, so carefully gathered from the sky by special lenses in the hotel tower above, is pouring down and animating the thick dust upon the tabletop. Some magic that I've never understood causes that dust to rise and form, in sparkling three dimensions, a precise, silvery model of Eerie-on-Sea, complete with houses, streets, an illuminated pier and even the rolling ocean.

At least, that's what it normally does.

Right now, though, the dust is dancing chaotically, making nightmare shapes on the table and spilling over onto the floor, as if something is very wrong with it.

Lady Kraken's vast French windows – the ones that lead out onto her balcony – are wide open. The rising fog has already reached them, creeping into the apartment, bringing with it blooms of hoar frost.

But the most astonishing thing of all is not the magical workings of the faulty cameraluna. Neither is it the rolling mist that swirls around the furnishings like ghostly tentacles. No, it is Lady Kraken herself, seated in her wheelchair like an empress on a throne, bolt upright, stiff as an oar, a look of shock on her turtle face, her eyes filled with moonlight.

Yes, you heard that right.

Her eyes are full of moonlight! Glowing like two ice-cold crystals.

"Lady Kraken!" I shout, rushing over to her and waving my hand in front of her face.

She doesn't respond; doesn't even seem to see me.

"What can we do?" I say to Violet.

"Look!" Violet points to Her Ladyship's hand, which is gripping a lever on the control panel on the arm of her chair. This panel operates the chair itself and several gadgets in her home. And also the cameraluna.

Lady Kraken is holding this lever so tightly that her hand is shaking.

"Help me get her off this!" I cry, seizing Lady K's stick-like fingers and trying to force them open. "When did she get so strong!"

"I think it's a seizure," Vi replies. "Or electric shock maybe."

At these words I let go – I don't plan to get fried by electricity myself. Instead, I jam my fist down on a big red button on the control panel, which – fingers crossed! – is the off switch.

The cone of moonlight instantly winks out. The writhing dust on the table collapses, and the room is plunged into darkness.

Apart, that is, from the eerie glow of Her Ladyship's eyes.

"I'll shut the windows," says Violet, running to do just that while I try waving my hands in front of Lady K's face again.

Already the light in her eyes is fading. Her body is looser now, and I have to prop her up with pillows to stop her from tipping over. Soon there is a little purple colour coming back to her wrinkly eye sockets, and a blush of ghastly yellow in her sunken cheeks, which, for Her Ladyship, is the nearest thing to a sign of robust health we can expect.

Violet, who has already turned on the lights, is making a hasty search of the apartment.

"There's nothing here," she says. "Will Lady K be all right?"

"I don't know. But her eyes are nearly back to normal. And listen – do you hear that?"

Violet listens.

"Is that –" she looks surprised – "snoring?"

I nod. Lady Kraken is fast asleep, her snores surprisingly delicate for such a dried-up old bundle of bones and bad temper.

"We should get out of here," I whisper. The last thing in the world I want to do is wake my employer up and have to explain.

Violet looks unsure. "Shouldn't we tell someone?"

"Let's tuck her into her chair with some blankets," I suggest. "I'll try to find out how she is in the morning."

"Do you think she's behind that weird hum?" Violet asks as we push Lady Kraken into her bedchamber.

"No," I say flatly. "Do you?"

"Not really. But…"

"But what?" I ask.

"Nothing," says Violet as we tiptoe back to the door. But I spot her eyeing the cameraluna trapdoor in the ceiling with a look of suspicion.

"I don't understand it!" Violet says the next morning, pacing the floor of my Lost-and-Foundery. She stayed over last night, as we'd already arranged, but there wasn't as much sleep on this particular sleepover as a Lost-and-Founder likes. "Why would the malamander be searching for its long-lost mate in the town, Herbie? That's never been part of the legend."

Well, I don't know, do I? I've already been not answering questions like this for hours.

"I'm more worried about what I'm going to say to Mollusc next time I see him," I say, behind a massive yawn. "We made a racket in the hotel last night, Vi. He's bound to guess it was us."

There's a cough and a horrible wheezing sound.

We both look over at Erwin who, I am sure, has just tried once more to speak. But, instead, the cat looks sick, his whiskers pointing downwards.

"Oh, Erwin." Violet gently lifts the bookshop cat. "What *is* the matter?"

Then, when the cat doesn't respond, she looks at me.

"Have you ever seen him like this before?"

I confess that I haven't.

"Then I think we should take him to Dr Thalassi," she decides. "Before we do anything else. We can check up on Lady Kraken afterwards."

"OK," I reply. Then I add, "Oh, is, er, that watch still running, Vi? The one that was handed in yesterday?"

"Yes." Violet sighs, suddenly impatient. "Here!" And she slips the battered old thing off her wrist and hands it over. "I know you've been itching to write out a Lost-and-Founder's label for it, Herbie, for a rightful owner who will never come."

And she's right – that is exactly what I should do. But, instead, I buckle the watch onto my own wrist.

"You, um, you never know when we might need to tell the time today." I shrug. "That's all."

Violet looks even more exasperated, as if she can't fathom the ways of Lost-and-Founders, and finally realizes that she never will. Instead, she wraps the poorly cat in a blanket.

And the three of us climb out of my basement window and into the cold light of an Eerie-on-Sea morning.

When we reach Dr Thalassi's surgery, which is on the ground floor of the castle, we see a lonely light in the window. But after ringing the bell, it isn't Dr Thalassi – curator of the museum, medical man about town and, in the absence of an actual vet, animal doctor when needed – but Jenny Hanniver, keeper of the Eerie Book Dispensary, who looks out of the door.

"Violet!" she cries, pleased to see her ward. "And Herbie. You two are up early. How was the sleepover? Oh, you have my cat with you. Though why I call him 'mine', I don't know, since these days he spends most of his time with you two."

"Is the doc in?" says Violet, giving her guardian a hug.

"No," Jenny replies, pulling her shawl close. "I've been waiting for half an hour to see him myself. I don't know where he is. But come in out of the cold, both of you. What's the matter?"

"I'm really worried about Erwin," says Violet as we shuffle into the empty surgery. She places the bundled blanket on the examination table and opens it a little. Erwin peers out and gives a hoarse little cough.

"He does look a bit peaky, doesn't he?" Jenny agrees. "What's wrong exactly?"

"Well, he can't…" I begin. Then I stop.

I look at Violet. We have never let on to Jenny that we

know Erwin can talk, but we have always imagined she must be aware. He's the bookshop cat, after all, and has lived with Jenny for years. Now it comes to it, though, it seems a bit of a weird thing to say out loud. What if Jenny *doesn't* know and thinks we're potty?

"He's..." Violet tries to rescue me, but seems to be struggling with the same sudden doubt. "He's just not himself. That's all."

"Hmm," says Jenny, looking at us both in turn and – I suspect – seeing everything. Then she strokes the cat, tips his head back and looks into each of his eyes.

"How long has he, ah, not been himself?" she asks. "Would you say?"

"A few days," I answer. "Maybe a week. I know because..."

"Yes?"

"Because, um, I've also been a bit not myself," I say, not sure if I should mention my own attacks of fuzzy-in-the-head wooziness either. "As it happens," I add, "for about a week."

"Hmm," says Jenny again, laying her hand across my forehead.

"Why are you here?" Violet asks Jenny then. "You're not not-yourself too, are you?"

"Me?" Jenny laughs. "No, I'm fine. I'm here to see the doctor about a mechanical matter. The mermonkey has been playing up. It hasn't been working properly – not for, well..."

"About a week?" Violet suggests.

Jenny gives a frown, then nods.

"I don't mean the usual creaking joints and dodgy electrics," she says. "Sometimes the mermonkey refuses to dispense anything. Or it dispenses two books as if it can't decide. It has never done anything like that before. I've run out of ideas, and specialist tools, so I thought Dr Thalassi could take a look. Eerie-on-Sea wouldn't be Eerie-on-Sea if I have to shut the book dispensary down."

"Shut it *down*?" Vi and I cry together.

Erwin can't talk, Lady K's cameraluna is misfiring weirdly, and now the mermonkey is going wrong. Everything we know and love seems to be falling apart.

And I'm woozy!

"Can we leave Erwin with you, Jenny?" Violet says then, briskly. "There's something we need to do at the hotel. But I promise I'll be home soon."

"Oh," her guardian replies. "Yes, of course. But no need to hurry back to the shop, Violet. This afternoon will be fine. Bring Herbie, too," she adds, with a significant look at me.

"We'll be there on time," I reply, tapping my new-old wristwatch.

"On time for what?" asks Violet, looking confused, but I steer her away. Together we step out into the cold and head back to the hotel.

"What are you thinking?" I say as we hop up the hotel steps.

"We said we'd check on Lady Kraken, remember?" Violet replies. "Well, that's the perfect excuse to find out more about the Kraken gold."

"Could that," I ask, "be connected with all these things going wrong?"

Violet gives a huge shrug.

"All I know is that every time something has gone wrong before, Sebastian Eels has been at the bottom of it. And I'm beginning to think it's not just the professor who needs to know the truth about him. It's time we did too."

And I can't argue with that, can I? Plus, I add quietly to myself, I can also nip to the hotel kitchens to retrieve some leftovers for breakfast, which is, thanks to Mr Mollusc, the only breakfast I'm allowed. But, leftovers or not, we need to keep our strength up for the investigations.

"You're not concerned about using the front door?" I say. "After all the noise we made in the hotel last night?"

"You worry too much, Herbie," Vi replies, pushing into the revolving hotel doors. "I bet no one even noticed."

But the moment we enter the hotel lobby, before I can even turn towards the kitchen and my longed-for breakfast, I'm stopped by a voice.

"Excuse me. Yes, you. The boy with the funny cap. From last night? Hubert, wasn't it? You couldn't plug this in for us, could you?"

And suddenly I'm rubbing my eyes at an extraordinary sight.

SCOPES AND GADGETS

IT WAS ANGELA SONG WHO SPOKE, from *Phlopicus Sarcophagus* (or whatever it's called). She is standing beside the great fireplace, dressed mysteriously in black, looking every bit the paranormal investigator. Beside her is Sound man Mike, busily unpacking various pieces of equipment onto the ornate mahogany coffee table. And there is Dr Thalassi! His sleeves are rolled up, his hands are full of equipment too, and he is in close conversation with Professor Newtiss. Angela waggles the plug of a power cable at me hopefully.

I glance over to Reception.

The receptionist, Amber Griss, smiles good morning to me from her chair at the desk, and shrugs a *why not?* about the cable. So, I take the plug, spool the cable out across the gleaming marble floor and plug it in beside her.

"What's going on?" I ask.

"Something extraordinary happened in the hotel last night, apparently," Amber replies. "People running around, shouting, doorbells ringing. And trouble in the town, too. Mr Mollusc is in a towering rage about it. He's gone up to tell Lady Kraken. Didn't you hear all the noise?"

"Nope," I reply quickly. "I don't have a clue what you're talking about, Amber – I slept through the whole thing."

And I yawn, enormously.

"Well, anyway." Amber peers at me through her severe spectacles. "These podcast people are calling it 'an exciting development'. It seems they picked up something on their scopes. They want to use the hotel lobby as a base of operations from now on. Mr Mollusc is in a rage about that, too."

By now the monster hunters have transformed the reception area into a cross between a recording studio and an incident room. Beside an enormous loudspeaker, there's a green display screen with a grid on it, which hums with power. On the grid there are electronic lines of light – the sort of lines that would jump up and down if you were measuring someone's heartbeat. Right now, though, they're more like the kind of lines you'd get if you were measuring pancakes. In other words, flat.

"What do you think they've found?" Violet whispers.

"Let's go over and ask," I whisper in reply.

"Are you sure about this?" we hear Angela ask Fluffy Mike as we approach.

The sound man gives a very positive double thumbs-up before tweaking some dials on a control deck. The speaker powers on with a deep background rumble.

"And you picked up something yourself, Doctor?" says

Angela, arching one perfect eyebrow at Dr Thalassi.

"I have a seismograph in the museum," says the doc. "Very sensitive. I've been noticing mysterious fluctuations on it for a while now. Well, for about..."

"A week?" Violet suggests, glancing at me.

"Yes." The doc blinks at her. "Good morning, Violet; good morning, Herbie. And yes, it was about a week ago it started, now you come to mention it. I was investigating it myself just this morning when I bumped into Professor Newtiss here, and his team."

"And we're pleased to have your help, Doctor," says Angela, who doesn't look too impressed at being relegated to "team". "But you're sure it's not just interference –" she turns back to Mike – "or static, or feedback? We need to be sure before broadcasting this. You know what our listeners are like."

"But *what* is it?" asks Violet. "What did you record?"

"Last night, on the beach, we picked up a strange sound," Angela says. "A strange sound, which—"

"Now, now, Angela," comes the booming voice of Professor Newtiss. "Let's not spoil the surprise, eh?"

"I'm alarmed to hear that anyone was on the beach last night," says Dr Thalassi. "I can't think of anything more reckless in this weather. I hope none of the locals were irresponsible enough to have been acting as a guide."

I say nothing as loudly as I can, and Violet does the same. Behind the doc, Fluffy Mike, who is holding a big pair of headphones to one ear, gives Angela an A-OK sign.

"Professor, who are all these people?" Angela asks quietly. "I thought you didn't want to make this public too soon?"

By now a ragtag bunch has gathered in the hotel lobby, including curious hotel staff, and even a fisherman or three. Everyone is staring at the equipment in confused expectation.

"Relax," Herman Newtiss replies, stroking his beard. "It's just a few locals. You wanted to interview some, didn't you? Well, we'll record them now, too. A reaction take of *ooh*s and *aah*s when we do our big reveal."

Then he puts his hat back on, shoves his hands into the pockets of his tweed hunting jacket and turns to the small audience.

"Ladies and gentlemen, as you know, you are fortunate to have the *Anomalous Phenomena* podcast in town."

He pauses here, as if expecting some kind of response, but everyone just looks politely confused, so he pushes on.

"Well, anyway, while searching for the famous malamander of Eerie-on-Sea ..."

Dr Thalassi gives a little snort of amusement at this.

"... we inadvertently captured something else entirely and made what we believe is a dramatic discovery. A mysterious sound, a – a *vibration*, if you will, a..."

"A hum?" I suggest, remembering what Violet called it in my basement last night. I feel a little shy as everyone looks round at me, but I press on. "An eerie, um, *hum*? Perhaps?"

"Yes!" declares Professor Newtiss, pointing at me dramatically. "That is it exactly. The Eerie Hum! Perfect,

Herbie! That'll look great on a T-shirt. And we, at *Anomalous Phenomena*, discovered it first."

"Our subscribers are going to love that," says Angela, her eyes flashing with excitement. Then she nods to Fluffy Mike and says, "Punch it!"

Mike doesn't punch anything that I can see, but he does flip some switches.

Instantly, the hotel lobby is filled with a hiss and crackle from the loudspeaker. We hear the surging tide, the gusting of the wind and the faint murmur of our voices recorded during the monster hunt the night before. And, as the recording plays, the flat lines on the green screen start to twitch up and down. Mike, still listening to one half of an enormous pair of headphones, begins to fast-forward the recording, turning a big yellow dial. Then he holds up his finger.

We go quiet as the recording resumes. You could hear a pin drop in the hotel now. Then we hear something else.

"Help!" comes the surprisingly high-pitched voice of Professor Newtiss. *"Help me, I'm sinking!"*

"Er – OK, can we just skip that part?" says the man himself, his ears pinking with embarrassment as sniggers run around the lobby.

Mike gives a smile of apology, then dials forward again, until … he stops. Now, through the speakers, we hear the unmistakable sound of the distant moan – the wail that legend says is the malamander calling for its long-lost mate. Even now, in the warmth and comforting everydayness of this hotel morning, the sound chills me to the core. On the screen, the monstrous roar is represented by a sweeping peak of eerie green light.

"Dismal's beard!" gasps a fisherman. "The malamander!"

"The wind," Dr Thalassi corrects him. "Nothing more."

"It's a good, clean recording," says Angela, in a business-like voice. "Whatever it is. But let's listen to what comes next."

On the green screen the lines have dropped back down again to be almost flat, as the recorded wail dies away. Now there is nothing on the recording but tide sounds, faint murmuring voices, snaps and crackles and pops...

But then, as we're all straining to *hear* what is about to come, something *appears* instead – a riot of jagged lines on the green screen. These lines – the ones I said were like the lines that record heartbeats in hospital – suddenly become a vast, jagged mountain range on the graph. If this *were* someone's heartbeat, I reckon their chest would have just exploded. The lines leap and spike exactly as if some deafening, ear-shattering roar is taking place on the recording. But from the speaker comes no sound at all.

Except, that is, for a faint, almost imperceptible hum.

Then the lines go flat again.

"What was *that*?" Violet demands. "The lines went crazy, but I didn't hear a thing. And I don't remember hearing another sound last night either."

"You wouldn't," says Angela. "This was a sound outside the range of human hearing. We can't hear it at all, even though, according to the instruments, it was loud enough to carry right across Eerie Bay."

"Infrasound," booms the professor. "Incredibly loud. But you'd feel it, Violet, before hearing it."

"Good heavens!" says Dr Thalassi. "What could be causing it?"

"That," says Angela, "is precisely what we are going to find out."

"But what *is* it?" Violet asks. "Can't you, you know, twiddle some knobs and flip some switches till we *can* hear the sound? Like they do in the movies?"

"What do you think?" says Angela, turning back to Fluffy Mike. "Can you bring that sound into normal hearing range?"

Mike gives a cautious nod, and then twiddles some more knobs and flips some more switches, the headphones still clamped to one ear. It's a tense moment as we all wait in silence. Then Mike gives another nod, more definite this time. He rewinds the tape and starts the recording again.

From the speaker comes the crackle of the recording once more, but it's different now; the sounds of the sea and wind are almost too low to hear at all, and make the speaker vibrate horribly.

"Ugh!" says the professor, who appears to be slipping something into his ears. "Too far. Dial it back it bit."

Fluffy Mike twiddles his dials a bit more.

And then we hear something new.

THE OCEAN SPEAKS

FROM THE LOUDSPEAKER comes a thin, high note, like a distant voice.

Like a voice that is singing – a voice that is almost human. Almost…

"What is that?" Angela whispers, but no one answers. No one seems able to speak.

The sound – the singing, if that's what it is – is growing clearer. I can hear it in my ears, but I can also *feel* it in my, well, my somewhere-deep-down. I almost want to say I can feel it in my soul.

As I've felt it before.

Because suddenly I know, without doubt, that this is not the first time I've heard this singing.

Around me, everyone is still as statues, as if straining to catch every note of the eerie song as tendrils of sound twist around us. Even over at the reception desk, Amber Griss is staring at the speaker, transfixed. With an effort I swivel my gaze towards Violet, and I'm shocked to see that while her eyes are as wide as scallop shells, the pupils in them have shrunk to almost nothing.

"Vi?" I try to say, but the sound sticks in my throat. I can hardly even open my mouth. The singing is in my head, in my *everywhere*: filling my mind, bringing with it images – no, *memories* – of people screaming, of water rushing, of hands grasping at me in the water, of waves, of dark sky and the sea...

And of a face.

In my mind.

A face, haloed by hair-like tendrils.

A face with black, fathomless eyes that stare into mine as time turns into ages.

"Boy..."

A voice seems to be calling me.

"Shipwreck Boy..."

Click!

The sudden brutal end of the recording cuts through my hypnotic trance. I return to the present to find myself sitting on the floor of the lobby, with dribble on my chin.

Over by the loudspeaker, the professor's hand is on the power switch, and I realize it was he who turned off the recording. I see him remove something from his ears.

"Gah!" Angela splutters, shaking her head clear, as all around people rub their eyes and look dazed. "That singing – it made me want to..."

"Want to what?" asks the professor.

But Angela just shakes her head again.

"That sound," she says, "was in the malamander's roar?"

"No," the professor answers, looking delighted with what he has just witnessed. "Not in the malamander's roar, Angela, but in the sound that came *after* it. It's what the Eerie Hum would be like if we could hear it without the aid of technology. It's not made by the malamander at all, but by—"

"The malamander's mate," Violet says, her voice still dreamy. "The monster has called for years. And now, finally, something is calling back."

"What?" Angela stares at Violet.

Professor Newtiss peers at her too, through his tiny spectacles.

"But that would be extraordinary!" Angela cries. "Let's play it again."

"Er!" I declare, with as much authority as a small but smartly uniformed Lost-and-Founder can muster. "Or maybe let's not? At least, not right now? Not here? Maybe there shouldn't be any more public playing of unknown eerie sounds until you've scienced them a bit more, and worked out if they're safe. Don't you think?"

Angela seems to see the sense of this. The podcast trio huddle over their equipment now, talking in excited whispers.

Dr Thalassi walks unsteadily over to Vi and me.

"Are you OK, Doc?" I ask.

"But there is no such thing as a malamander," he says

firmly, trying but failing to straighten his bow tie. Then he adds, as if he can't believe he's asking, "Is there?"

"Jenny's waiting in your surgery, Doctor," says Violet kindly. "With Erwin. I'd love it if you took a look at him, please. He isn't well. Oh, and it sounds like the mermonkey is on the blink again."

"Right," replies Dr Thalassi, clearly grateful to be thrown a lifeline to practical matters that he is used to understanding. "I'd better get back then. See you both this afternoon."

And with a look of profound distraction on his face, the doctor leaves the lobby.

"What did he mean, *see you both this afternoon*?" Violet turns to me.

"Do you really believe what you said?" I ask her, changing the subject. "About the malamander's mate?"

"What else can it be? And, Herbie, do you see what this means?"

"No," I reply. "But then I rarely do. And *never* before breakfast..."

"If I'm right," Vi explains impatiently, "if this really is the malamander's mate calling, then that explains why the malamander was so active last night. Herbie, he was looking for her! Or him, or them, or who-or-whatever it was making that singing sound. And since the malamander was in town, that must mean..."

"That whatever made that sound," I reply, finishing for Violet, "is in the town too."

"Not just in the town, Herbie; it must be in the hotel—"

"Not for long it won't be," an angry voice cuts across us then, and we turn to find Mr Mollusc striding across the lobby, a look of poisonous fury above his horrible moustache. "Whatever *it* is. This time you have gone too far, Lemon!"

"Sir?" I say, wishing I could go even further. "What do you mean, sir?"

"I've just been to see Her Ladyship." The hotel manager looms over me, trembling all over with indignation, but also with – I can't help noticing – a kind of dark delight. "All is known, Herbert Lemon. Someone broke into Lady Kraken's private quarters last night. And I believe it was you!"

"Sir!" I squeak. "I can explain…!"

"So," hisses Mr Mollusc in triumph, "it *was* you! You as good as admit it. I have you at last, Lemon." He pokes me in the button with a mean finger. "You're finished, washed up, high and dry, out on your shrimpy little ear…"

Saying the word *ear* seems to give him an idea, because Mr Mollusc grabs hold of my actual ear, and pulls it towards the hotel lift. Obviously, I have no choice but to go too, hopping along with a "yike, yike, yike!" When the elevator doors open, I'm shoved inside.

"Sir!"

"Oh, just wait till Her Ladyship hears I've caught the culprit already." Mr Mollusc chuckles to himself as the lift doors close on us. "She is furious, and her punishment will be terrible to behold. I might take pictures."

"But, SIR!" I cry. "Is Lady K OK? Alive and well, I mean, and not, er, glowing?"

"What are you blathering on about?" the manager says. "Of course she's alive and well."

"Phew!" I mutter as I rub my ear.

"You, boy, have nothing to be relieved about," the manager snaps as the elevator rises. "That's your problem, Lemon. You seem to think the world owes you something – that you have a *right* to wear that uniform."

"That's not fair, sir," I protest. "I haven't done anything wrong. I mean, not deliberately..."

Mr Mollusc swings around and lowers his face to mine so that I can feel his moustache bristling against my nose.

"The WORLD," he declares, with profound bitterness, "isn't fair! The sooner you realize that, boy, the better. Now, silence!"

So, I go silent.

We arrive at the sixth floor. I am marched along the corridor beneath the disapproving glares of the illustrious Kraken family portraits, who seem, if possible, even more disgusted at the sight of me than last time.

Then I am once more in front of the large wooden doors of the Jules Verne suite.

Mr Mollusc tugs the bell pull, and we hear the distant sound of the ship's bell. At least Violet didn't break it when she yanked it around last night. The little light beside the doors flickers on to say *COME IN.*

And the doors swing quietly open.

"What now?" comes a creaky voice from the darkness within. "This had better be good, Godfrey."

"Oh, it is, Your Ladyship," declares Mr Mollusc, propelling me into the room ahead of him. "I have found the culprit! He needs to be vigorously punished, and—"

But before the manager can continue, there's a swishing sound behind me, and a *bang*, as the great wooden doors of the apartment slam shut, locking him out.

And trapping me within!

"Herbert Lemon," comes the voice again, laced with barely controlled fury.

"Your Ladyness?" I say, not sure if I should add an "I can explain!" or not. The curtains are drawn and everything in the Jules Verne suite is in darkness.

There's a whirr of antique electric motors and a shape moves in the shadows. Lady Kraken, barely visible, is hunched in her bronze-and-wicker wheelchair. Even in the gloom I can see that she has a packet of frozen peas on her head, held in place by a hastily wrapped turban.

"So, *you* are to blame, are you?" says Lady Kraken. "Dunderbrained boy! After all I've done for you! *This* is how you repay me?"

"I can explain!" I cry. "I mean, I'm sorry we rang your bell in the night, and broke in, but we were worried. Yes, *worried*! About *you*! Because last night, me and Violet, we *saw*—"

"What?" snaps Lady K, coming to a halt. "What precisely

did you see in the night, Mr Lemon? Something that explains your terrible behaviour? Something that explains – this?"

The old lady clicks on an antique standard lamp, flooding the room with slow, treacly light.

I see the large circular table on which the cameraluna usually displays. It is covered in drifts of dust that are tumbling over the edge and onto the Persian rug on the floor.

Then I notice something else on that floor – something that Vi and I didn't spot the night before.

I do my third gulp of the day.

BIRTHRIGHT OF
THE KRAKENS

THERE, IN THE DUST on Lady Kraken's rug, is an enormous webbed and monstrous footprint. And beside it, running in all directions, are much smaller footprints that can only have been made by Vi and me.

"Um," I say, deciding that only my most professional manner will fit the occasion. "Would you like me to adjust your peas? They seem to be slipping."

"Forget my peas!" Lady Kraken slaps the arm of her wheelchair. "I have awoken from the strangest dreams to find even stranger footprints in my home, Mr Lemon, and if my manager is to be believed, it has something to do with you."

I drop down on my hands and knees to examine the three-toed foot mark close up. There is no mistaking it. I can't help wondering what Angela would say if she saw such conclusive evidence of a legendary monster's existence. Or what she wouldn't pay to get her hands on this rug. I crawl along the floor on all fours, trying to work out where the creature that made these footprints went.

"Mr Lemon," Lady K says, watching my antics with fascination. "If I required a sniffer dog, I would have rung for one. Instead, I am waiting for an explanation."

"It didn't leave by the window," I say, returning to my employer's side and straightening my cap. "So, it must have gone out the same way it came in: through the ceiling."

And I point up to where the edges of the cameraluna trapdoor can be seen above the round table.

"*What* didn't leave by the window?" Lady Kraken demands. "*What* came through the ceiling? Answer me, boy!"

"The, um," I say, because now there's no way to avoid saying it, "the malamander, Your Ladyness."

"So!" Lady Kraken's eyes narrow in her turtle face. "It is as I feared."

I try a grin.

It doesn't seem to work.

"And *you* have done this?" Lady K continues, pointing a crooked finger at me. "*You* have stirred up once more that which must not be stirred, and awakened again what must not be awoken?"

"Er," I reply, trying to work out this extraordinary sentence on my fingers, "well, something strange *did* happen in the hotel last night. But I swear by my cap it wasn't awokened or astirred by me or Violet."

"And your break-in?" she demands. "Your illegal entry into my private quarters?"

"Like I said, we were worried. We thought you might have been eaten! And when we got in, you were a bit … you know. Do you remember, Your Ladyness, being a bit … you know?"

"Hmmm." Lady Kraken taps her tooth with one long fingernail as if considering whether or not to solve the situation by just eating me herself. But then she flaps her hands in exasperation.

"Oh, to blazes with it all!" she declares. "And as for Violet, I wish you'd brought her with you, boy. I might have got a clearer answer to this strange business if you had. Instead, all I have are footprints on my rug, a pounding headache, and you! And no memory of how any of it happened."

"But what do you remember?" I venture.

"As for that," Lady Kraken continues, "I was merely consulting my cameraluna, as I am in the habit of doing when the moonlight allows – to watch over the doings of our strange little town – when I appear to have been the victim of some sort of accident."

"Accident?"

"That's what I said, isn't it?" she snaps. "Well, a strange sound, at any rate. Actually, more of a hum. Whatever it was, it seemed to come from the lenses of my cameraluna itself, and just grew louder and louder till it made the whole room shake. But when I grabbed the lever to shut the blasted thing down, I felt that hum seep right through my skeleton, till

I could hear it – *hear* it, I tell you! – ringing like a bell in my skull! Only, it was more like – like…"

"Singing?" I suggest.

"In point of fact –" Lady Kraken narrows her eyes at me again – "it *was* like singing."

"The sort of singing," I continue, "that you hear sometimes in a dream, but which slips from your memory as soon as you wake, leaving you feeling you've been in the presence of something wondrous that you desperately want to hear again, but never can? That sort?"

Lady K blinks at me in surprise.

"Yes," she croaks, after a moment. "Yes, Mr Lemon, that is *exactly* what it was."

"And may I ask, Lady Kraken, what you were watching last night? With your cameraluna? When the, er, the *singing* started?"

"You!" The lady bobs her head towards me accusingly. "I saw you, Mr Lemon, with Violet, and that Blaze Westerley boy, all down on the beach with a gaggle of hotel guests – *my* hotel guests – filling their heads up with nonsense about our private legends, on an unauthorized monster hunt."

"You know about that?"

"Of course I know about that! But that is not what I was really watching," she continues. "That scoundrel Sebastian Eels was also on the beach last night. Now, what do you know about *that*?"

"I don't know much about that," I say. "I was hoping you could tell me."

"I?" Lady Kraken looks shocked. "Tell you? I cannot tell you what he was doing. He has a small boat tied up secretly at the edge of Maw Rocks, and he's been going out in it for weeks. But I lose him every time, and don't know where he goes. I'll keep at it though, don't you worry. I'll make sure that bounder doesn't put a step out of line."

"Actually, Lady Kraken," I say, taking my chance, "I was wondering – there's something about Sebastian Eels that Vi and I would like to know."

"Oh?" The suspicion is back again, written in a thousand wrinkles.

"Can you tell me, please, what happened to him when he was twelve years old?"

Lady Kraken sits bolt upright. The bag of frozen peas finally slides off completely and lands on the floor.

"Why on earth would you ask me that?" she demands, recovering herself. "Unless..."

She grabs the controls of her chair in one claw-like hand, and starts to advance towards me. "Are you trying to double-cross me, boy? Are you trying to pique my sympathy for the villain? Are you trying to make me feel ...?"

By now she's backed me up against the table, pressing forward with her chair so that I cannot move.

"... *guilty*?"

"No!" I cry. "I just heard that something happened to him when he was a boy, and I thought, well, I just *thought*..."

I glance at the watch on my wrist.

"Bladderwracks, would you look at the time!" I cry. "Must dash!"

And I slip out from where I'm trapped and run to the doors. Which are, of course, still locked.

"I am very disappointed in you, Herbert Lemon," Lady Kraken says, whirring her chair around to face me again. "Didn't you agree to be my eyes and ears? To look in all the dark corners where my cameraluna cannot see? To report back if anything strange happens? And instead, you ask me this? About Sebastian Eels?"

"I just wondered," I say, backed against the door, "why Sebastian Eels would think he'd sold his soul for Kraken gold when he was only twelve years old. That's all!"

Lady Kraken goes still.

She stares at me, her beaky mouth open in astonishment.

"I see," she says eventually. "Well, in that case, you may go, Mr Lemon."

"I may?"

"Yes," Lady Kraken slips into reverse and begins receding into the shadows. "Just remember, you are still my eyes and ears, Herbert Lemon. In my hotel, and out in the town. My eyes and ears. Now, go!"

The doors open behind me.

And I can't get out of there fast enough.

EMPTY BUCKET

VIOLET TURNS OUT NOT to be in the lobby, or even in my Lost-and-Foundery, and it takes some time to find her. But there she is, down on the beach, standing alone on the wet sand, just beyond the pier.

Staring out to sea.

I hurry down the steps to join her under the leaden, seagull-filled sky, a freshly left-over croissant – grabbed hastily from the kitchen on my escape from Lady Kraken – in each hand.

"You've heard that strange singing before, haven't you?" says Violet a little while later, as we munch together. "I can tell. But how is that possible?"

I reply with a shrug.

"Are you getting your memories back?"

"Not exactly," I admit. "But this isn't the first time we've come across something that I felt I'd experienced before. Remember Pandora from our Festergrimm adventure? I was almost sure I knew her somehow, even though that seemed impossible too."

Violet throws the last of her croissant into the air, where it is caught by a seagull with a scrap of blue plastic bag on his leg. This is Bagfoot, also from our Festergrimm adventure.

By now we are crunching our way beyond the shingle and out to the rock pools again. It's funny how in daylight the midwinter beach doesn't hold quite the same terror it does in the darkness of night. And yet, as I snatch my foot back from an invisible patch of quicksand, I'm reminded that Eerie Beach is always a dangerous place to be.

"Whatever the truth of it, one thing is sure," says Violet then, "Sebastian Eels knows more about you than he's letting on. Just as he knows more about me."

"You think there might be some connection?"

"Don't you, Herbie?" she replies. "People get lost in this town, but sometimes people get found. You are the Lost-and-Founder, and I am the girl who was found when her parents got lost. There does seem to be a bit of a theme."

"Your parents set off in a rowing boat to find you and were never seen again," I say, "but you're right not to give up hope, Vi. They could turn up again one day, no matter how impossible it must seem. *If the impossible is possible anywhere …*"

"*It'll be possible,*" Violet completes Erwin's quote, "*in Eerie-on-Sea.* Thank you, Herbie."

"Halloo-oo-oo!"

We hear a call on the wind, and look up to find a figure

advancing towards us across the sand – a figure made round with several coats, and multiple hats tied on her head with a piece of string.

"Hallooo!" Mrs Fossil calls again, as she reaches us. "Mornin', me dears."

"Hello, Mrs F," I reply. "How's the beachcombing today?" I add, eyeing her bucket, which she carries swinging at her side.

Mrs Fossil finds the most amazing things at low tide, and sells them, too, in her shop. So, it's always worth taking a peek in her bucket if you spot her out and about on the foreshore. But today, the beachcomber's cheery, snaggle-toothed grin fades at my question, as she holds out her bucket for us to see.

It's empty.

"Oh," says Violet. "Have you only just started?"

"Been at it for hours." Mrs F shakes her head, looking in the bucket herself, as if expecting something interesting to suddenly appear. "I don't understand it. I mean, I'm getting plenty of plastic tat," she adds, pulling a fistful of burst balloons and squashed water bottles from her voluminous pockets. "I always get that, and straight in the bin it goes. But there's nothing *good* out here. Not even a crumb of sea glass, or the ghost of an ammonite. Not even those bright yellow periwinkles I make into necklaces, and you *always* get those. Nothing but squat!"

"I remember when I first met you," says Violet. "It was

almost exactly a year ago, and you had treasures galore in your bucket that day."

"Oh!" Mrs F smiles again. "I remember it too! Like it was yesterday. Was so lovely to meet you, Violet, and to see that Herbie had a friend at last."

"Maybe the weather's not right?" I suggest, reddening. "For finding treasures on the beach, I mean."

"And *then* ..." Mrs Fossil ignores my attempt to change the subject ... "I found out who you were. *The* Violet Parma! Peter's little girl! Who I last held as a baby, snug in my coat, at midwinter time, all those years ago."

"Ah, yes." Violet looks a little embarrassed herself now. Then she adds brightly, "Did you ever want children of your own, Wendy?"

Mrs Fossil's face, which is as changeable as the sea, shifts again into a look I can barely describe. She stares at Violet before giving a single word in reply.

"Once."

A cold wind buffets us. Wendy Fossil holds her empty bucket in a hug.

And now I think everyone wants to change the subject!

I look out across the surf, to where the great iron wreck of the battleship *Leviathan* jags from the surging waters, inaccessible at all but the lowest tides. Something catches my eye on the beach – a point of aqua light. I run over and stoop to pick up a beautiful pebble of blue-green sea glass, large as a walnut and tide-rolled to random perfection. I hold it in my hand, marvelling that such treasures can be found in the world. Then I run back to the others.

"Oh, Herbie, that's a lovely bit." Mrs Fossil's eyes light up when she sees what I have. "Best thing I've seen on the beach all week. Clever boy! Gives me hope my luck will change."

"You can have it, Mrs F," I say.

And I drop the aqua gem in the beachcomber's bucket.

"Oh, thank you, thank you!" Mrs Fossil beams at us both. "Now at least I won't go home empty-handed. But home I shall go. Got some baking to do, eh, Herbie? Eh?" And she gives me such an exaggerated wink that it must look to Violet like we're up to something.

"Are you up to something?" Violet asks me as we watch Mrs Fossil make her way back up the beach.

I do an innocent grin.

"Eels has a boat," I say instead, with a glance at my watch. "Hidden among the rocks somewhere."

And I tell Violet what Lady Kraken told me.

"That must be where he'd been last night," says Violet. "I think we should take a look, don't you?"

It's an hour later, and I'm looking at my wristwatch again.

"We can't keep searching forever," I say as Vi and I clamber over yet another spur of rock beneath the cliffs, only to find yet another empty bank of shingle beyond it, and no sign of a hidden boat.

"What's the hurry?" Violet demands, "We've got all day, haven't we?"

"I do have a job to do, you know," I reply. "And the tide's coming in already."

I look back towards the town, which is now hidden beyond a bend in the coastline. The base of the cliffs we're searching is covered in water at high tide, which is *not* a reassuring thought! By now we have climbed way beyond where anyone sensible would go, and we have nothing to show for it. I'm just about to start properly protesting when we climb another rocky spur and finally come across a cave. And from the mouth of the cave tumbles a shingle bank that would be the perfect place to pull up a small vessel.

"This must be it!" says Vi, looking down at a gully that still has seawater in it, despite the low tide. "Where Eels hides his boat."

"Could be," I concede. "No boat here now, though. Maybe he's taken it out?" I add, wishing I'd thought of this earlier and saved us a lot of bother and climbing.

"We should still take a quick look in that cave," says Violet, predictably, "since we're here."

I cast another nervous glimpse at my watch, and then follow as Violet slides down the seaweedy rock to the cave.

Actually, *cave* isn't the best word, I realize when we get there. It's more of a deep cavern, sheltered from the elements, where so much shingle has been piled by the waves that it would never get flooded. We find here, among the driftwood, several empty wooden crates. A couple of these have been placed side by side to make a rough workbench. And on that bench are tools, cables, a battery lamp and the remains of several recent meals.

"Bingo!" cries Vi, her voice echoing in the cavern. "Eels' secret hideout."

"I doubt it's that secret." I shrug. "There are smugglers' caves all along the base of these cliffs. The fisherfolk know them all."

"There's no way out of this one, except by the sea," Vi points out, looking up at the solid rock wall at the end of the cavern. "You'd get stuck here, Herbie. If the tide came in."

And that's when a sound reaches us.

It's the roar of an engine.

We look around, and out in the bay – approaching fast – we see a motorboat.

"Oops," says Vi, winning the prize for understatement.

Even at a distance there's no mistaking the tall, brooding form of Sebastian Eels, standing at the wheel of his boat. Powering straight towards us.

NO LAW AGAINST MAGIC

FOR A MOMENT I THINK we're going to have to hide behind the workbench, and I don't like our chances of staying concealed there. But Violet runs instead towards a hump of rock that sticks up from the shingle bank, just inside the entrance of the cavern. I follow, and in a few seconds we've thrown ourselves behind it, though we need to lie flat on the pebbles to stay out of sight.

"Newer, braver Herbie," Violet hisses to me, "remember?"

I do a desperate thumbs-up that Fluffy Mike would be proud of.

We hear the final roar of the boat arriving, beaching on the stones, then the sound of Sebastian Eels jumping out and crunching up the shingle in the cavern, pulling a length of rope. He goes behind the workbench and threads the rope through an iron ring set into the rock there. Using an electric winch on the back of the boat, he begins to pull the vessel out of the water.

I look at Vi, lying flat in the dark beside me. I see a gleam from her eye as she looks back. We cannot make a single move without giving ourselves away, so we have no chance to escape while Eels is here.

Which is why it's so very annoying when he shows no sign of leaving at all. He fetches a few things from his craft, and opens the bag he brought with him. He takes something out and slips it onto his head.

It's a metal band, like a crown of bright silver.

Sebastian Eels turns, holding the gleaming band in place over his temples with the tips of his fingers, and stares out to sea.

What, by all that's bonkers, is he doing? And can he finish soon, please? I can feel a cramp creeping up my left leg!

Still wearing the silver band, Eels sinks down on the shingle, till he's sitting, legs apart. He puts his head in his hands.

I cast a desperate look at Violet, and see that she's as bemused as I am.

What *is* he doing?

Then we hear a sound.

It's echoey, the sound, so maybe I'm mistaken. But if I *wasn't* mistaken, I'd say that sound – which we hear again now – was something very like a sob.

I look at Vi again, to check it's not her, but she just blinks at me in equal confusion.

We look back at Sebastian Eels.

It wasn't *him*, was it?

Crying?

And yet, even as we watch, captivated by the astonishing sight, I see the shoulders of our arch-enemy heave, his face hidden behind his hands. Then, after a final gasp, he rubs his eyes and sits back. Sebastian Eels removes the silver band and in a moment his face is composed once again.

I move my leg.

I can't help it; my cramp is getting really bad!

My leg moves a second time, despite the urgent signals from my brain for it to do no such thing, and a single pebble rolls down the shingle bank.

Eels snaps his head in our direction, and peers into the dark.

I go still, despite the pain, but the damage has been done. Sebastian Eels gets to his feet.

"Who is there?"

And suddenly I know for sure that we are going to get caught here, in a dead-end cavern, by our mortal enemy. As if to ensure this very outcome, my leg gives an almighty twitch, and about a million pebbles slide down into the sea. I'm just thinking desperately that if we both run – or hop, in my case – maybe at least one of us will be able to escape, when Violet does what Violet always does in sticky situations like this: namely, the unexpected. And in this case, the unexpected thing she does is stand up.

"Caught you!" she says, looking at Eels defiantly.

"What?" The man goggles back at her, disbelieving. "But I – I caught *you*!"

"And me," I say, getting to my feet, and rubbing my sore leg. "Ow!"

"We heard you," Violet says, still looking defiant. "You can't deny it. We heard you..." She stops, as if unable to believe what she is about to say.

"Crying," I add, helpfully. But when I see the look on Eels' face, I think that maybe I shouldn't have.

Beneath his scruffy black hair – which is streaked with more grey now than it was when he and Violet first crossed paths a year ago – the eyes of Sebastian Eels go hard with anger.

"You think this is all a game, don't you?" Eels says, keeping his eyes on us and reaching for his workbench. His hand closes on the haft of a long adjustable spanner. "Child's play. But you don't know me at all. You never have. You know *nothing* about me!"

He begins walking towards us, swinging his makeshift weapon.

"Wait!" says Vi, holding up her hands. Amazingly, Eels stops. "We – we know you are in a lot of trouble, that you've stolen things, hurt people, lied and cheated. Do you really want to make things worse by threatening a couple of kids?"

"If you two pipsqueaks know all that," Eels replies, "then perhaps you know too much..."

He starts forward again, menacingly.

"Kraken gold!" I cry.

I suppose, strictly speaking, I should cry those words as part of a sentence – you know, with grammar and stuff – but in all the excitement they just sort of burst out on their own and echo around the cavern.

"What did you say?" Eels demands in a shocked tone, stumbling to a halt once more.

"*When I was only twelve years old,*" I recite from memory, in the unsqueakiest voice I can manage, "*I sold my soul for Kraken gold.* Or rather, *you* did."

Sebastian Eels clutches the front of his coat as if he is choking.

"How – how do you know about *that?*"

"Does it matter how we know?" Violet shoots back, trying to hit home now I've accidentally caught the man off guard. "Whatever it means, we can tell it's true just by your reaction. And it will all catch up with you in the end. Things always do. They say you've even committed…"

But Violet stops, unable to quite bring herself to say it, even though I'm sure all three of us hear the unspoken word *murder* in our heads.

Several expressions pass over Eels' face in quick succession – from shock to fear to disbelief to just plain feeling sick in the stomach. But then the man's face resolves itself into a single look of fixed fury.

"You're so convinced of my villainy," he spits, "but are you really so sure you have it the right way around? There are many, especially among the fisherfolk, who think *I* am a hero in this town."

"If you have done that most terrible thing," Violet declares, pointing an accusing finger, "then you can *never* be a hero."

Eels shrinks back as if Violet's words hurt him more than anything she could physically throw. He looks at the spanner in his hands and then flings it down onto the shingle as if it had suddenly become white-hot.

"No!" says Eels. "No, there *is* a way. A way to fix things. Fix even that. If..."

But he stops himself.

"If what?" Violet demands. She still sounds like someone put her in charge of this whole situation – which is pretty amazing when you think about it, though very Violet – but I can also see confusion in her face and hear doubt creep into her voice.

"If –" Eels stares at his hands as if talking to them now, and not us – "if, when you *did* kill someone, you could bring them back again to life."

"What?" Vi gasps. And right now, I'd say she's gasping for the both of us.

"Would that still count as murder?" Eels, looking up, seems to be genuinely interested in our answer. "*Real* murder, I mean. If you could magic them back? It'd be a little *inconvenient*, I grant you – for the killed person, that is – but it's not *that* bad, is it? It's not like it's even illegal, since the law doesn't recognize the existence of magic. And no court could convict a murderer if the apparent murder victim could be brought back again later, alive and well..."

He trails off, looking at us with a pleading light in his eyes.

"Bladderwracks!" I whisper. "Sebastian Eels, what have you done?"

"Of course it's bad!" Violet cries before Eels can reply. "It's horrible!"

The light in Eels' eyes changes.

"I might have known Peter Parma's daughter wouldn't understand. Too holier-than-thou! But here's one thing you should consider: if I did have the power to return someone from the dead, I might not be able to resist getting rid of you pair of shrimps for a week or two, and only bring you back later when you can't interfere with my plans. What do you think of *that*?"

"You're mad!" Violet shouts, her commanding tone crumbling finally in the face of such utter bonkersness. But, mad or not, Eels dives for the adjustable spanner.

"Run!" I shout.

And then we are crashing down the shingle beach in a storm of pebbles, and throwing ourselves over the slippery rocks, and running and running, back towards the town, and safety.

THE DAY OF THE BERTH

BY THE TIME we reach the town steps, we have run ourselves empty. We climb to the top, gasping for breath and looking fearfully over our shoulders, but the beach is empty. Sebastian Eels, for all we know, is still in his dingy cavern.

"Unbelievable!" says Vi as we slump, exhausted, on the seawall. "He's really lost the plot this time."

"Unless..." I start.

"Unless what?"

"Unless that's the Deepest Secret of Eerie-on-Sea," I say, wondering at the idea. "Some enchanted gizmo or other that brings people back from the dead?"

"I suppose," says Vi, but she's shaking her head as she says it. Our time in this strange little town has shown us that the normal rules of nature don't always apply here, but a magical object with the power over life and death? That seems too far-fetched even for Eerie-on-Sea. "Or maybe he's finally lost all grip on reality," she adds. "I'm not sure we can take anything that Eels says seriously any more, Herbie."

"Agreed," I reply. "We'll just have to keep well out of his way from now on, that's all."

Then I glance at my watch. "Wowzers!" I cry, seeing the time. "We have to go!"

"Do we? Can't we just lie low in your Lost-and-Foundery for a bit, and talk about it all over snacks?"

"Nope!" I say. "We have to go somewhere, Violet. *Right now!*"

And so, that's how we end up wending our way through the narrow streets of the town, putting the beach, and our weird experience, behind us. It has started snowing again – big, fat flakes this time – muffling all to silence. The windows of the seaside houses glow with the warmth of indoor light as snow settles on the sills and shutters. We hurry along, our breath puffing out as sparkling clouds, silently praying that we don't bump into Sebastian Eels again for a very long time.

"What's the hurry, Herbie?" Violet demands. "Where are we going?"

"It's just a thing," I reply, in my vaguest way, "that we can't be late for. That's all."

"What *kind* of thing?" Violet demands, but I just press on, jogging up the last flight of steps that lead into Dolphin Square.

"Are we going to the bookshop?" Violet asks as we cross the square. The bronze dolphin in its centre grins his chilly grin as we pass. "It doesn't look like there's anyone in."

"Doesn't it?" I reply, though we can both see that the windows of the Eerie Book Dispensary are dark and empty. "Oh well, never mind."

"Actually, that's a bit weird," Violet says, looking concerned. "Jenny should be there. It's not closing time yet. I hope nothing's happened!"

Even close to, we can't see much inside the book dispensary. The snow is getting heavier, and the short day is ending. And yet, a little light from somewhere manages to gleam in the glass eyes of the mermonkey, sitting almost invisible in the dark of the shop window, waiting for some unwary reader to dare to throw a coin in its hat.

"I don't even have *my key*!" Violet slaps her coat pockets then, as she suddenly realizes this. "Oh, Herbie, I left it in your basement. But I didn't think I would be *locked out* of my own home."

"You aren't, Vi," I reassure her. "Look!"

With a final glance at my watch to see that it's 4 p.m. exactly, I turn the handle and open the bookshop door.

And I indicate "after you" to Violet.

"Why are you being so funny today?" Violet looks at me with great suspicion. "I've got a good mind to go off looking for Jenny right now—"

"No, no, no," I insist, grabbing Violet by the elbows and steering her up the steps and into the book dispensary.

Which is dark.

And cold, with no fire roaring in the hearth.

And yet, weirdly, the place doesn't feel empty. There's even a faint shuffling sound from somewhere, and something else that might be the squeak of a wellington boot.

"Herbie!" Violet whispers, alarmed. Then …

… the bookshop lights come on in a sudden blaze.

"SURPRISE!" comes the roar of a collective voice, and we see that everyone is there: Jenny Hanniver, in a glittery shawl; Dr Thalassi, in the tartan bow tie he keeps for the very best occasions; Mrs Fossil, only wearing one hat now, though a good one, with a party feather in it; Blaze Westerley with his Uncle Squint, neither of whom look like they go to parties in bookshops much, but who seem delighted to be at one now. Amber Griss is there too, clapping and saying "Surprise!" and "Happy Berthday, Violet!" with the rest of them. And even some of the regular hotel guests have come – the Colonel and Mrs Crabwise are waving cheerily – along with many neighbours, fisherfolk and faithful customers of the Eerie Book Dispensary who have particularly warmed to the "book girl" who has spent the last year helping them retrieve the tomes dispensed by the famous mermonkey.

Last but not least, Erwin is there too – sickly-looking still, but bravely sitting on the mantelpiece as the lights of an enormous Christmas tree flicker on.

The doc throws a match on a well-laid fire in the hearth, which roars into life, and the guests part to reveal a table groaning with party food: cake, sandwiches, nibbles, cake, carrot sticks, more cake and large jugs of fruit punch and mulled wine. Also, there is cake! In fact, there is an especially large Victoria sponge in the centre of it all, covered in violet-coloured buttercream letters, spelling:

HAPPY
BERTHDAY
VIOLET

"Wow." Violet blinks as if unsure what to say. "I'm not sure what to say. Except…"

"What?" asks Jenny Hanniver, coming over and wrapping her in a huge hug. "You don't mind surprises, do you?"

"No, but …" Violet manages to reply from somewhere inside the hug, "it isn't actually my birthday."

"Not *birth*day," says Uncle Squint, with a knowing wink at his nephew. *Berth*day."

"That's what I said," says Violet. "Isn't it?"

"They mean BERTH-day," I grin, pointing at the cake. "As in B-*E*-R-T-H."

"A berth is the place where you moor your boat," says Blaze, looking like he can't believe he has to explain. "*And* the place where a sailor hangs her hammock aboard it. It's a tradition with us fisherfolk to celebrate a 'berthday', when someone new comes to town and earns our respect. This is your first berthday party, Violet, so many happy returns! To your *berth*, that is."

"Exactly." Jenny laughs, and everyone else joins in with cheers. "And you certainly found your berth here, Violet. A year ago tonight."

"Well!" I say, feeling that a *little* extra detail is called for. "It's certainly a year since she sneaked in through my basement window and made my life a lot more interesting than it was. But it's quite an honour, Vi, if the fisherfolk want to throw you a proper berthday party. I never got one!"

"Aye, well –" Uncle Squint peers at me piratically – "'tis true, young Herbie, and no doubt we should. We fishers haven't always been as welcoming of outsiders as we could be. But we owe this young lady something special after Gargantis woke last winter, and everything changed for us. She has earned her place in Eerie, and no mistake."

And there's an *arr* of agreement from all the fisherfolk there.

Violet looks like she might actually explode, though in a good way. She rushes over to Uncle Squint and throws her arms around him, making him go an interesting shade of sea-pink.

"Now, now," says the old sailor, patting Violet awkwardly on the shoulder. "Less of that, missy, or you'll be getting me all misty in the eye, and that won't do."

"Can we eat now?" I ask, already holding a paper plate. "I can't help noticing there's cake."

And that's when the party really gets started.

"I'm amazed all these people are here," Violet says to me.

"People love you, Vi," I reply, giving Uncle Squint the side-eye as he loads his plate. "Come and have something to eat while you still can."

Soon the party is in full swing, and even Erwin brightens up a little bit.

"Sebastian Eels isn't here, though," says Violet, with a wink at me, just as I'm manoeuvring a second slice of berthday cake towards my tonsils.

"Not funny!" I splutter, spraying crumbs everywhere.

By now Mrs Fossil has got her hurdy-gurdy out, and a jaunty sea jig fills the air as people begin to dance.

Then a bulky shadow falls over us.

"Congratulations!" says a booming voice, and we look up to see that Professor Newtiss has somehow wangled an invitation to Violet's party too.

"So much local culture!" he says, his plate piled with sausage rolls and his beard full of crumbs. "We'll definitely cover this 'berthday' business in an episode of the podcast. So quaint! But first," he adds, steering us away from the heart of the party, "I wondered if you'd managed to find out anything?"

By now we're standing beside the mermonkey, sitting strange and hairy in the snowy window.

"A little," Violet replies, before explaining to the professor about Sebastian Eels' hidden boat.

"Good work." He nods, seemingly genuinely impressed. "And you, Herbie? You went to see Lady Kraken, didn't you?

She refuses to see me. That was the perfect moment for you to find out about Kraken gold."

"I did," I say. "But – I didn't."

"Hmm." The professor regards me doubtfully, before popping another sausage roll into his mouth. "You need to try harder. Both of you. No one will tell us outsiders a thing about it."

Just then Fluffy Mike walks slowly past us in his enormous headphones, his face bathed in light from an extraordinary gadget slung over his shoulder. It has a smaller version of the screen of jumping green lines we saw yesterday, and a control unit covered in knobs and dials. In one hand the sound man holds a radar microphone – attached to the device by a coily flex – which he sweeps from side to side as he disappears into the back of the shop.

"A portable Eerie Hum detector!" The professor chuckles. "What will Angela come up with next, eh? We'll be taking it out onto the beach later, all the way to the wreck."

"You mustn't!" Violet hisses. "It's too dangerous. The malamander is real! You have to stay away."

"Ah." Professor Newtiss sighs. "Shame I wasn't recording that. Would have made a great quote for the episode. But anyway, keep digging, you two. Don't forget, I have information for you if you can find out more for me."

And he pats the pocket of his tweed jacket, where, I guess, his notebook must be.

"Wait…" I start to say, but the professor strolls off, taking his "information" – and what's left of the sausage rolls – with him.

"They saw a sprightning, didn't they?" Violet turns to me. "How can he be so sure there's no such thing as magic? Herbie, they are going to get themselves eaten!"

But, before I can reply, Jenny comes over and leads Violet back to the crowds to mingle. Leaving me alone with the mermonkey.

And my cake.

At last!

But it's just as I'm taking a really big bite that I see something. There, reflected in the shiny metal plate on the back of the mermonkey's antique typewriter, is me and my cake. But behind us, looking over my shoulder, is a face!

The reflected face of someone peering in through the shop window. A pale face, with something indescribable in his eyes.

It's too late to abort the bite, so I splutter on cake again, sending bits of it shooting out in all directions as I spin round to look.

"Herbie!" says Amber Griss, who was just coming over to chat and who gets crumbs all over her party frock instead. "Honestly!"

"Forry!" I reply, brushing down the front of my uniform. I put my plate down and head to the window, pressing my face to the glass. There is nothing out there now but the silent tumble of snow.

"What is it?" says Amber.

"I thought I saw someone," I explain, though that's not quite true – I *definitely* saw someone.

"Really?" the receptionist replies. "Who?"

I shrug. I'm not quite sure what to make of it. With everything that's happened today, my money would be on Sebastian Eels peering in on a party he'd never be invited to. But as I glance up at the mermonkey, grinning down at me, hunched and terrible at its typewriter, I realize he must have seen the face too. And I reckon we both know it wasn't Sebastian Eels.

THE MERMONKEY'S PAW

I'VE BEEN TO A FEW PARTIES in the Eerie Book Dispensary in my time. Jenny says that bookshops and parties go together like custard and cream, and you won't find me disagreeing. Vi's berthday party is probably the best one yet, though, and it takes a long time for people to start leaving. But leave they finally do, muffling up against the weather and waving happily as they trudge off through the snow to their homes. Soon there only remains Jenny, the doc, Mrs Fossil, Vi and me.

"And Erwin," says Violet, gathering up the cat in her arms. "Poor puss. Still not yourself, are you?"

There's a lot of tidying to do. There's also only one slice of berthday cake left, but even I don't dare take that, so I start edging away from the table. Unfortunately, Dr Thalassi sees me and blocks my escape. He lowers his caterpillar brows and nods towards the mess, rolling up his own sleeves. I sigh and pick up a stray balloon.

"Thank you so much for everything," Violet says, helping Mrs Fossil to clear the plates. "I especially love your Christmas tree."

"Oh, I am glad," Mrs F grins. "But it's your tree now."

The tree in question is a white, salt-bleached thing set in the corner to one side of the fireplace. It was obviously in the sea a good while before Mrs F rescued it, and has long-since lost its bark and needles. But the shape is unmistakable. And now it's covered in dozens of colourful little decorations that Mrs Fossil has made herself from beachcombed bits: snippets of fishing net, sea-glass gems and driftwood, all tangled through with an old garland of coloured lights.

"It washed up months back," Mrs Fossil says. "I thought it would be festive, what with midwinter almost here *and* Christmas coming up."

"There's just one more thing left to do, Violet," says Jenny Hanniver then, taking the plates from Violet's hands, "to make this a proper berthday."

"Really?" says Violet.

"Of course," Jenny replies. "You must consult the mermonkey. This is a special occasion. As you begin your second year in the town, aren't you curious to see what book the mermonkey chooses for you?"

"I thought it wasn't working properly." Violet eyes the creature across the room with concern. "Like lots of things round here lately."

"I called in earlier," says Dr Thalassi, helping himself to

another glass of mulled wine now that the party doesn't seem to be quite over. "With my tool bag. Had a little tinker with the brute. Should be functioning normally again now. If you can ever call a mermonkey 'normal' that is."

"Thanks again, Doctor," Jenny says. "I've had those podcast people asking about it too. They want to come and film me operating the mermonkey tomorrow," she adds, fiddling self-consciously with her hair. "I ought to have the old thing running at its best for that. Apparently it will help them get 'clicks' and 'likes', whatever they are."

"Do you think there's something brewing?" Violet asks then, exchanging glances with me. "In the town? It feels like things are changing, and not in a good way."

"Only thing I can sense brewing is a nice cup of tea." Mrs Fossil gives us her snaggle-toothed grin. "Who wants one?"

But Violet isn't in the mood for tea. Instead, she walks round to face the mermonkey, which sits as still and hairy as ever, one hand poised over the keyboard of its typewriter, the other holding out its top hat for a donation.

"It does seem like a big moment," Violet agrees.

"Here." Jenny comes over with the tip jar full of coins from the bookshop counter. "Help yourself."

And now everyone gathers around, as people always do when they witness the functioning of the marvellous, mechanical mermonkey. There is something endlessly fascinating about what is about to happen, and a sense that no one – not even Jenny – really knows how it happens at all.

Violet fishes out a coin.

"Make a wish," says Mrs Fossil, "as you throw the coin in. That's what I always do."

"Really?" Violet says.

Jenny nods. Violet holds out the coin, but pauses.

"Herbie, do it with me," she says then, beckoning me over. "Hold the coin too, and let's make the wish together."

"It's your moment, Vi," I reply.

"But I owe you a lot for making my year unforgettable. And it seems like a moment I want to share."

"OK." I shrug. "But does the mermonkey work like that? *Shared* books, I mean?"

I look up at the mechanical creature. It grins down at me with tombstone teeth and glass-bulb eyes, and somehow that seems like answer enough.

I hold the coin with Violet.

"Ready, Herbie?" she whispers. "On the count of three… One…"

I close my eyes and make a wish. I can feel Violet making hers beside me.

"Two…"

Suddenly it occurs to me that we are probably both wishing for the same thing.

"Three!" Violet cries.

And, together, we let go of the coin.

There's a thud.

Not a very impressive one.

I open one eye to see that the coin has missed!

Well, not exactly missed, but it has hit the rim of the top hat and looks like it is about to drop over the side. But then, almost as if the hat has been tipped slightly to keep the coin in play – which can only have been done by the mermonkey itself – the coin starts to roll. It makes a complete orbit of the rim of the hat, before plopping down into the black hole in the middle.

There's a moment of silence.

Then we hear a *click*.

With a series of ratchety, clatchety sounds, the mermonkey's hairy arm judders up and up until it places the hat upon its head. The coin rattles down into the mechanism inside, and the creature's eye bulbs light up.

For one long, suspenseful moment the mermonkey stares right into our eyes, one after the other, as if checking that it can really see what it thinks it sees there.

Then it lets out a terrible scream.

The creature reaches out one crooked paw and starts to type, crashing its index finger down with great deliberation onto the keys.

Click!

Clack!

CLICK!

"It's really going for it!" I shout, to be heard over the noise.

"Noisier than ever!" Violet agrees as the mermonkey jabs the keys with increasing force.

The screaming grows louder and louder, and soon the creature's head is wreathed in acrid smoke.

"What's happening?" cries Mrs Fossil, her hands over her ears. "Oh help, it's going wrong!"

Then fire – *actual flames!* – erupts from the mermonkey's neck.

"Get back!" yells Dr Thalassi. He lunges forward and pulls Violet and me behind him.

The mermonkey is hammering on the typewriter with both paws now, with both *fists*, balled as if in fury. And it shrieks like it's actually burning to death. Jenny dives to pull the plug from the wall, while the doc hoicks a small fire extinguisher out from behind the bookshop counter and shoots a spout of foam over the blazing machine.

With a few final mechanical heaves, the mermonkey judders to a stop. One eye bulb blows out with a *POP!* The other stays alight, but grows dimmer and dimmer until it fades to nothing. Then the mermonkey, white with foam but also black with soot, slumps forward over the typewriter as if dead.

THE VERY LAST SLICE

THE SHOCKED SILENCE that follows the mermonkey's spectacular demise is suddenly broken by a loud *PING!* as the battered typewriter ejects the prescription card the mechanical creature had been typing on.

The card flutters uncertainly around the room, till it lands on top of Mrs Fossil's Christmas tree and wedges there, next to the star.

"Are you all right?" Jenny gasps as Vi and I cower in the bow window. "Anyone hurt?"

"Only that poor beast," says Mrs Fossil, pointing to the stricken mermonkey. "Oh, what happened?"

"I fear," says Dr Thalassi, "that despite my best efforts, the old thing has finally given up the ghost. It was always likely to happen, Jenny, what with it being so very old. Didn't I always say it would be better to retire the machine to the museum, and find some kind of modern replacement?"

"It *can't* be replaced," Jenny wails, approaching the

mermonkey cautiously, her arms out as if she wants to give it a hug. "It's ruined!"

"It can be fixed though, can't it?" says Violet, who looks almost as distraught as Jenny at this sudden, catastrophic loss. The mermonkey is such an essential part of Eerie-on-Sea life that the thought of doing without it seems impossible.

"We'll get it cleaned up and see," says Dr Thalassi, putting an arm around Jenny's shoulders and giving her an encouraging squeeze. "Maybe it's not as bad as it looks. Remember last summer? When that tourist child filled its hat with bubble-gum ice cream? We fixed it after that, didn't we?"

"What about the card?" I say, pointing to it but unable to quite reach.

Jenny plucks it from the top of the Christmas tree, and shakes her head at what she sees there.

"I'm sorry." She hands the card to Violet. "You'll have to try again when it's fixed."

Violet stares at the card in her hand – the prescription card the mermonkey types its book code onto. But instead of the usual orderly code telling you which floor of the shop your book is on, then which room, then which wall in that room, then which shelf, and *then* – with a final number – which book on that shelf has been chosen for you, the card is a sooty, smudgy mess. And in the centre, hammered into the card with enormous force, is a jumble of meaningless letters:

Or maybe not *completely* meaningless.

"MRDEMDUS…" I say, trying to read the card over Vi's shoulder. "MERMUSDER … or is it…?"

Then I gasp as I see it – a word in the chaos. And like the song in the Eerie Hum, this is a word I've heard before.

"Mer-med-us-a," I say in a hushed whisper.

There's a crash from the fireplace. We all turn, startled, to find that Erwin has jumped off and run deep into the shop, leaving a broken wine glass on the hearth.

"What is a mermedusa?" Violet asks, but I suddenly realize – despite the strange sense of recognition – that I am entirely unable to answer.

"I've never heard of such a thing," says Dr Thalassi, in a voice that suggests he hates having to admit as much.

"Neither have I," Jenny agrees.

"Sounds a bit scary," Mrs Fossil adds. "Like a creature of some kind."

I get a brief flash of memory in my mind – an image of two dark eyes surrounded by a halo of hair-like tendrils. The face that I've been seeing in my queasy moments. I shake my head clear and find that Violet is watching me with a significant look. She and I will need to talk about all this. I slip the mermonkey card into my pocket for later.

By now the party mood has vanished altogether.

The ruined mermonkey is covered by a cloth, and we get back to the tedious business of clearing up.

"I was wondering," Violet says as we're finishing, "is there somewhere I can find out more about Sebastian Eels? About his childhood, I mean?"

"Oh, Violet!" Jenny throws her hands up in despair. "Why do you want to know about him? Haven't we been through enough with that man over the last year? You just need to stay away from him."

"Yes, but..."

"It's that professor, isn't it?" Jenny continues. "He was asking me about Eels too. I don't think we should tell him anything, just for some silly podcast."

"But what if I *needed* to know?" Violet insists. "What if I needed to find out about something that happened to Eels when he was a boy? When he was, say, twelve years old?"

Mrs Fossil and the rest stop what they are doing and look at Vi. The doc's cup of hot wine pauses just in front of his mouth.

"Why would you need to know that?" says Jenny quietly.

"So, something did happen!" cries Vi. "I knew it."

"Now, look," the doc growls. "Eels may be a trouble-maker, but he at least deserves some respect for the tragedy that befell his family."

"Tragedy?" Vi and I say together.

"I don't suppose it can hurt if they know," says Jenny then, with a sigh. "But you mustn't repeat it, especially to these pod people. It was a long time ago, anyway. The fact is, Violet, Sebastian Eels wasn't an only child. He had a sister once. And, from what I've been told, when Eels was twelve, his sister died."

Violet looks at me, amazed. "I – I didn't know."

"Well, why should you?" says Mrs Fossil. "Horrid business, but all in the past and long forgotten now."

"I doubt Sebastian has forgotten," says Jenny, with a brief look of compassion on her face, and I remember that she and Eels were friends once.

"How did it happen?" Violet asks, but the doc shakes his head.

"Enough," he says firmly. "The details are private, I expect. This was years before I came to town, so there's no point asking me, anyway."

"Nor me," says Jenny. "Before my time too."

"Well, I was here." Mrs Fossil rocks on her wellies as if uncomfortable with the subject. "But Eels was never one of my friends. He didn't even go to the school here in Eerie. There's only one person I can think of who knew Eels at the time, though I'm not sure even they were best childhood buddies."

"Who's that?" I ask.

"Him, up at the hotel," says Mrs F. "Godfrey. Though I wouldn't go asking him about it, miserable old coot."

"What?" My cap nearly flies off my head. "Godfrey? Godfrey Mollusc? You mean Sebastian Eels was friends with *Mr Mollusc*? As *children*? I didn't think Mr Mollusc was ever a child. I thought he just popped into existence one rainy day, already annoying and old!"

"That's a mean thing to say, Herbie," says Jenny, suppressing a smirk. "I know Mr Mollusc is a grumpy sort, and I imagine it's not much fun working for him ..."

"Pfft!" I go, folding my arms.

"... but he was as young as you once. You might even have got along with each other if you had been boys together. I always got the feeling he had a sad and difficult childhood."

"I don't think he likes *me*, anyway," says Violet. "I doubt he'd have come to my birth— sorry, *berth*day party, even if you'd invited him."

"We did invite him, didn't we?" says Dr Thalassi then, helping himself to yet another cup of mulled wine. "We invited everyone – all the hotel staff."

"Yes, but I'm not surprised he didn't come," Jenny replies. "Anyway, let's please talk of happier things."

But I don't hear what those happier things might be because my mind is suddenly full of something else.

"Herbie?"

I hear my name being called, and I realize it has been called a few times and I haven't responded.

"Hmm?" I reply, returning to the room.

"Are you all right?" Jenny asks. "You were staring out of the shop window like you'd seen a ghost."

I want to reply "Maybe I did", but I decide it's easier to ask a question of my own.

"I wonder," I say, "if maybe I, er, could perhaps take that last slice of berthday cake, please?"

Jenny laughs. "Haven't you had enough already?"

"It's not for me," I add quickly. "I think maybe there's someone who would like it."

And before anyone can say anything to dissuade me, I slide the last piece of Victoria sponge onto a clean paper plate and cover it with a bowl. With cheery nods to all, I pull on my coat and leave the bookshop, with Violet running to catch me up.

"Herbie, what are you doing?" she says as we head back across Dolphin Square.

"I have an idea," I reply. "A weird one, it's true. But I think this last slice of cake might just be the key to something."

And I tell her about the face at the window as we head down the snowy stone steps, back towards the Grand Nautilus Hotel.

WHAT MOLLUSCS
LIKE BEST

"YOU SAW HIM?"

I nod. "In a way, I think maybe I saw him properly for the first time."

"Mr Mollusc? Looking in through the window?" Violet clearly can't believe what I'm saying. "At *my* berthday party?"

"And the expression on his face," I say, "made him look like…"

"Like what?"

"Like – like someone who, deep down – and maybe sometimes not so deep down – like someone who wishes he was someone else," I reply. "If you see what I mean."

"I'm not sure I do," replies Vi, and we walk the rest of the way in silence.

When we reach the hotel, I take a moment to straighten my uniform and set my cap straight. Violet still looks disbelieving about this whole situation, but she makes an effort to look a bit smarter, too.

Then we walk up the main steps and through the great revolving doors of the Grand Nautilus Hotel.

"Herbie!" says Amber Griss, smiling a greeting from behind the vast reception desk. She's still wearing a little paper hat from the party. "Violet! Hello again. I'd be careful if I were you. Especially you, Herbie. Mr Mollusc is in one of his moods."

"I know," I say. "Actually, and I can't believe I'm asking this, but do you know where old Moll— I mean, where *Mr* Mollusc is? We've, um, we've brought him a slice of berthday cake."

Amber's eyebrows spring up so high her specs slip down her nose.

"Really, Herbie," she says, pushing them back up with one perfectly manicured finger, "this is not the time for one of your tricks."

"It's no trick," I say. "Lost-and-Founder's honour. I'll just go straight to his office, shall I?"

Amber shakes her head, then points with her pen towards the dining room, still looking like she thinks I'm making a huge mistake.

I put my head round the dining room door. The great room is empty now, unless you count large tropical plants and a lingering whiff of this evening's dinner. Well, almost empty. At a second glance I see that someone is sitting alone at a private window seat, looking out across the snowy pier.

It's Mr Mollusc.

And beside him is a half-empty whisky bottle and a completely empty glass.

I push the door, wincing as it creaks. Mr Mollusc looks round but doesn't react – his eyes are concealed in the shadow beneath his brow. His moustache does twitch, though. Twice.

I suppress a gulp. And the urge to try one of my grins. It's hard to believe, I know, but I sometimes wonder if *all* my grins annoy the manager one way or another. Vi and I walk over and stand before the table.

"These seats are taken," says Mr Mollusc, in a low and dangerous voice, even though they obviously aren't. "Now, get back to work!"

"It's past closing time at the Lost-and-Foundery, sir," I say. "And I, well, *we*, brought you this."

I put the plate on the table in front of him. Violet takes the bowl off, revealing the sugary treasure within.

"It's a piece of berthday cake," Vi explains. "From my berthday party. I'm – that is, *we're* – sorry you couldn't come."

Mr Mollusc looks at the paper plate.

The slice of cake, a bit squished now after being carried across town, looks back at him.

Mr Mollusc gets to his feet. Slowly.

"Is this your idea of *fun*, boy?" he asks me, his voice quieter and more threatening than ever. "Is this your idea," he adds, "of a *joke*?"

I shrink back a bit, and so does Vi. We must have been mad to think this would work!

"We're just trying to be nice," says Violet. "That's the last slice and everything."

Mr Mollusc clenches his fists. Both veins in his forehead begin to pulse, and even I've never seen a double-barrelled eruption from the hotel manager before.

"We just thought it was a shame you couldn't be there!" I blurt-squeak. "What with all your hard work at the hotel, sir. We just thought it wasn't *fair*!"

Mollusc towers over us now, trembling, eyes bulging from their sockets.

"*What* did you say?" he hisses.

"Fair, sir. It's not fair that you missed the cake. But, if you really don't want it, I suppose I *could* take it on myself. Just to help out…"

Mr Mollusc slams his hand down between me and the plate of cake, making me leap back.

"*You?*" he says. "*You* thought that? About *me*?"

"I thought it too!" says Vi, closer to a squeak of her own than I've ever heard.

Slowly, and with a stiffness seemingly brought on by confusion and disbelief, Mr Mollusc slumps back into his chair.

"Cake fork?" I suggest, sliding one across the snowy-white tablecloth. "Or would you prefer to spoon it? It's quite sticky."

Mr Mollusc picks up the silver cake fork as if it's a priceless artefact he has just discovered in an ancient tomb. He stares at the slice of cake. Then he swoops in, scoops up a big bit, and shoves it in beneath his moustache in one large golollop.

Then Mr Mollusc looks up at the ceiling and closes his eyes, and his tongue goes round and round his chops, in case he has left any outside, and a peaceful smile comes over his face as he says, "Berthday cake!"

It doesn't take long for the last slice of Violet's cake to depart this world. Soon Mr Mollusc is scraping the paper plate to get every last crumb. The cake fork, by the time it's finally put down, is licked so clean it could be put straight back in the cutlery trolley, and no one would know (but don't worry, I won't).

The hotel manager sits back and shakes his head.

"The best cake," he says, "I believe I have *ever* tasted."

Then he fixes us both with a narrow eye, as if he just remembered we are there, and his mouth starts to twitch.

A strange sound emerges from Mr Mollusc's throat, and I begin to fear he's choking on a crumb. I'm about to run round and give the man a life-saving wallop on the back, when I realize he is actually trying to form two words that I have never heard him say to me before.

"Th-th..." he says. "Th-*ank* you. Thank you, *both*, v-very much."

Then the area beneath his horrible moustache arranges itself into an equally unfamiliar configuration, as Mr Mollusc breaks into a smile.

I don't know what to say. The smile is *terrifying*! But then I see that Violet has discreetly sat down at the table, so I do the same.

"It was – kind of you," Mr Mollusc says, "to bring me that. It's a long time since – since…"

And then, to my horror, I see a gleam appear in one of his eyes.

I look at Violet. Not *again*!

"We'll be off!" I say, but Violet puts her hand on my arm.

"Didn't you ever go to a berthday party when you were a boy?" she asks the manager, as gently as she can. "You're from Eerie originally, aren't you? You grew up here?"

Mr Mollusc nods and wipes the gleam away.

"It's quite a rare thing, you know?" he replies. "The fisherfolk must really like you. That must be nice. But I did have normal *birth*day parties, of course. Mother always made a cake…"

And he drifts off, staring at some memory in his mind's eye.

"What was Eerie-on-Sea like?" Violet asks. "Back then? You must have known Wendy Fossil when she was a girl."

"Oh, I did." Mr Mollusc nods, his smile full of memories now. "Always collecting things from the beach, she was. Even back then. Ah, but there are so few of us left now."

"And Sebastian Eels?" Violet asks casually. "What was he like before he got all grand and famous?"

Mr Mollusc peers at Violet, with a sudden return of his usual suspicion.

"Well, as for him," he says, "I could tell you a tale about Sebastian that would keep you up at night. I don't know how *he* sleeps, at any rate, after what he did."

"Really?" says Violet. "Ooh, I'd love to hear about that. You'd love to hear about that too, wouldn't you, Herbie?"

All I can do is grin as Mr Mollusc licks a last dollop of icing from his moustache and nods.

ODDFREY

"**WE WEREN'T SCHOOL FRIENDS,**" says Mr Mollusc, "Sebastian Eels and me. He didn't go to school, and neither did his sister. They had a tutor come to their fancy house. I only got to know them at sea."

Mr Mollusc pauses to pour himself a large drink from the whisky bottle. A waiter appears as he does this and gives a small cough. Amazingly, Mr Mollusc sends him away with a lemonade order for us.

"At sea?" Violet asks, eager to keep the story going.

"Sailing," Mollusc explains, after gulping down half his glass. "There was a proper sailing club in Eerie back then. I loved it. Had my first sailing dinghy when I was eight years old. Only a little one. My parents got her from one of the fisherfolk families, all patched up. She was called *Seahorse*. Finest little boat in the bay."

Violet and I exchange disbelieving glances, as he swigs again from his glass.

"So, you took Sebastian out in your boat?" asks Vi, but Mr Mollusc snorts.

"Hardly. He had his own, didn't he? Much bigger than mine. Room for two, you see. Sebastian and his sister, Sabrina. *Gemini* was their boat's name. Made sense, I suppose, what with them being twins."

It's probably just as well the lemonade arrives then, because I don't know who looks more astonished at this news, me or Vi, because *twins*?

"I had no idea," says Violet as Mr Mollusc drains his glass and fills it up again.

"No," says Mr Mollusc. "I doubt many remember it now. Even back then they were such a secretive family. But believe me, Seb had a twin sister. They looked alike, they even dressed alike, but they weren't …"

"Yes?" asks Vi. "… weren't what?"

"Weren't *really* alike," Mr Mollusc finishes. "Not really. Sebastian was always an arrogant little … always so sure of himself, I mean. Sabrina was confident too – rich-girl confident, I suppose you'd call it – but she didn't have to grind your nose in the sand if she thought you were getting too big for your boots. Or put a crab in your pocket. Or stamp on the watch your grandfather gave you."

And he takes another gulp of whisky. I'm beginning to wonder if I should engineer a little accident for that whisky bottle, or we'll never get to the end of this story!

"No, Seb always had a cruel streak in him," the manager

continues. "Sabby was the nice one. But you couldn't be friends with one without being friends with both, see? And they could sail like champions! I didn't mind coming in behind them. I didn't expect to win any prizes in my little *Seahorse*. I just loved being part of it."

"Prizes?" I say. "Part of *it*? What do you mean?"

Mr Mollusc peers at me. At the sound of my voice, it almost looks like he's tempted to revert to form and send me back to my cubbyhole with a flea in my ear. I slurp my lemonade and try to look as unannoying as possible.

"The Eerie Bay Treasure Hunt, of course," Mr Mollusc says then, into the bottom of his glass. "It was the biggest sailing event in these parts. It's a shame they stopped it. When I was a boy, it was the highlight of the summer."

"I've heard of it," I say to Violet. "There was treasure hidden on one of the islands in the bay, and contestants had to sail from place to place, solving clues to find it."

"The fisherfolk usually won," says Mollusc with another faraway look. "But that didn't stop a few of us from the sailing club having a go. We all wanted that Golden Nautilus for ourselves."

"Golden Nautilus?"

"That was the prize," Mollusc replies, holding up his empty hands exactly as if they contained a small, solid-gold nautilus, about the size of a golf ball. "The Kraken family donated one, every year."

I'm halfway through another slurp when I hear this,

which threatens to turn into a spray of lemonade.

Kraken gold!

Violet nudges me in the ribs to calm down, but I can tell she's thinking the same thing as me.

"Sounds like an adventure," she says. "I'd love to go on a treasure hunt like that. I wonder why they stopped it."

"You'd have to ask Her Ladyship," replies Mr Mollusc. "The last Eerie Bay Treasure Hunt was also the first she presided over. This was the year she inherited the hotel, and she took her responsibilities seriously. The clues for the treasure hunt were carefully worked out and hidden in the hotel safe. The treasure itself had been discreetly concealed out in the bay weeks before. It was going to be the best treasure hunt ever, or so I thought. I was twelve years old by then, experienced on the water and determined to out-sail the fisherfolk if I could."

I'm tempted to ask how he knew the clues were in the hotel safe, but something tells me I shouldn't. Actually, I should probably let Vi do all the talking from now on.

"But something happened, didn't it?" Violet asks softly. "Something that stopped it from being the best treasure hunt ever."

Mr Mollusc tops up his glass yet again, his hand unsteady. But then he simply stares into it, looking sad.

"You asked me if I was friends with Sebastian," he says, "but the truth is, the only true friend I had in the world was Sabrina."

Then he looks at me and Vi, together, in such a way that I suddenly understand something about Mr Mollusc and his long-lost friendship that I never would have guessed. And as he tells us the rest of his tale, it's almost like I can see it...

"Ahoy there, Godders!" calls Sabrina Eels as a twelve-year-old Godfrey Mollusc runs down the beach towards her. Her boat, Gemini, is pulled a little way up the shingle beach, near the pier in Eerie-on-Sea, awaiting the tide.

"Ahoy, yourself!" Godfrey calls back. "Going out, Sabby?"

"Of course!" Sabrina replies, jumping down to meet her friend. "Last day before the big race tomorrow. You?"

"Same," Godfrey replies with a grin.

"Hello, ODDfrey," comes a third voice, and a tall boy with a shock of black hair and what can only be described as a handsome sneer stands up in the boat and looks down on the newcomer. "I thought we'd be seeing you."

"Sebastian." Godfrey raises one hand in greeting, deciding to ignore the "Oddfrey" insult. "Yeah, thought I'd take Seahorse around the rocks a bit. Check the repairs are OK. Can we go out together?"

"Course!" Sabrina says again. "Race you to Shifting Sands and back! You can time us."

It takes a while to get Seahorse ready, and by the time she is, the tide is high enough. The three friends shove their vessels out into the waves, and leap aboard.

And then they are off.

There's a sharp wind, and the boats pick up speed as they tack out into the bay, sailing in wide zigzags, putting the ancient town behind them and approaching the treacherous shore known as Shifting Sands. Godfrey Mollusc wants to warn the others to keep their distance – the Sands are a notorious danger for boats, and well named – but he knows they won't listen. The Eels twins are brilliant on the water.

Gemini sweeps in perilously close to the sandbanks, while Godfrey holds Seahorse back, keeping her safe but also conceding the race.

"Loser!" shouts Sebastian as the two boats head back out to open water, earning himself a punch on the arm from his sister.

"Picnic?" calls Sabrina, and Godfrey gives an enthusiastic thumbs-up.

Most of the islands that make up Maw Rocks are tooth-like spikes, but a few have lost their peaks, and offer a flatter place for three friends to come ashore. Gemini is already heading towards the nearest of these. Godfrey switches position, swinging the boom of his small sailing boat around so that her sail fills with wind. Oh, how he'd love to get there first for once, and "loser!" Sebastian back. And now the race is well and truly on.

In reality, there is never any doubt about the winner. Seahorse is no match for the much larger and better-built Gemini. Even so, Godfrey snatches every scrap of wind he can as he strains to keep up. The two boats skip over the waves as they cross the expanse of Eerie Bay and approach the jagged field of islands, to lie under the sky and eat whatever they have brought with them, their boats tied close by, while dreaming of winning the Golden Nautilus at tomorrow's Eerie Bay Treasure Hunt.

"Maybe there's a way we can ALL win," says Godfrey, biting into an apple. "If we work together, maybe we can even beat the fisher families for once. Imagine actually holding the solid gold nautilus in your hand. And getting to keep it!"

"Not sure how that would work," Sabrina replies. "Neither boat can carry three. Nice thought though."

"We can't share it," says Sebastian. "There's only one prize."

"We'd have to share it if we won," his sister reminds him. "Gemini carries two. We'd be winning together, Seb."

"Hmm," Sebastian replies, pulling his sunhat over his face.

"I'd love to win," sighs Sabrina. "More than anything!"

Looking at his friend as she stares up at the clouds, Godfrey Mollusc thinks he'd love to see that more than anything too.

"I won't win, anyway," he says then. "Something's still up with Seahorse. I'll have to adjust the trim again and hope for the best. But I'm determined to be there if you two get the prize."

"Do you want me to take a look?" Sabrina replies. "Tell you what, let me sail her back, and I'll see what I think.

She's a fine boat, Seahorse, and deserves to sail her best. Even if she'll never quite catch Gemini, *ha!"*

Godfrey wants to say yes, but something makes him hesitate.

"What's wrong, Oddfrey?" says Sebastian, peering darkly from beneath his hat. "Not excited about sailing home with me?"

And the fact is, this is entirely correct. But also not something Godfrey can possibly admit. It's not until Sabrina is sailing off, heading for home in Godfrey's precious Seahorse, that Sebastian Eels speaks again.

"I know you prefer her to me," he says.

"No, no..." says Godfrey, searching quickly for a polite reply.

"Ah, save your breath," Sebastian sneers. "You two would have all the adventures together, wouldn't you? Solve ALL the mysteries. A right little dynamic duo you'd be, I'm sure, if I wasn't here. But never forget, Oddfrey – she's my sister. She's my TWIN. I could turn her against you, if I chose. If you want to be with her, you have to be with me, and nothing will ever change that. Got it?"

"Look, Seb..." Godfrey begins, but Sebastian grabs him by the scruff of his T-shirt, and almost lifts him off the ground.

"No, you look!" he replies. "Have you any idea how pathetic you sound with your 'I won't win, Sabby, but I don't mind if you do' act? Where's your drive, Oddfrey? Don't you dream, every day, of winning? Of being the big man, with the world at your feet?"

"I WOULD like to win," says Godfrey, gasping for breath, "but..."

"It's that 'but'," says Sebastian Eels, releasing the other boy and letting him sink to the rocky ground, "that makes you the little person you will always be. It's why you'll end up in some dead-end job one day, while I..."

"While you what?" snaps Godfrey, angry at being pushed around like this.

"WHILE I WIN!" Sebastian shouts, roaring it out across the bay. Then he leans down over his friend. "Win the Golden Nautilus! And I won't share it with anyone."

"What about Sabrina? What about your sister?"

But at these words Sebastian Eels glares at the other boy with such a terrible look on his face that Godfrey Mollusc is shocked into silence.

"Of COURSE I'll share with her." Seb chuckles then, suddenly giving a lighter smile. He reaches down and helps his friend up. "And you can be part of it, Oddfrey. You can still share in the glory when I claim the prize tomorrow."

"Really?" Godfrey says. "How?"

"Easy!" replies Sebastian. "Because I'm going to cheat. I'm going to steal the treasure hunt clues before the race. I'm going to steal them tonight."

"No!" Godfrey is shocked.

"Actually, yes," comes the reply. "And, if you want to make my sister happy, you're going to help me."

GOLDEN NAUTILUS

"WHAT HAPPENED?" VIOLET ASKS as Mr Mollusc pauses his story to fill up his glass yet again, but the whisky bottle is empty. Immediately the waiter places a new one beside the manager.

"Maybe a glass of water instead..." Violet tries to suggest, but the waiter is already gone.

"What happened, what happened...?" Mr Mollusc opens the new bottle and aims it uncertainly at his glass. "The worst thing happened, that's what! The worst..."

"Sabrina?" Violet suggests.

Mr Godfrey Mollusc stares desperately into his glass and nods.

"Shouldn'a done it, of course," he slurs. "Cheating. But my dad worked in the hotel. You probably didn't know that, Lemon –" he looks at me with glassy eyes – "but this hotel has been in my family too, in a way. Dad was head waiter. And before that – well, he had another job. When he was a boy."

And he tries to fix his gaze on my Lost-and-Founder's cap for a moment.

"Anyway," he says eventually, "where was I?"

"Your dad worked in the hotel," Violet reminds him. "So, did that mean you could get in without arousing suspicion?"

Mr Mollusc nods vigorously.

"Getting into the hotel was easy but getting near the safe, ah, that was a bit harder." He grins. "I did it, though. As for the combination, well, the old manager kept the safe code on a piece of paper, pinned to the cork board in his office. Can you believe it? What a fool!"

"I can believe it," says Vi. "So, you got into the safe?"

"Had to pick my moment and hide under the desk when I heard people passing, but yes – I got the Eerie Bay Treasure Hunt clues and solutions, the map with X marks the spot, everything. Gave it to Seb. But I did it for Sabrina really."

"He was pretty pleased, I imagine," suggests Vi. "Seb."

"No," Mollusc replies. "He was furious!"

"What have you done, you little IDIOT?" Sebastian Eels shouts. It is midnight, the night before the treasure hunt. "These are the originals!" He waves the stolen papers. "What will Lady Kraken say when she finds them missing? I meant for you to COPY them! You're such a loser, Oddfrey."

The two boys are outside the wooden beach hut that the Eels family owns on the seafront. The hut is full of sailing equipment and serves as an unofficial clubhouse for the friends when the weather is bad.

"Where's Sabrina?" Godfrey demands, snatching back the papers. "Let's see how much of a loser I am when I tell her what you've done."

Eels shoves the shorter boy to the ground. Then he stamps hard on his wrist, grinding it into the sandy wet shingle, forcing his hand open.

"What YOU'VE done, you mean?" he spits, grabbing the papers back. "You're the thief. But never mind, I have a good memory."

And with this he sits on an upturned barrel to memorize the clues and co-ordinates. Godfrey gets to his feet, rubbing his sore arm.

"There you are!" calls a voice shortly after, as Sabrina comes around the hut and finds the two of them. "Seb, it's late. Mum and Dad want you back home. Surely we're all set for the race now."

"Oh, I'm all set," says Eels, thrusting the papers back into Godfrey's hands. "You're all set, too, aren't you, Oddfrey?"

And this is the moment when Godfrey Mollusc could have changed everything. If he came clean to Sabrina, there and then, Sebastian's plan would be ruined. And he, Godfrey, could probably spin the whole thing as a prank. Sabrina liked a prank as much as anyone. Nevertheless, catching Seb's eye, Godfrey also knew that if he let Sebastian Eels down now, he'd make an enemy for life.

"All set," says Godfrey Mollusc, hiding the papers behind his back. "See you tomorrow!"

And he ran all the way back to the Grand Nautilus Hotel, to return the things to the safe. For better or worse, it was done, and too late to go back now.

The next day dawns with an ominous sky and a nasty gusting wind that would normally spell a day on land for Godfrey and his friends. But this is the day of the Eerie Bay Treasure Hunt, and bunting is already flying wildly over the pier, while a carnival atmosphere attempts to hold itself together in the face of the worst weather so far that summer.

The boats that will compete that day are bobbing crazily around, just beyond the end of the pier, where two bright orange floats mark the start line. As usual, most of the treasure hunters are Eerie fisherfolk, in an array of vessels, mostly powered by diesel engines. The fishers who man them are a surly and cheerless lot, and look down on the few sailing boats there, especially those belonging to the junior members of the Eerie Sailing Club.

"I can't believe there's no rule about engines," says Sabrina, as she readies Gemini for the off. "It's virtually cheating! You can't beat good honest wind and canvas."

"Except," Godfrey replies in a quiet voice, "they usually do."

"Not this year they won't," asserts Sebastian Eels, standing confidently in Gemini despite the snatchy wind and angry sea.

Lady Kraken, emerging from the colourful circus tent that has been erected for the occasion, walks slowly – a walking stick in each hand – to the very end of the pier. A great crowd of townsfolk and tourists alike have gathered on the beach and promenade to watch the famous event. There's a brass band playing. Children run and laugh, and refuse to put on suncream. All around are the smells of fish and chips, candyfloss and the sea.

Then Lady Kraken rings the great bronze starting gong.

The race has begun!

With a roar of their engines, the fishing vessels power forward, churning up the already wild sea and sending swathes of black exhaust smoke across the cheering spectators. Godfrey heaves on his tiny sail and feels Seahorse *kick forward as she catches the wind. Ahead of him,* Gemini *is already picking up speed, cresting the waves the fishing boats are leaving in their wake.*

"Good luck, Godders!" calls Sabrina, her face full of excitement at the adventure. "Keep up this time, eh?"

"You too!" Godfrey yells back. He is looking forward to seeing the joy on his friend's face when she wins the Golden Nautilus. Because now, with her cheating brother at her side, there's no way she can lose.

The Eerie Bay Treasure Hunt follows no set course. The route is defined by clues that are placed at each destination, culminating in the final location – the designated "treasure island" for that year – where the Golden Nautilus waits for the first contestant to arrive. But, of course, everyone's been given the very first clue already, in a sealed envelope, just ahead of the start. Those who have already solved the clue make for the first destination, while those who can't work it out watch what everyone else is doing and decide who to follow.

This year, the first clue is pretty easy and the entire pack of racers turns towards a small island out in the bay, famous for being the shape of a puffin, where the second clue will be found. It'll be chaos when they reach it, so everyone strains to be at the front. Gemini takes a slight lead, skimming over the sea, as Sabrina and her brother lean far out over the side to keep their sail full.

Even so, it's a diesel-powered fishing boat that makes the island first. One of the crew dives into the water, swims to the island and is reading the clue – painted in small letters on a plank of wood – even as Gemini arrives. The fisherman is still staring at the clue, shaking his head in confusion, when Sebastian steps smartly ashore, strolls up to the sign, glances at it for a second, then jumps back into Gemini.

Together, the Eels twins begin sailing hard for the next stop in the race, leaving the other contestants, all at Puffin Island now, torn between trying to solve the second clue themselves, or following Gemini. But it seems impossible that anyone could have worked out the answer so quickly. Instead, the contestants clamber onto the tiny island, jostling each other as they try to work out where to sail next.

But Godfrey knows the truth, of course. Without wasting any time on Puffin Island, he brings Seahorse about and gives chase.

As the day wears on and the race continues, the pack of vessels breaks up. The boats begin to head in different directions, some on the right track, others following a wild-goose chase. Gemini, flying with the wind, is way ahead, and barely stopping at each island. It must look like the Eels twins have given up and are just sailing for the fun of it. Only Godfrey Mollusc trails them now.

Then, as the skies darken and the waves turn truly nasty, Godfrey hears a whoop from his friends ahead, and he knows they are heading for their final destination: the treasure island … and the prize. They are far ahead of Seahorse, but Godfrey's determined to be there at the moment of triumph, to see Sabrina's face.

He could hardly have known then that he'd never see that face again.

WINNER TAKES IT ALL

MR MOLLUSC MAKES A GRAB for the whisky bottle, but misses it. The waiter steps forward smartly, catches the bottle as it falls, and pours out another glass for his manager. Mr Mollusc drains it, then bangs his empty glass down for more.

"But why?" Violet asks, as gently as possible, though also with a hint of urgency. It's clear we're reaching the most important part of the story, but Mr Mollusc is at risk of drowning his sorrows before he can share them with us. "*Why* was it the last time? What happened, er, Godders?"

And she places her hand encouragingly on the man's arm.

Mr Mollusc tries to focus on her.

"Shabrina?" he says woozily. "Ah, Sabrina. I should *never* have done it. You never would. I know it's all my fault! But it's Sebastian who's really to blame. He's the one who did it! When he arrived at the treasure island…"

Sebastian Eels jumps onto the island and climbs the steps to the lighthouse. Only a few of the jagged islands that make up Maw Rocks have lighthouses on them, and this one — known as Dismal Beacon — is the furthest from the town. The lighthouse has recently been automated, so there's no keeper now, though an old lighthouse keeper's rowing boat is still there, pulled up out of the sea. As for the race, none of the other boats are anywhere close, so only Godfrey Mollusc, approaching as fast as little Seahorse can sail, sees what happens next.

Sebastian beckons for his sister to join him, pointing excitedly into the open door of the lighthouse. There's no mistaking his body language — he's found the Golden Nautilus! Sabrina, securing Gemini beside the old keeper's boat, runs up the steps to the lighthouse. Her brother indicates for her to go first, and she enters the building.

But instead of following, Sebastian runs back down the steps and jumps into Gemini. In a moment he's cast off, and is quickly catching wind and pulling away from Dismal Beacon. Sabrina comes back out of the lighthouse like a rocket, but her brother is already some distance away, holding one hand in the air — a hand that gives off the unmistakable glint of gold.

"Seb!" cries Sabrina. "Seb, get back here!"

"Oddfrey will pick you up," Sebastian Eels calls back. "Catch me if you can!"

And at this, finally, Godfrey sees red.

How can Sebastian do this to his own sister? His own TWIN? He has not only cheated, but also STOLEN the prize from under her nose. And worst of all, he, Godfrey, is part of it! There's no glory to share here, only shame.

But now Godfrey Mollusc burns with anger as well as guilt.

"Sebastian!" he roars, his voice carrying with the fierce wind.

He sails straight past the island, without even looking at Sabrina, and rushes at Gemini.

Sebastian Eels, who hasn't made much speed yet with all the triumphant waving he's been doing, hastily stuffs the Golden Nautilus in his pocket, and scrambles to brace the sail. But it's too late. Sailing faster than she's ever sailed before, Seahorse closes on Gemini, and Godfrey Mollusc makes ready to throw himself at the treacherous boy aboard.

"You were supposed to pick her up!" shouts Sebastian, alarm on his face. "You left my sister!"

"YOU left her!" Godfrey yells back. "YOU!"

And he jumps.

But the sea is rough, and Sebastian quick. And just as Godfrey jumps, Gemini turns.

Godfrey Mollusc misses the boat and falls into the choppy sea.

"Stop messing about, Oddfrey!" Sebastian Eels laughs then, looking down at him in the water. "This is no time for a swim."

"How could you cheat her like this?" Godfrey shouts, *bobbing crazily in the water in his life jacket, trying to locate his boat, which has sailed on without him. "How could you LEAVE her? Your own sister!"*

"Oh, Odders, don't you know a joke when you see one?" Seb calls back. "Just get back in your boat and pick her up. I've got a victory parade to lead. We'll all laugh about this tomorrow, you'll see."

And with that he races away, setting sail for Eerie-on-Sea, distantly visible on the horizon.

"But you couldn't get back on board?" Violet suggests as Mr Mollusc pauses again. "Back on board *Seahorse*?"

He shakes his head.

Then the hotel manager, the whisky finally catching up with him, slumps forward, spilling himself across the table in a drunken stupor, his head lolling, his eyes closed.

I'm about to try and pull him upright and call the waiter to help when Violet stops me. She puts her fingers to her lips. The man is still talking in a mumbly half-voice. Vi and I lean forward to listen.

"She was caught in the currents," Mr Mollusc is saying, his eyes still closed. "My *Seahorse* – lost! Weather getting worse – just couldn't get near – then – pulled out by one of the fishing crews. Tried telling them – have to go back for Sabrina! They thought I was raving. Been in the sea a long time. So cold! They told me there was no one on the island – one of the other boats must've picked her up. It was the treasure island after all. So – taken back to Eerie alone. Promised myself – *promised* I'd come clean to Sabrina 'bout what I'd done – make it all right. But, when I got back, Sabrina not there. Sabrina not anywhere! Sebastian – strutting around on the pier, enjoying the cheers – being fussed over by Lady Kraken and the rest, but his sister – vanished. Gone!"

"I'm so sorry," Violet whispers. "What did you do?"

"Told the race people, didn't I? Tried to raise the alarm. But no one listened. *Gemini* had set out – *Gemini* had come back. And I was only twelve. So, in the end – just one person I could turn to."

"Sebastian Eels," I whisper too.

"When I told him 'bout Sabby," Mr Mollusc continues, murmuring now, "he went whiter than I'd ever seen him. Thought he'd hit me, but instead, he *clung* to me, pleaded for help. All the nastiness – just vanished. He needed me desperately. And course I helped. We sailed back out in *Gemini*, in terrible weather, to Dismal Beacon. Place deserted – lighthouse empty. But – we found…"

He goes silent now, before the beginnings of a snore reaches our ears.

"What?" Violet shakes the man gently. "What did you find?"

"Little rowing boat…" comes the answer as if from far, far away. "Lighthouse keeper's rowing boat…"

"Yes?"

"It was gone."

Then the snoring begins in earnest, and all the shaking in Rattle and Roll Land wouldn't wake Mr Mollusc now.

And me?

Well, I think back over everything we've just heard. I remember how Eels stamped on Godfrey Mollusc's wrist one midnight, many years ago, on the wet, sandy beach – Godfrey, whose father worked in the hotel restaurant, where a broken wristwatch was found many years later, behind the radiator, where I now guess it had been left to dry.

I take that very same battered watch off my arm and, as gently as I can, I strap it on the sleeping manager's wrist.

"Are you sure, Herbie?" Violet says, still whispering.

"If I'm wrong –" I shrug – "he'll just hand it back in to the Lost-and-Foundery tomorrow, and shout at me. But I reckon I'm right, don't you?"

"It's all so horrible," Violet says then. "Sabrina Eels! Yet another person missing in Eerie-on-Sea. But we still don't really know what happened, do we?"

"Perhaps I can help with that," comes a booming voice we recognize, and a large shadow, concealed in the next bay window, leans forward. It's Professor Newtiss, who hands the waiter a crisply folded banknote.

"You!" I gasp. "You – you got him drunk deliberately?"

"I may be good at research, Herbie," the professor twinkles darkly behind his tiny specs, notebook and pen in hand, "but sometimes the old-fashioned ways are the best.

He refused to tell me that story – and when I asked him so nicely, too."

"How much did you hear?" Violet demands. "And how much did you know already?"

"I knew a little," the professor replies, joining us at the table. "I guessed something must have happened during that sailing race, but I just couldn't find out what. Nicely handled, by the way." He grins through his beard at Violet. "With the cake? You found the old misery's soft spot, and gave it a jolly good poke, eh? I like that."

"We were just trying to be nice!" Violet looks disgusted. "Not trying to trick him."

The professor gives a shrug. "Either way, it'll make a pretty sensational episode of the podcast. Maybe we'll call it *'The Hotel Manager Who Was Once a Thief!'* Wait, no, not paranormal enough. How about *'The Twin Sister Left to Drown!'* Much spookier. Our listeners will love it."

And he jots down his ideas.

"But these are private things!" Violet protests. "Real people's lives. You can't broadcast them."

"Just watch me," Professor Newtiss replies with a chuckle. "Anyway, I think I can fill in what happened next. Lady Kraken found out about the cheating, it seems, so she probably also knew how Sabrina came to be marooned on the island. I imagine a remorseful Godfrey would have confessed it all to her, to try and make things right. Her Ladyship rewarded him with a job in the hotel, but – no doubt due to his theft from the hotel safe – not the one special job he'd always dreamed of."

And here Professor Newtiss nods at my Lost-and-Founder's cap.

"Mr Mollusc wanted to be Lost-and-Founder?" Violet gasps, but I say nothing. Somehow, I've always known this was true.

"Ended up as kitchen boy instead," the professor explains. "Worked his way up from there."

"But what happened with Sabrina?" Violet asks. "How can someone go missing, and no one care?"

"Oh, I should think people cared," says Professor Newtiss. "But these ridiculous little seaside towns are all the same. Everyone knows everyone else, and Lady Kraken would have been well placed to hush things up. And there is a long history of people going missing in Eerie-on-Sea, is there not?"

Violet, whose lost parents are never far from her mind, goes quiet.

"This must be why the Eels family left town," the professor continues. "Sebastian Eels himself didn't return until he had grown up and inherited his childhood home."

"How does any of this," I demand to know, "help you find out about the Deepest Secret of Eerie-on-Sea?"

The professor shrugs.

"At least now we know that whatever Eels is after, it probably has something to do with his long-lost sister," he says. "We just need to work out what."

"We?"

"Yes, *we*, Herbie," the man says. "We're a team, aren't we? I can even get you on an episode if you like. You're part of this now, whether you like it or not."

COLD, DARK BOTTOM

"**WE'VE HELPED YOU ENOUGH**," I say to Professor Newtiss. "It's time for you to help *us*. What do you know about me, and my past?"

"And my missing parents?" Violet adds.

Professor Newtiss adjusts his spectacles and looks a bit shifty.

"Hmm," he says, "I suppose I should give you a little something, to keep our arrangement sweet. Herbie, in your case there seems to be a link between your past and a book written by Sebastian Eels. A book called…"

"*The Cold, Dark Bottom of the Sea*," I finish for him. "Yes, we know that already."

This is the book the mermonkey dispensed to me when I first came to town, and I've long thought it was some sort of clue. The book itself is the tale of a luxury ocean liner called the SS *Fabulous* that hit an iceberg and sank far out in the ocean.

"But we've already established there's no record of a ship called *Fabulous* going down," says Violet, as if reading my mind. "Not for a hundred years."

"You don't know anything about us at all, do you?" I say, suddenly realizing it. "You tricked us!"

The professor opens his mouth to protest, but then freezes, holding his hand up for silence. All I can hear is the steady snoring of the hotel manager.

"What?" Violet whispers.

"Make yourselves scarce!" cries Professor Newtiss. He snaps his notebook shut, darts out of his chair and hurries away to the hotel bar.

"Hey!" says Vi.

But then I hear it too: steady, crisp footsteps crossing the polished floor of the hotel lobby. I look through the interior dining room windows and see someone passing the reception desk, heading straight for the dining room.

"Down!" I gasp, and slip beneath the table where Mr Mollusc has passed out. Violet joins me there in a flash. We stare round the curly legs of the tables and chairs and see a pair of leather boots enter. The boots start to cross the dining room but then stop, swing around, and head our way.

"Well, well, well," says the voice of Sebastian Eels as the boots come to a halt right beside our table. "Godfrey Mollusc. Still looking for answers in a whisky bottle, I see."

Mr Mollusc has only snores to give in answer. But, as I crouch under the table, trying not to breathe, part of my brain is still thinking about the tragic story we've just heard of three twelve-year-old friends, long ago, and is amazed to realize that these two unpleasant men with us now are the same people, all grown up.

"You'll always be a loser, Oddfrey," says Sebastian Eels then, and he turns to walk away.

"Sabrina…"

This reply comes in a muffled voice, and I'm amazed to hear the snoring Mr Mollusc say anything at all. Then I look at Violet and realize it wasn't the hotel manager who spoke. It was Vi! Making her voice as deep as it will go and mumbling into her sleeve, *Violet* was the one who said "Sabrina!"

Sebastian Eels stops and turns back. This is bad enough, but then I'm horrified to see that Violet is preparing to say something else!

Now, the thing about my friend Violet is this: she's genuinely amazing. Honestly, when it comes to detecting mysteries and solving clues and all that, many's the time I've said, "Herbie, Violet's just done something you'd *never* do, and in doing it she's bust this mystery wide open." It's a real skill that she has, and, like I said, it's amazing.

But if there's one thing Vi's not *quite* so good at – one little flaw in her otherwise flaw-free Violetness – it's this: she doesn't always know when to stop. And many's also the time when Vi and I have barely escaped from certain doom by the skin of our whiskers after she's gone too far and been caught at her tricks. Like, for example, being discovered under a table doing the voice of a drunk man who is *clearly fast asleep*.

So that's why I grab Violet's arm to stop her from saying *anything more*, and hope that the horrified look in my eyes is enough to explain why. The booted feet of Sebastian Eels, returning to the table, should also add a little urgency to the situation.

Vi makes a face but also nods.

We both go still and hold the breaths we are already holding a little tighter.

"You dare say that to me?" says Sebastian Eels.

Nothing but snores from Mollusc.

"You, who are responsible for her loss," Eels snarls, *"dare* to speak my sister's name?"

Snores again, including one of those really loud ones people sometimes do.

"Pathetic!" Eels cries in disgust, and he gives Mr Mollusc a kick in the shins.

"When I have her back," he continues, "when Sabby is returned to me and I have fixed it all, I promise, Godfrey Mollusc, that I will make you pay for what you did, once and for all."

And with this he spins on his heel and strides away towards the hotel bar.

"Did you hear that?" Vi whispers. "He really does think he's going to get his sister back!"

"I heard," I reply. "But what I'd really like to hear is what's going on in there." And I point to the hotel bar. Not only is

Professor Newtiss still in there, but I now see that Angela Song and Fluffy Mike have been there all along. "We need to get closer."

We creep out from beneath the table and approach the bar. Fortunately, there's a large potted fern near the door to hide in. Now we can see – and, crucially, hear – the podcast trio as they greet Sebastian Eels.

"Of course we know who you are," says Angela Song, shaking Eels energetically by the hand and giving up her seat. "I've read all your books. And you saved our sound man's life. It's such an honour to properly meet Eerie-on-Sea's most famous resident at last!"

"You are too kind," says Sebastian Eels stiffly. Then he shakes hands all round, as introductions are made. "I hear you have been asking a lot of questions. And that you are carrying out investigations."

"Oh, yes," says Professor Newtiss, looking a little alarmed, but mostly managing to hide it beneath his large beard. "For our podcast. Starting with the legend of the malamander."

At this point, I'm leaning so far out of the fern I almost fall over. Does Eels, who once stole from Professor Newtiss, still recognize him after all these years?

"Ah, the malamander," says Sebastian Eels. "So, you are interested in that, are you?"

"There are rumours you went looking for it once," the professor says after a pause. "What'll you drink, Mr Eels? We'd love to hear your stories."

Sebastian Eels turns a narrow look onto the larger man. But if he does recognize him, he is covering it well.

"Thank you, but I can't stay," Eels replies, taking up a central position in the group anyway. "However, the fisherfolk tell me you have made a discovery."

"We have," declares Angela, proudly patting an instrument resting on the bar. "We call it the Eerie Hum. We have some excellent recordings."

The instrument in question is the very same portable hum detector we saw earlier at Violet's berthday party. Right now though, the lines are trembling flatly across the bottom of the green screen, as the instrument waits to pick up the mysterious infrasound once more.

"We'll detect it again soon," Angela continues, though the look on the professor's face suggests he really wishes she wouldn't. "And once we do, we'll be able to track the Eerie Hum right to its source. We're on the verge of a sensational discovery, Mr Eels. And we'd love to interview you about it."

"Fascinating," says Sebastian Eels in a neutral tone. "How very clever of you. And what do you think is causing it, would you say? This so-called Eerie Hum?"

"Well, my money is on vibrations from the hotel lift," Angela replies. "Resonating through the building. Have you seen how old everything here is? We can still spin that into something exciting for the podcast, of course, especially with the professor here to talk up the spooky monster angle first. We'll make sure our listeners know that the malamander calls for its long-lost mate, and all the details."

"Indeed." Sebastian Eels looks again at the professor. "And you will be sharing all this with how many subscribers, exactly?"

"Oh, just fifteen million," Angela says like it's nothing. "And about the same again on our video channels."

"I see." Sebastian Eels radiates such coldness now that I'm surprised the room doesn't fill with icicles. "That is a lot of people finding out about Eerie-on-Sea, isn't it? Well, well."

"Sure is," Angela agrees. "But when they hear our theory that the Eerie Hum might actually be the malamander's long-lost mate calling back—"

"You know, perhaps I will have that drink after all," Sebastian Eels interrupts. "But I'm sure you would all be much more comfortable back at my place. My house isn't far, and I can tell you a tale or two about the malamander that you won't hear anywhere else."

"Really?" Angela looks delighted. "Are you sure?"

"Of course!" declares Sebastian Eels. "I won't take no for an answer. And if it's spooky material you want, did you know that there are miles of tunnels beneath the town? I happen to have access to them through my own cellar. I can give you a private tour tonight, and explain how they, too, relate to the legend of the malamander."

This is met with such enthusiasm from Angela and Fluffy Mike that glasses are drained and coats are grabbed. Mike hitches the hum detector over his shoulder. The last thing we see as they leave is the look on the face of Professor Newtiss as he follows his fellow podcasters and Sebastian Eels out of the bar.

"It looks to me," I say to Violet, once we are alone, "like the professor thinks he's just hit the jackpot and is about to find out everything he wants to know."

"He might think that," Violet replies, "but knowing Eels like we do, it's more likely that the *Anomalous Phenomena* podcast will never broadcast another episode again."

SPARK AND EMBER

"SHOULDN'T WE DO SOMETHING?" I say when we are safely back in my lost-property cellar. "Shouldn't we warn them? The podcasters?"

"What can we say?" Violet replies. "I don't see how we can do anything without coming face to face with Eels again, *and* admitting we were eavesdropping."

"But Eels is – *Eels*!" I cry. "A villain to his fingertips. You said it yourself, *Anonymous Whatever-It-Is* is in danger."

"Yes, but at least there are three of them," says Violet. "Surely Eels can't hurt them all, can he? And the professor, at least, knows exactly what he's like."

I also feel guilty about leaving Mr Mollusc still slumped at his table in the restaurant above. But something tells me this won't be the first time the waiters have found him like this when they arrive for work in the morning. I wonder if he'll even remember giving us this glimpse into his tragic childhood.

Or what he'll say when he sees the watch.

"It just gets murkier and murkier," says Violet then. The wood-burning stove has almost gone out, and it feels to me more like bedtime than talking-over-clues-and-working-out-what-to-do-next time. "But," Vi continues, "ever since this Eerie Hum started, things have been going wrong in Eerie-on-Sea. First, the cameraluna broke down, and now the mermonkey may never work again. And I still haven't heard Erwin say *anything*, not for days!"

I look over to where the bookshop cat is half dozing in a box of lost scarves. It's shocking to see him so ill-looking. He peers back at us, gives a sickly little cough, then curls around to go back to sleep.

"Sebastian Eels is behind it all, Herbie." Violet gathers blankets around her on the armchair. "He always is. And, once again, it's up to us to find out why before something really disastrous happens. So, *that's* why ..."

"Yes?"

"... that's why I'd like to see this island for myself."

"Island?" I ask. "What island?"

"The one with the lighthouse," Vi says impatiently, from deep in her makeshift bed. "Dismal Beacon. The one where Godfrey Mollusc last saw Sabrina alive. I think we should go tomorrow."

"Huh?" I'm stunned.

"And I also think," Violet adds sleepily, "that we should borrow Sebastian Eels' boat to do it."

"What?!"

"Goodnight, Herbie," Vi says, exactly as if she hasn't just dropped a bombshell.

"So!" I slump into my beanbag. "Let me just get this straight, Vi: tomorrow, which is *actually* midwinter, and therefore the *most insanely bonkers time* to be on the beach – let alone bobbing about in a boat – you want to set sail to *a dangerous and remote island*, where people have *actually vanished*. And you think we should steal our *arch-enemy's boat* to do it? Is that right?"

"You make it sound quite exciting," replies Violet Parma. "OK, I agree. Count me in."

"What? No, I didn't mean..."

"Oh, Herbie, I know it sounds dangerous." Violet throws back the blanket and looks me straight in the eye. "But can't you see? There's a connection here, there *must* be. Between you and your strange story, me and my missing parents, Sabrina Eels getting lost, and others who have vanished over the years. Like little Pandora Festergrimm."

I gently remove my cap and look inside to where Clermit, my clockwork hermit crab, sleeps.

"People get lost in Eerie-on-Sea," Vi continues. "But sometimes people get found. You're the Lost-and-Founder at the Grand Nautilus Hotel. Don't you want to know why?"

Well, I can't say no to *that*, can I?

"Anyway, I was actually thinking of asking Blaze," Violet adds.

"Blaze? Has he lost someone too?"

"Well, yes," Violet replies. "His parents, remember? That's why he lives with his uncle. But that's not what I meant. While I like your idea of stealing Sebastian Eels' motorboat, Herbie, maybe it would be a bit less risky to ask Blaze and Uncle Squint to take us in theirs. I just feel sure there is a clue out there, somewhere, waiting to be found – and we won't find it sitting here, will we?"

And so, whether I like it or not, it seems to be all decided.

The next day dawns strange and icily still, and almost threatens never to get light at all. But we can still make out the unmistakable shape of the *Jornty Spark* bobbing gently in the gloom, beside the harbour wall.

"Ahoy!" cries Violet as we approach. "Ahoy there, *Jornty Spark*!"

"You sound like you've lived in a seaside town all your life," I say with a grin.

Violet grins back.

"Well, I have just had my first official berthday. I'm honorary fisherfolk now."

"Who's that?" comes a gruff voice, and a grizzled head appears through a hatch in the deck of the fishing boat and peers up at us.

"Arr, it's you two," says Uncle Squint. "And your feline," he adds, seeing Erwin in Violet's arms. Despite the cat being under the weather, or probably because of it, Violet didn't want to leave him behind. "Come aboard – we were just toasting a sardine or three for our breakfast."

"Sounds, er, yummy," I reply. Then I hold up a paper bag of stale pastries from the hotel kitchen. "Let's make a feast of it."

Vi and I climb down the harbour wall, using the ancient and sea-nibbled iron steps embedded in it, and onto the deck of the *Jornty Spark*. Towards the prow of the boat (that's the pointy end) sits the wheelhouse with its dials and widgets, while at the stern (that's the roundy end at the back) stands the peculiar contraption that marks the *Spark* out from the other boats in Eerie's ragtag fishing fleet: a wooden mast – hinged and geared so it can be raised and lowered – on top of which is a wind turbine. Even though there is barely enough wind to turn the turbine now, this device keeps the boat's mighty electric battery nicely topped up with power. She's the only electric fishing boat for miles around, and one of the wonders of Eerie-on-Sea.

"Arr, she's a bit crotchety at the mo, though," says Uncle Squint, seeing me eyeing the turbine with admiration. "The tinkering never ends with a boat like this. Come below and grab a cuppa."

We descend into the oily warmth and toasty smells of below deck, and see Blaze at the stove, tossing things around in a frying pan, while the kettle begins to sing. In the dark, sitting between the swinging hammocks of Blaze and his uncle, is the great ceramic battery, fizzing with electrical power.

"I still can't believe you have a sprightning," I say at the sight of little Ember, buzzing and flitting around the battery. Erwin can't resist stalking her, but he knows better than to leap, I hope. A sprightning's high-voltage sting is no joke, believe me! Especially for a sickly cat.

"Does she really follow you everywhere?" asks Violet, a hint of envy in her voice.

"Aye," Blaze replies with a grin, "latched on to us good and proper, she has. Like she's *Spark*'s lucky charm."

"Here for a free feed from our battery, more like," says Uncle Squint gruffly, but he glances at the little electrical sprite with affection enough.

"Have the monster hunters left town yet?" asks Blaze then, as he pours us each a tin cup of black tea and eyes the croissants appreciatively. "The pod people? I don't dare go ashore in case they ask me to take them out again."

"They're still here," Vi replies, "but..."

"But what?"

"Well," I explain, "there was no sign of them at breakfast this morning. And they seem to have found a new guide: Sebastian Eels!"

"Him!" Uncle Squint snaps, before dunking a fried sardine in his piping hot tea. "That man's a menace. Mark my words, if he doesn't get himself killed, he'll be the end of someone else."

"What makes you say that?" Vi asks.

"Seen him out in his boat," Uncle Squint replies. "At night! In winter, too. And far too close to Maw Rocks. If he wants to get himself drowned, he's going about it the right way."

"You've seen him sailing?"

"Not exactly sailing, Herbie." Blaze laughs. "He's got a motorboat. Fast one, too."

"Have you ever followed him?" Violet asks.

"Why would we do that, lass?" Uncle Squint retorts grumpily. The bad feeling between him and Eels goes way back, and I'm glad when Violet changes the subject.

"We were wondering," she says, "could you take us out somewhere, please? In the *Spark*? If you're not doing anything today, that is. There's an island in the bay we'd like to visit."

"Is there now?" says Uncle Squint. "And which island might that be?"

Violet ducks beneath the swinging lamp and crosses to an ancient chart pinned to the wall. It's a map of Eerie Bay we've seen before, showing the vast field of tiny islands that make up Maw Rocks. And the dangerous water channels between them. Drawn on the chart, in the centre of the Rocks, is the great shipwrecking whirlpool known as the Vortiss. But, fortunately, we're not going anywhere near that.

"Here," Vi says, after a moment of searching. She points at a small speck on the chart, way out on the furthest edge of Maw Rocks. "This island. With the lighthouse."

"Dismal Beacon," says Squint Westerley, proving the

aptness of his name by frowning hard at us, each in turn. "Now, why in the name of all that's eerie would you be wanting to go there?"

Violet opens her mouth to say something. But nothing comes out. I suddenly wonder how we can possibly explain ourselves. Then I remember what Vi said before, about all the people who have vanished in Eerie-on-Sea over the years.

"It's for important Lost-and-Founder business," I say.

And I straighten my cap as I say it.

MAW ROCKS

ONCE BREAKFAST IS DONE, the crew of the *Jornty Spark* – plus me and Vi – prepare for the voyage. The deck is cleared, the galley kitchen stowed and Erwin settled below deck, curled up on the warm battery, but keeping one wary ice-blue eye on Ember, who is showing a tendency to tease him. At the press of a button, the wind turbine blades snap together, and the pylon it sits on is lowered clankingly to the deck.

"Do the honours, Mr Westerley," says Uncle Squint, wedging his skipper's hat firmly on his head.

"Aye, Cap'n," his nephew replies from his place at the wheel. He turns a key and the dials on the *Spark*'s control panel flicker on, glowing with a steady blue light.

"Untie us, if you please, Ms Parma."

"Aye, aye!" replies Vi, climbing the harbour wall, unlooping the rope from an iron ring, then jumping back on deck.

"Shove off, Mr Lemon!" barks Captain Squint, handing me an oar.

"But," I reply, "I only just got here."

For some reason no one laughs at my joke. Instead, Violet picks up a second oar and together we push off from the harbour wall. Soon we are far enough out for Blaze to safely engage the *Spark*'s engine, and – with a kick forward from the propeller – we begin to ease out into the choppy waters of Eerie Bay.

The enormous carved horn on the boat's prow – which Vi and I discovered on our Gargantis adventure is not a horn at all – slices the cold air ahead of us as the *Jornty Spark* picks up speed.

"So, Dismal Beacon," says Blaze, steadying the wheel and raising his voice over the sound of our wake. "That's the very last of Maw Rocks before the open ocean. What's the big mystery? Someone lost their socks there?"

He nods at my cap as he says this, and I see the hint of a grin. I'm sorry to say that Blaze Westerley doesn't take my job very seriously.

"Have you ever heard of Sebastian Eels' sister?" Violet asks him.

"Sister?" Blaze looks surprised. "I had no idea he had one."

"He doesn't," Vi replies. "Not any more. But he did. Dismal Beacon is where she was last seen."

Blaze nods as if he isn't surprised.

"Mighty currents in those waters. Go too far one way and you'll be pulled deeper and deeper into Maw Rocks till the Vortiss'll get you. Go too far the other, and a whole different set of currents will push you towards the cliffs of Eerie Rock and wreck you to smithereens. You can only approach those parts safely from the open sea."

"If someone was on that island," I ask, "on Dismal Beacon, I mean, and they wanted to row back to town, how long would it take?"

"Row?" Blaze whistles. "What idiot would be rowing way out there?"

"The lighthouse keeper?" I suggest. "Back when there was one. He had a rowing boat, didn't he?"

"Only to get around the island." Blaze shakes his head. "I suppose, if the tide was rising, and you *had* to row, you might be lucky and reach home in a couple of hours. But if the tide was going out…"

"What?" I ask.

"You wouldn't get there at all," says Blaze, simply. "And, like I said, if you got caught in the currents you'd be finished, anyway. A rowing boat has little chance of surviving those waters. And if the weather was rough…"

But here he just whistles again.

Violet goes silent, and I say nothing more. Vi's parents set out from Eerie-on-Sea in a rowing boat and were never seen again. But she doesn't need me to remind her.

"Take her down a peg, Blaze, lad," comes the voice of Uncle Squint then as he joins us in the wheelhouse. "Fog bank ahead. Better run her slow from here."

Sure enough, across the horizon a swathe of dense green

mist has appeared while we were talking, rising from the sea like an ethereal cliff.

"Bring her closer to Maw Rocks," Squint commands. "We'll keep the islands on our starboard side, and navigate by sight. Not *too* close, mind."

"Aye, aye," says Blaze, turning the wheel. To starboard (that's our right side, if you're wondering), the field of rocky islands spike up from the sea like the monstrous teeth they are named after, promising doom to careless sailors. We approach the sheer peak of the nearest, jutting black and frost-touched from of the sea.

"Bladderwracks," I say under my breath as the massive rock slides silently by. I clutch the icy handrail, remembering why I was once so terrified of travelling by sea. And then the mist rolls over us.

Our faces and hands are chilled as freezing fog fills the air around the boat. The islands vanish into the mist. Soon we can see little beyond a tiny patch of choppy sea around us.

"Easy, Blaze. Easy," says Uncle Squint, his voice dull in the thick air.

"Did you see that?" says Vi suddenly, pointing. "Ah, it's already lost in the mist."

"What?"

"I'm not sure, Herbie," Vi replies. "I thought I saw – in a break in the fog—"

Then she gasps.

"Quick! Shut off the engine!"

"Eh?" says Blaze.

"Do it, lad," says Uncle Squint. "Better to do first and ask later out in these waters," he adds as his nephew powers down the electric engine, and we start to drift.

"What did you see, lass?" asks Uncle Squint.

"Over there," says Violet, pointing into the fog. "I thought I saw someone."

"Someone?" Blaze looks doubtful.

"Yes," says Vi. "No. Oh, I don't know."

Uncle Squint looks at us for a moment. Then he slips a small brass telescope from his pocket, snaps it open and peers ahead into the drifting fog.

"Nudge us on a bit, lad," he says, lowering the telescope. "But slow! We don't want to be seen. This is a sea souper and no mistake, but the fog is patchy. If there is something, I'd like a glimpse of it so we know what we're dealing with."

"It's midwinter," I say. "What do you think we're dealing with?"

"No need for that talk," Uncle Squint snaps, dismissing my fears rather too quickly for my liking. "Now," he adds in a whisper, "there's another break in the fog – all stop, lad."

Blaze powers down again. The electric engine is quiet at slow speeds, but even so, once we stop, the eeriest silence falls over us. Even the lapping of the sea against the hull seems to quieten. The mist, which was as thick as smoke a moment ago, goes wispy and allows us glimpses of shapes and shadows ahead, and…

A boat!

Much closer than we were expecting.

It's a motor launch, with an open top. And in the boat someone stands, peering out into the mist.

Squint raises his telescope again, but I don't need a magnifying lens to recognize who it is.

It's Sebastian Eels!

THE FLYING SAUCER

"EASE US BACK, BLAZE, LAD," says Uncle Squint softly. "Nice and slow."

Blaze Westerley puts the *Spark* into reverse, and the figure on the boat starts to fade as we recede into the mist. I reckon we'd escape undetected, too, if the thing that happens next didn't happen. But it does!

There's a sudden crash of copper pots from below deck, followed by the kind of sound you'd hear if, say, a pesky bookshop cat had finally given in to temptation, jumped at an electric fairy and got zapped on the nose. Ember shoots up out of the hatchway and buzzes around the boat, spitting sparks of indignation and lighting up the mist.

Blaze takes off his hat and quickly swipes the little sprightning out of the air.

But, in the silence that follows, we hear a sound.

A petrol engine starting up.

"Blasted imp!" growls Uncle Squint as Blaze gently scoops

Ember onto the end of his finger, where she crackles with crossness. "Get that firefly stowed, Mr Westerley," he snaps, taking the wheel himself and spinning it hard to port.

The *Jornty Spark* turns as Squint throttles forward, sending the needle up the speed gauge. We begin moving swiftly through the water now, kicking up a spray either side of the prow and skipping the waves. Vi and I lean out the back of the boat, and peer into the mist.

"Are we followed?" demands Uncle Squint.

"Can't see anything," Violet calls back.

"We can hear him though," I add, because sure enough the growl of the motorboat reaches us from somewhere.

Then Violet says to me, "Get down!"

She hits the deck, dragging me with her as – with the roar of a powerful engine – the motorboat emerges from the fog beside us.

There's a hole in the side of the *Spark* – let's face it, there are *lots* of holes in the old boat – but it does mean that Vi and I can get a good look at Eels from our hiding place as he draws up alongside, matching our speed, standing at the wheel of his sleek launch. He is dressed for action – like the way the professor dresses, but more serious, as if – in Eels' case – he really does expect to be hunting monsters.

"Squint Westerley!" he calls across the water. "What brings you out on such a foul day?"

"Fish," replies Uncle Squint as tersely as any of the fisherfolk of Eerie-on-Sea.

"Not carrying any passengers, are you?" Eels replies. "Not *snooping*, are you? By any chance?"

"Fisherfolk don't snoop," Squint barks, "and we never take passengers, as well you know."

I notice that during this bad-tempered exchange, we are getting closer and closer to Eels' boat. It seems that Uncle Squint is easing over towards her, and forcing Eels to keep steering a little to starboard, to keep distance.

"Watch it!" snaps Sebastian Eels. "Look where you're going!"

"No," says Squint Westerley, standing firm in his wheelhouse. "*You* look where you're going."

And suddenly, out of the mist ahead looms an enormous mass of rock, its peak jutting so high it is lost in the fog. Now I realize why Squint was forcing Eels to keep changing course – he was pushing him steadily into Maw Rocks.

Eels spins his own wheel in panic, cursing loudly, as his boat turns and narrowly misses the island. In the mist behind us, he vanishes from view. Uncle Squint slams the throttle forward, opening up the *Spark*'s mighty electric engine, full power.

"Hold on!" cries Squint, rather too late as Vi and I are almost thrown overboard. But we cling on, at the head of a great V-shape of sea spray as our boat races out into the ocean.

Eventually Squint throttles back down to a moderate speed.

"Can't see him, Uncle," Blaze says, back again on the

deck and surveying the fog all around. "Can't see much of anything, though."

"Can't hear anything, either," says Vi, "which is more important. We've lost him."

"But where are we?" I ask, looking at the tiny patch of choppy and mist-circled sea that seems to be our whole world now. "Maybe we've lost ourselves."

"By my reckoning," says Uncle Squint, handing the wheel back to his nephew. He licks his finger and holds it up into the frosty air, "we should be – just about…"

"There!" Violet cries, pointing off into the mist. "Something in the sky. Something – flying?"

"Flying?" I say, straining to see.

"In the mist," Violet says. "It looks like – like a flying…"

"Saucer!" I gasp, suddenly seeing it too. "It's a UFO!"

Well, it's more like a flying *hat*, if I'm honest, so not a *completely* Unidentified Flying Object. But is an Identified Flying Hat a thing? An IFH? Anyway, whatever you want to call it, a hat-like object is hovering low in the misty sky off to starboard, ready to vaporize us all with its alien death ray.

"Arr, don't be a ninny, Herbie," says Uncle Squint with a chuckle. "'Tisn't *flying* at all. 'Tis the top of the lighthouse. Look!"

Sure enough, as Blaze corrects our course and eases us towards the strange shape in the mist, we see that the hat-like object is indeed attached to the top of a tall tower that rises from a rocky island becoming dimly visible in the parting mist.

"Dismal Beacon," says Squint with satisfaction. "We've arrived." Then he adds, as we approach, "Bring her in, Mr Westerley. There's an old stone quay below the lighthouse, around the other side."

As we approach the island, I am filled with a creeping sense of dread. I've seen the chart of Eerie Bay, so I know how very far out at sea we are – how distant we are from the town. And this long-forsaken and barnacled rocky speck, blooming with frost crystals and wreathed in greenish-fog, seems more desolate than anything I could have imagined in the cosy warmth of my Lost-and-Foundery. To think a lighthouse keeper lived here once.

"When did the last keeper leave?" asks Violet then, her own thoughts seemingly matching my own.

"Years past now," says Squint as we make our final approach to the quay. "Ease us in, Blaze, lad. Look lively with the rope there, lass. Make ready with the bad jokes, Mr Lemon."

"Eye eye, Cap'n *Squint*," I reply, though I guess you'd have to read that one to find it funny.

I grab the boathook as we rock up to the roughly built quay. Violet jumps onto the island and loops the rope through a sea-gnawed iron ring. She braces herself, holding the *Spark* in place, and calls me over. Muttering a "bladderwracks!" or two beneath my breath, I jump onto the quay beside her.

The lighthouse is white with red stripes, but it is coloured all over with salt-spray, corrosion and neglect. It looms over us in the drifting mist, making me dizzy when I look up. The top of the tower is exactly what you would expect from a lighthouse: a lantern room with wide glass windows beneath a domed cap. The light is not on, presumably because now is technically daytime. However, with the dark of midwinter and the thickness of the fog, it's hard to tell what time it is.

"Well?" says Uncle Squint. "What now?"

Violet looks around at the empty rock, seemingly at a loss.

"We just need to do a bit of exploring," she says. "Could you come back and pick us up again in an hour or two?"

"Hardly!" Uncle Squint scoffs. "I'm not leaving you two here alone."

"But if you stay tied up here," Violet protests, "Eels might see the *Spark* and come to investigate."

"Aye, we are a bit noticeable," agrees Blaze. "Maybe we can pull back into the fog bank and wait close by?"

"I don't like it," says Uncle Squint, but you can tell he sees the sense in what we're saying.

"We can signal with our torch when we're ready to be picked up," says Vi. "You have got your torch, haven't you, Herbie?"

I fish a flashlight out of my coat pocket, and snap it on and off.

"Careful!" says Vi. "Eels could see."

"Right," I reply, quickly putting the torch away. "Sorry."

"We'll tie a lantern to the prow of the *Spark*," says Blaze, "so you can spot us coming. And if Eels happens upon us, well, we'll say we're baiting garsharks, won't we, Uncle?"

"Aye." Uncle Squint rubs his stubbly chin. "Aye, that we could, lad. All right then. But you have one hour sharp, and that's all. We'll be close by the whole time. And don't be afraid to holler, Eels or no Eels. Understood?"

"Aye aye," says Violet, doing a quick salute. She unloops the rope again and tosses it back aboard the *Spark*.

"One hour, mind," grumbles Squint, tapping the face of a battered old pocket watch from his waistcoat. "Not a minute more."

But the *Spark* is already falling away from our lonely shore, carried by the strange currents out beyond Maw Rocks, and soon all we can see is a faint speck of light from the lantern that Blaze hangs at the prow. And then, as the fog-bank closes over the boat, we can't even see that.

Vi and I are on a tiny rocky island.

Far out in Eerie Bay.

Alone.

DISMAL BEACON

"SO, WHAT *ARE* WE DOING HERE?" I ask.

"Herbie, this is our chance to investigate another Eerie disappearance," Violet replies. "There must be *some* clue to what happened to Sabrina."

"But, Vi, what happened to Sabrina happened years ago. Decades. Look at this place now. What clues can there be after all this time?"

Violet doesn't answer. Instead, she climbs the barnacled steps to the lighthouse. The island levels out here, so we can walk all around the circular base of the building, which is green with seaweed, and crawling with tiny crabs and even tinier hopping things. At high tide the sea must cover all this, I realize with a gulp, leaving the lighthouse itself lapped by the waves. No wonder Sabrina Eels didn't wait to be rescued.

"The keeper's boat must have been tied there?" says Violet when we get back to where we started. She points to a small alcove in the rock, above the quay. "Imagine being alone here, Herbie, and marooned, and thinking your only chance was to set off back to shore in a small rowing boat."

Well, I don't want to imagine this, do I?

"It's hard to think of this place as the treasure island," I reply, with a shudder, remembering how the prize of a Golden Nautilus was once hidden here, in the last-ever Eerie Bay Treasure Hunt, all those years ago.

"It's also hard to imagine Mr Mollusc as a boy, sailing close by," Violet puts in, gesturing out to the ocean, "but he was. And he did. Actually," she adds, "we could throw a piece of driftwood in the sea, and watch where the current takes it. That might tell us which way Sabrina went."

"Do you have a piece of driftwood?" I ask, looking around and seeing nothing like this at all.

"Blast it!" says Vi. Then she adds, more to herself than to me. "Well, that just leaves the lighthouse itself. That's the only place that won't have been altered by the tide since the vanishing of Sabrina Eels."

But, of course, the door of the lighthouse is locked. In fact, it's covered in a heavy sheet of pitted iron that is bolted to the lighthouse wall in a way that even Clermit is unlikely to budge. On the metal sheet are the words KEEP OUT, painted in sun-bleached letters, for all trespassers to see.

"Double blast it!" says Violet again, giving the door a kick.

I'm just wondering if I should take Violet's words literally, because nothing would be more Violet than actually trying to blow off the door with dynamite, when I see something that makes me shout.

"Look out!"

And I dive at my friend, knocking her to the seaweedy ground as behind us the heavy iron panel that blocks the door crashes down onto the step where we were just standing with an ear-splitting *CLANG!*

We stagger to our feet.

"Did I do that?" asks Vi, staring at her boots in surprise.

"I hate to disappoint you, Vi, but that panel came down because someone has cut through the bolts. And recently, too. Look!" And I point to the freshly sheared metal. "The whole thing was just wedged back on for show."

Beneath the iron panel is the normal door of the lighthouse, sealed by a normal lock.

Without a word, I raise my cap and slip Clermit out. He should still be nicely wound up from before, so I give a polite knock on his pearlescent shell.

"Hey there, little buddy," I say, as Clermit clicks up to speed and extends his scissor claw in greeting. "It's another door, I'm afraid. Can you help us get in?"

And I place him on the ground.

In a clockwork moment, Clermit has scuttled up and picked the lock. The lighthouse door swings creakingly open. The cold stench of oilskin coats, neglected fishiness and old mouldy rope hits us.

"This clue had better be worth it," I say through my sleeve as I welcome Clermit back under my cap. "Smells like a zombie keeps his underpants here."

And clicking on the torch, we enter the cluttered ground floor of the lighthouse. Around the circular wall is a flight of stone steps, leading to a wooden trapdoor in the ceiling. Violet climbs the stairs and pushes the trapdoor open a crack.

"A kitchen!" she says, shining the torch around. "This must be the lighthouse keeper's home."

We emerge into another circular room, with a coal-burning stove, a tall cupboard of pots and pans, a sink and a rickety table with a single chair beside it, all covered in a fur of dust and the cobwebs of some very well-travelled spiders. In the middle of the space is an iron spiral staircase, rising to another trapdoor.

"So?" I say as we look around. "What now? There's nothing here, Vi."

"No?" she replies. "What's that, then?"

And she points to the first step of the spiral stairs, where a long narrow footprint is clearly visible on the dusty metal.

"Someone *has* been here," says Vi. "Recently."

"Maybe there's a caretaker," I point out. "The lighthouse may be automatic, but it still needs looking after, surely."

Even as I say this, though, I know it's not that. You don't need to be a genius to guess the connection between this broken-into lighthouse and Sebastian Eels making secret nocturnal trips into Eerie Bay in his motorboat.

"But what's he been doing here?" asks Vi, clearly thinking the same as me.

She starts to climb, leaving me little choice but to follow.

Pushing open the next trapdoor, we discover that the room above is the keeper's bedroom. There are even the remains of an old iron bed frame and several empty crates. Outside the small windows, the sea mist swirls thicker than ever.

The spiral staircase rises to a third trapdoor, and beyond that it continues up and up the inside of the open tower, until it reaches the very top of the lighthouse.

Without a word, Violet continues upwards. The metal stairs creak and wobble, flakes of rust dropping around me as I follow. The lighthouse gets narrower and narrower the higher we go, and soon I can almost touch the walls. Then we reach the lamp room at the top.

"The light!" says Vi, clicking off the torch as we emerge into a round room walled entirely by windows. She taps the magnifying lens of the great lantern that stands in the centre of the room. At its base is the clunky old mechanism that rotates the lamp so it can shine out to sea. "It must be visible for miles around."

"That," I say, "is kind of the point, Vi."

I examine the cables and wires of the mechanism. Something about it all seems a bit odd to me, but this is my first lighthouse, so I put the thought aside.

"Can't see a thing," says Vi, looking out of the window

into the swirl of the mist. In places it thins slightly, offering tantalizing glimpses of the sea far below, only to close up again with eerie green fog.

"Now what?" I say. "It's just … a lighthouse."

Violet sighs. This is beginning to feel like a wasted trip, and I can tell she's thinking the same thing.

"Do you know what's different about this adventure, Herbie?" she says, turning to me. "Different from all the others? The mermonkey, that's what. We always get a clue from the mermonkey. But this time, he let us down."

"We got something from him," I remind her.

I fish around in my coat pocket and pull out the book prescription card that the mermonkey dispensed when he went haywire after the berthday party.

"That?" Violet says. "But it's not even a code."

I hold the card up and look again at the smudgy jumble of characters that are stamped over one another so chaotically.

"The mermonkey doesn't type for nothing," I say. "I still think it says *mermedusa*, don't you?"

As I say this, a whisper echoes around the lantern room, as if the great magnifying lens just vibrated.

DUSA-usa-usa.

Violet looks at me, her eyes fearful suddenly.

I'm about to say something else when I catch a glimpse, through the window, of a dark shape gliding past the rocky island far below.

"Let's signal to the *Spark*." I pick up the torch. "It was

worth a try, Vi, but there's nothing here. I – I don't think we should have come here at all."

I put the torch against the glass, and start clicking it on and off.

"No!" says Vi, snatching the torch back. "We can't go yet."

"But the boat's just there," I protest, waving down to where, sure enough, a long, sleek shape is coming into sight again, from the other way.

"Well, they'll just have to wait, won't they?" Vi replies. "It hasn't been an hour yet. There's a clue in this lighthouse, Herbie. I just know there is."

And Violet starts examining the room more closely.

I wave again at the *Jornty Spark*, where she is emerging from the fog. I'm looking forward to getting back in the warm cabin. But then I see something that chills me more than an unheated lighthouse in winter.

It isn't the Westerleys' boat!

Below, becoming horribly visible as he draws near, is the face of Sebastian Eels. He looks up at us from his open-top motor launch. He must see me, too, because he grins as he holds up some sort of device, from which he extends a telescopic aerial.

Then he presses a button.

YOWZERS!

IT FEELS LIKE I am hit by a duvet.

A duvet travelling at the speed of light.

A duvet, travelling at the speed of light, that has wrapped itself around my head in an eiderdown death grip of doom.

I fall to the ground, my hands clamped to my ears, and stare bug-eyed at Violet, who is doing the same. A terrible sensation quivers right through my body, as if hit by a great roaring sound, and yet there is nothing to hear at all. I feel the stone of the lighthouse vibrate powerfully through my hands as I force myself to my feet.

"V-v-V-v-V—" I try to say, reaching out to my friend, but then immediately clamping my hand back to my head. Vi is trying to speak too, but I can't hear her words. I stumble towards her, but it's only as I crash into the great lighthouse lantern that I realize I *can* hear something after all: a terrible, bone-shaking, stomach-shredding, *world-wrenching* hum.

And that's when, despite the boggling of my bamboozled

brain in the grip of a storm of infrasound, I understand what's so strange about the lighthouse lamp. Among the old cables and cast-iron parts of the mechanism is something much more modern. Something strapped to the great magnifying lens of the Dismal Beacon.

But already, my thoughts are getting runny and I'm falling into a trance. My mind fills with the strongest image I have yet experienced – since the Eerie Hum began – of infinite black eyes in a blank and awful face, surrounded by a halo of tendrils.

"Shipwreck Boy!" the face seems to say, in a hissing voice. "At la-a-as-st!"

"No!" I cry out loud.

I grab the modern device, even though it threatens to shake my arms to pieces, and tear it off the lens with all my strength. I fling it to the ground, still vibrating ferociously, and stamp down on it with my shoe as hard as I can, breaking it open.

And it's over.

The terrible resonance ends. The face in my mind dissolves once more, leaving my head ringing, my mind pinging and my bladder well-and-truly wracked.

"H-H-Herbie?" Vi manages to get out as she staggers to her feet. "W-w-hat just h-happened?"

I wobble back to the window and look down, just in time to see Sebastian Eels' motorboat vanish at great speed into the mist.

"No!" I cry, as a sudden, terrible realization dawns on me.

I snatch up the torch and begin signalling madly through the window.

"Herbie, that was the hum, wasn't it?" says Vi, a look of horror on her face. "So that means…"

"It was," I cry in reply. "And it *does*! Eels has turned the lens of Dismal Beacon lighthouse into a giant loudspeaker, and it has just broadcast the hum – the Eerie Hum! – right across the bay."

"But the hum *attracts* the malamander."

"Er, I know!" I reply, still at the window, desperately flicking the torch on and off again. "Which is why we need to get off this rock *right now*!"

"Blaze and his uncle might not see a torch in this mist, Herbie. How long before our hour is up?"

"I don't know!" I cry. "I returned the watch to its rightful owner, remember?"

Then, as I look back down at the rocky shore, I catch another movement in the mist: something big emerging from the water and darting across the rock to the base of the lighthouse.

"Oh, bladderwracks!" I gulp as the whole building seems to quiver.

Exactly as if something big has started climbing up it.

"The light!" says Vi. "The *lighthouse* light. Can we use it to signal the *Spark*?"

"It'll be on a timer," I reply. "We'll have to short-circuit the wires."

"How do we do that?"

Well, the answer to this is we need to cut into the two heavy-duty cables that we can see – one brown, one purple – and connect them together. Without electrocuting ourselves, that is, though I haven't a clue how we'll do that without special tools and protective gear, and ideally the help of someone like Dr Thalassi.

I shake my head in despair.

"Then we'll just have to make a run for it," Violet says, dashing to the top of the spiral stairs. By now the whole lighthouse is shaking, and we can actually hear the sound of claws in brick. I remember how easily the malamander scaled the Grand Nautilus Hotel.

"It's coming!" I croak, feeling my knees going weak.

And that's when, with a sickening slap, a great webbed hand smacks against the window. The malamander scrapes its claws into the storm-proof glass with a teeth-edging screech and pulls itself up to look in – its spines bristling, its scales quivering in rage, and its fishy tooth-filled mouth hanging open.

Violet and I are completely exposed, side by side in the lantern room at the top of the lighthouse, with nowhere to hide.

"Don' moof," I hear Violet say from the corner of her mouth.

"'Kay!" I say back, from the corner of mine.

And will this work? Will keeping perfectly still really

get us out of this situation?

The malamander presses its terrible scaly face against the glass and begins to growl.

"Clermit," I whisper, keeping my lips as still as I can. "Clermit, we need you."

The malamander's eyes flick to my face as I feel a movement beneath my cap.

"Climb down my back," I whisper, hoping Clermit can hear me. "We need to get the light on…"

Whether it's the panic in my sideways voice or the stiff way I'm standing, I don't know, but Clermit seems to understand the danger of the moment. I feel my cap lift very slowly. Then Clermit scuttles down my back, out of sight, making me twitch. The malamander's eyes narrow even further. Surely it can see me move! The creature digs its talons deeper into the glass, sending cracks criss-crossing the window.

"Join the brown wire to the purple wire," I instruct Clermit. "But don't let him …"

Clermit scuttles out from behind my foot and clambers up the lamp mechanism, in full view of everyone.

"… see you!" I finish, far too late.

The malamander's eyes focus instantly on the shiny brass and pearlescent shell of the hermit crab, who is seizing the wires.

It gives out a great roar of fury and smashes the lighthouse windows.

Vi and I drop to the ground, curling up against the flying glass.

And now the malamander is inside, filling the lamp room, glaring down at us in triumph – as it opens its venomous mouth.

"Now, Clermit!" I yell, covering my eyes.

Clermit snips into the purple cable with one claw and the brown cable with the other, till he reaches the copper wire within – connecting the two by channelling electricity directly through his own metal limbs.

The lighthouse lantern blazes on.

The malamander, exposed suddenly to the heat and ferocity of the Dismal Beacon light, bellows in shock and surprise, jumping backwards. It leaps out into the air high above the sea and is gone.

Vi and I are left sprawled on our backs amid the chunks of shattered storm-proof glass, chests heaving, squinting up at the steady rotation of the lighthouse lantern.

"Thank you, Clermit," I manage feebly. "That's enough now."

There comes the sound of scissor claws un-snipping, and the mighty light winks out. Then there's the tinkle of metal on stone as my little wind-up helper, frazzled by a gazillion volts, folds his limbs away and falls over. I replace him gratefully beneath my cap.

"Get up!" says Vi, on her feet and already looking down at me. "We need to go, Herbie. It might come back."

"Do you think Blaze and his uncle saw the light?" I ask as we head back to the spiral stairs.

"I hope so. Unless the malamander got them first."

And so, with this cheery thought, we race down the stairs and burst back out of the lighthouse.

I fill my lungs with enough sea air to do a few loud *AHOY!s* and maybe even a *HELP!* or two, but Vi clamps her hand over my mouth, so actually I don't do anything but squeak.

"It might still be out there," she whispers into my ear. "Waiting."

"I thought the malamander was afraid of daylight," I whisper back, when I can speak again.

"It's midwinter," Vi replies, "and with this fog it's about as dark as the daytime ever gets. And it has just heard the sound it most wants to hear – the call of its long-lost mate. It's still out there, Herbie, believe me."

Then, muffled by the fog but just audible above the lapping of the waves, we hear the faint ringing of a ship's bell.

"The *Spark*!" I say. "It's them!"

Ahead, emerging like a Viking longship from the mist, comes the curved prow of the fishing boat. We see the pale face and shocking red hair of Blaze Westerley, with bright little Ember buzzing around him.

"Ahoy!" he shouts.

"Sssh!" Violet shushes across to the boat. "We need to get out of here!"

And before Uncle Squint can even get the boat alongside

the quay, Vi has already jumped aboard and is beckoning me
to do the same.

"Can't you get a *bit* closer?" I say, eyeing the gap.

"Newer, braver Herbie doesn't need 'a bit closer'," says
Violet. "Jump!"

I eye the gap again. Vi's right – I can do this. I take a run-
up, and leap for all I'm worth …

… just as something bursts up out of the sea, straight
at me.

It's the arm of the malamander! It swipes at me as I fly
through the air, catching my leg.

"AARGH!" I cry, since there no longer seems to be any
point shushing. Also, it really hurts. "YOWZERS!"

And I crash onto the deck.

"Dismal's beard!" cries Uncle Squint, his skipper's cap
almost flying off at the sight of that great scaly arm crashing
back into the sea in a riot of spray. "Hold on!" He yanks the
throttle into reverse, spinning the wheel – and therefore
the boat – in a desperate high-speed turn. Then he rams the
throttle forward, and we start to fly.

"Herbie!"

Violet drops beside me on the deck as we flee at top speed.
I look down at myself and see blood, and that a big bit of my
uniform leg isn't there any more.

Then I pass out.

SCYLLA AND CHARYBDIS

"HERBIE?"

"Gngn?" I reply as something rough seems to be trying to expose my cheekbones. Then I open my eyes and realize that the something rough is Erwin's tongue, licking me awake.

"Will I walk again?" I ask in a wobbly voice, not daring to look at the place where my leg used to be. "Will I need a wooden peg?"

"Don't worry, Long John Herbie," says Vi with a grin. "It's just a scratch. Whatever that uniform of yours is made of, I'd like a coat of the stuff. I bet it could stop bullets."

I look down. My lower leg, exposed, with part of my trousers missing, has a piece of white cloth bandaged around it. My brain sends a cautious signal to my toes to wriggle, just to make sure, and wriggle they do, like anything.

"You fainted," says Blaze, looking over from the wheelhouse like he's never heard of such a thing before.

"How long was I out?" I ask, sitting up. "What year is it?"

"It's about half an hour since we left Dismal Beacon," says Blaze. "Now, get yourself together – we're going to make another run for it. And this one has to count."

"Aye," says Uncle Squint quietly from the prow of the *Spark*, where he is surveying the misty seascape. "When the moment's right, Blaze, lad. The beast's still out there. Somewhere."

"Run for it?" I say, getting to my feet. "What's going on?"

"We've been trying to get back to Eerie-on-Sea," explains Vi. "But the malamander can hear the electric engine. It's attacked us twice! I'm amazed we dodged it."

"It's toying with us," says Squint. "Waiting to see what we'll do."

"I still say the *Spark*'s too fast for it," adds Blaze, patting the glowing blue dials. "But the battery's low. We'll only have one more chance."

"Why is it so angry with us, Vi," I say, lowering my voice so only she can hear. "We survived it last year. You even spoke to it! Why is it trying so hard to kill us now?"

"Eels has been teasing it with the hum," Violet replies. "It's probably never been more dangerous."

"Rigging up the lighthouse like that." I shake my head. "Eels might have done the same to all the Eerie Bay lighthouses. Anything with a large glass lens. Like he must have done with the cameraluna. But why? Why does he want to attract the malamander?"

"Hold on!" says Blaze before Violet can answer my question. "I think this is it."

And he reaches out to the controls.

"Now!" bellows Uncle Squint.

Blaze throws the throttle forward. The *Jornty Spark* lurches ahead, propelled through the waters of Eerie Bay by her great electric battery. The sea mist, which was so thick earlier, is lifting at last, and we can see the rocky islands racing by.

"It's spotted us!" cries Violet, pointing over the back of the boat.

I join her at the rail, clutching my cap to stop it flying off. Sure enough, behind us, beyond the churning of the sea in our wake, a rack of spines has broken the surface and is swimming after us, like the fin of some great pursuing shark.

"Give it all she's got, lad!" cries Squint Westerley, grabbing up the boathook and brandishing it like a weapon. "It's gaining!"

Despite our tremendous speed, the malamander closes fast, swerving and slicing through the water.

"What do we do?" I shout, looking helplessly at Violet.

"Get behind me!" Uncle Squint yells. "You too, lass. Here it comes!"

"Don't hurt it!" cries Violet. "It doesn't want to attack us."

"Doesn't it?" Squint looks incredulous. "You could have fooled me."

There's a splash as the creature breaks the surface, closer now than ever. Violet falls back behind Uncle Squint, grabbing one of the oars. There's not much for me to grab, so I pick up poor sickly Erwin and wonder how good his claws will be against sea monster's scales.

The malamander leaps, arcing right out of the water like some sort of prehistoric dolphin, and plunges back into the sea right behind the *Spark*'s bow.

"Look out!" roars Squint as the boat judders violently. "We're being attacked from below!"

The stern of the *Spark* is lifted clear above the water, and I fall, sprawling, Erwin and all, into the wheelhouse. I look up to see Blaze, eyes wide as he struggles to control the boat; Violet, as she fights to stay upright, still clutching the oar; Squint Westerley jabbing with his boathook at a great scaly hand that slaps down onto the deck of the boat. The malamander lifts its head over the side and bellows at us with such fury that even I, cowering in the wheelhouse, can feel the spray of its saliva and smell the fish-rotten tang of its monster breath.

"Avast!" yells Squint, throwing the boathook like a spear. But its point slides along the scales of the malamander's flank till it bounces off a spine and spins away into the water.

"Please stop!" pleads Violet, pressing the end of her oar against the creature's chest, trying to push it back into the sea. "We're not your enemy!"

Then she gasps and stops pushing. Beside the tip of the oar is an opening in the monster's scaly chest, and inside, pulsing for all to see, is the creature's heart.

The malamander's heart, which – as Violet and I and almost no one else knows – opens to the sea at midwinter, so that its beatings may be detected by the creature's desperately sought mate. A mate that the malamander thinks it can hear every time Sebastian Eels broadcasts the Eerie Hum.

"Please!" Violet cries.

But the malamander just roars and smacks the oar out of her hand, sending it spinning into the sea and Violet sprawling across the deck.

"Hold on!" yells Blaze, and he spins the boat's wheel with all his might.

The *Spark* turns, almost capsizing, and the malamander is sent flying off to one side, carried by its own momentum. Blaze brings us out of the spin with the prow set at the gap between two nearby islands, and he throws the throttle forward again, propelling us straight at it. In a moment we have passed between the rocks at high speed, and Blaze brings us to a stop, shutting down the engine. In the lapping ocean silence, we strain to hear if we are still pursued.

"Everyone in one piece?" calls Uncle Squint, climbing to his feet. "Nice work, Blaze, lad."

Violet stands again, the look on her face somewhere between fear and fury.

"I hate that we are fighting it!" she cries. "This isn't how the malamander should behave."

"Who made you an expert in these things?" says Uncle Squint, with a disbelieving snort.

But Violet just shakes her head and says nothing. I feel something squirm beneath me.

"E-ow!"

"Sorry, puss." I jump to my feet. "But thanks for the soft landing."

"Well, now what?" Blaze asks. Even though the engine has been shut down, I see that he's still steering, and realize that now we've entered Maw Rocks, we are being carried along in the dangerous currents between them. "Battery's at ten per cent. That's not enough to get home at anything more than a crawl."

"Can we lure the creature away?" I ask, but another look at Violet's face tells me she thinks the malamander has been interfered with enough already. Besides, the only thing we know that can attract it for sure is the hum.

"Maybe we've lost it," says Blaze.

"I wouldn't be so sure," says Uncle Squint, before shouting, "Look lively, lad!" as he points at a mass of rock that is suddenly right in front of us.

With a spin of the wheel, Blaze only just avoids it.

All about us the mist is rising, forming a ceiling of cloud till soon only the peaks of the rocky islands are hidden, and the sea becomes visible again. I look here and there, still clutching Erwin, straining for some sign of the malamander.

"We're picking up speed," Blaze warns from the wheel. "Can I engage again now? Slow us down a bit?"

"No," Squint replies. "Not yet."

"But the currents?" says Violet. "Won't we get pulled towards the Vortiss?"

"Not if Blaze keeps us on this heading," Squint says before stumbling as the boat lurches yet again. Blaze manoeuvres desperately, and we just miss crashing into another sheer rocky mass, scraping down the side of it instead with a sickening screech.

"It's getting harder to stay in control," says Blaze. "I can keep us away from the Vortiss, but the coastal currents will wreck us if I don't engage soon."

Already he's fighting to keep us clear of another spike of rock.

Pang!

The brass bell of the *Jornty Spark* suddenly rings.

"Come on, Ember!" says Blaze as the sprightning buzzes around it. "Stop messing about."

Ping! Pang!

The sprightning zaps against the bell again. Then...

PING! PANG! PING! PANG!

She goes berserk, ringing the bell like mad.

"Something's wrong!" cries Blaze, catching Ember in his hat so we can at least hear straight.

And then we see that wrecking rocks and catching currents are not the only dangers out here. Up ahead, right where we are being pulled by the sea, Sebastian Eels is waiting in his boat, holding position with his powerful engines.

But that's not what makes my knees knobble and my cap slip down. No, what's doing *that* is behind Eels: on top of the next island rock, hazy in the rising mist, something squats on scaly haunches, spiny tail swishing. A rack of dorsal spines quiver in anticipation as two pitiless pale eyes gaze down at us all.

The malamander!

And the sea is carrying us straight towards it.

"Engage!" yells Uncle Squint. "Do it, Blaze. Bring us about!"

Blaze, staring up in horror at the creature, doesn't need to be told twice. He turns the key, igniting the control panel lights, and putting us into hard reverse with every volt and amp we have left.

From his boat, Sebastian lets out a laugh and begins to give chase. And I realize he hasn't seen the monster on the rock.

I point and wave my arms in the universally recognized "watch out behind you!" signal, but the man just laughs again and speeds up.

We tip crazily then, as the thrust from our propeller meets the rush of the water, and for one horrible moment we seem to stay right where we are, spinning crazily. Then Blaze gets us straight, pointing back the way we came, and he opens up the engine against the current.

But, with the battery nearly drained, we can only crawl, and nothing will stop Eels from catching us now. Except, of course, the one thing that can.

Then Sebastian Eels, turning to look behind him, finally understands the danger he's in. A screeching roar cuts through the air as the malamander leaps from its rock and crashes down onto Eels' boat in an explosion of wood, glass and water. Eels himself can briefly be seen catapulted into the air before splashing down into the boiling sea, his boat utterly destroyed.

The spines of the malamander are briefly visible before it dives down after him.

ABYSS

UNCLE SQUINT PUSHES BLAZE ASIDE and firmly spins the wheel. In a moment we have turned again, combining our engine's remaining power *with* the current, not against it. We shoot forward and – holding our breaths in dread – pass *right over* where Eels was wrecked and where the monster dived.

And Sebastian Eels himself? Well, of him there is no sign, though Violet leans far over the side to look.

"Brace yourselves!" Squint cries. "This is going to get rough…"

I toss Erwin down into the hold, slam the hatch shut and grab on tight as the *Spark*'s desperate journey into the channels of Maw Rocks turns into some kind of nightmare fairground ride.

"Five per cent!" yells Blaze, staring down at the control panel. "We'll never escape the currents now."

"As long," gasps Squint, fighting with the wheel, "as we escape – the beastie!"

I turn and see that the malamander is following again, dolphin-leaping, eating up the distance between us. Already it's close enough to swipe, smashing a chunk of wood from the back of the boat and setting us rocking wildly as we rush headlong down channel after ever-narrowing channel, scraping the sides, cracking the hull, and spilling lobster pots overboard.

Ahead looms the mountainous mass of Eerie Rock itself – where our terrifying ride will have its end at the base of the jagged cliffs.

We're running out of sea!

The bell of the *Spark* rings on its own now, as we plunge and crash and career towards certain doom.

"Look out!" Blaze shouts, as – too late! – a shelf of rock appears right ahead of us. We hit it and now we're flying as the *Jornty Spark* becomes airborne. When we crash back into the sea, our prow sinks deep below the surface, and my nose and ears are filled with freezing water before we burst back up once more. I've barely blinked the saltiness from my eyes when we're out of the sea again, and this time free-falling, straight down.

"Aargh!" I hear myself cry, clinging to the boat as it drops into darkness, my hat and Clermit tumbling beside me.

Then we land in the unknown with an almighty crash.

The *Spark* is wedged.

Wedged upright between two spurs of rock, in the shaft of a vertical cave.

And I'm lying dazed on her deck, looking up as water tumbles all around us in a dozen waterfalls, with nothing but a dim patch of misty sky visible beyond a jagged hole, far above.

"Violet!" I shout, sitting up. "Vi!"

"Herbie!" comes Violet's voice, echoing from somewhere. I look around. Uncle Squint is slumped over the control panel in the wheelhouse, unconscious or worse, while Blaze is hanging miraculously by his dungarees from the tusk at the boat's prow, Ember buzzing urgently around him. He's also not moving.

But where is Violet?

"Herbie?" comes Violet's voice again.

With a great effort, I pull myself up and peer over the end of the boat. I see, way down below, something glinting. It's Violet, waving my Lost-and-Founder's cap, its badge catching the half-light. For a moment there seems to be something else there, too – like a pair of glowing eyes blinking up at me from a pool of water beyond Violet – but when I rub my own eyes to make sure, there's nothing there but the dark.

"Vi!" I call down. "The malamander?"

"No sign," she calls back. "It's gone."

"I'll throw down a rope," I reply, "hold on!"

I get to my feet, aching all over, and stumble to Uncle Squint. I manage to get him down into a sitting position.

"Blu-rbu-rble," he says, spitting out water. He has a bloody bash on the head, and I don't think he'll be on his feet any time soon.

Then I check on Blaze, who is already climbing down from the tusk.

"Oh!" he cries when he sees the state of his uncle. "Herbie, are you all right? Where's Violet? Where's the…?"

"Gone," I reply, answering the last question first. I explain about Violet being somewhere down below the boat.

"Where are we?" Blaze says then, marvelling at our situation. And it's quite a sight. We have fallen down a rocky shaft, where seawater cascades in torrents, but we have got ourselves wedged between two spurs of rock in the exact centre of it, so the curtains of falling water miss us. I can see parts of boats and bits of wreck further down, telling me we aren't the first to get pulled down here by the disastrous currents.

"Don't *you* know?" I reply. "I thought you fisherfolk knew all the sea around Eerie Bay."

"Aye, we do. But Maw Rocks is different. It's foolishness to venture here, and now you see why."

"This isn't the Vortiss, then?" I ask, even though I know, from previous adventures, that it can't be.

Blaze shakes his head.

"We've been swept the other way, into the cliffs of Eerie Rock. The town will be close by, but I'm bodgered if I see how we'll ever reach it from here."

"There are caves and passages all through Eerie Rock,"

I reply, "but wouldn't that be the quickest way out?"

I point up to the patch of sky above.

Blaze shrugs.

"If you think you can climb up a raging waterfall, Herbie, be my guest. I'm not leaving the *Spark*. Or my uncle."

I don't know what to say to this. Except to point out, Erwin-like, that if I can't go up then I will have to go down, won't I? Just as Blaze won't leave his family, there's also no way I'm leaving Violet down there on her own.

I open the hatch, letting a terrified Erwin out from the chaos of pots and pans below deck. He scrambles up onto my shoulders, looking sicker than ever with his fur all over the place. Then I pick up a coil of rope, tie it to a sturdy whatsit on the boat, and throw one end down towards Violet.

"Herbie!" I see the flash of her eyes. "Herbie, it's not long enough. I can't reach."

"No need," I call back. "I'll come to you."

And then I add to Blaze, "And we'll bring back help, for you and your uncle."

"Aye." Blaze nods, though with fear and doubt in his eyes, as the desperate nature of our predicament sinks in. "Aye, I know you will try."

And he shakes me by the hand. Then I, Herbert Lemon – Lost-and-Founder at the Grand Nautilus Hotel – climb over the back of the boat, and lower myself down into the unknown.

Of course, I knew when I started climbing down that there would be a drop at the bottom. If Violet can't reach the rope, then the only way Herbie is going to reach Violet is by letting go. And me with a bandaged leg already, and my cap gone from my head.

Clermit!

I suddenly remember that he fell when my cap flew off, and is gone. Does he have any spring left? Will he find me again, or will I find him down here in the dark, smashed beyond repair? I look up to where the hull of the *Spark* is wedged above me like Noah's Ark. Then I look down.

"Do you have Clermit?" I call to Violet, but she shakes her head.

"Drop Erwin down to me!" she says.

I can see Violet more clearly now, dimly visible on a rocky surface.

I let go with one arm, swinging wildly for one panicky moment, then scoop Erwin off my shoulders. He glares at me beneath flat ears.

"Don't give me that look," I say. "At least she can catch you."

I let go of Erwin, and he drops, upright – as cats do – into Violet's arms.

"Got him!" she calls. "But are you sure about this, Herbie?"

"No," I reply. "But I'm being that newer, braver Herbie, remember? So, let's pretend that I am."

"There's seaweed," Vi replies. "A big heap of it. It's what I landed in."

And she points to where something horrid-looking glistens in the little light that reaches this far down.

So, I swing, and when it feels like the moment, I let go and land with a seaweedy *splotch* and an *ooph!* of air from my lungs.

"Herbie!" Vi helps me to my feet. It looks for one alarming moment like she might hug me. "I was getting the jitters down here on my own. I don't have the torch. Do you have one?"

I reach into my pocket and pull out a tiny torch I always carry for emergencies, and click it on.

Nothing happens.

"It's too wet," I say. "Like the rest of me. Maybe it'll work better when it dries out. I know I will."

"Yes, but we can't do anything in the dark," Violet points out, handing me my cap. As I look about the faint puddle of extreme-range daylight we're standing in, surrounded on all sides by pitch black, I can't help but agree.

"Ahoy!" comes a voice from far above, and we look up to see Blaze leaning over the side of the *Spark*.

And below him, dropping in an energetic spiral around the rope, is little Ember, crackling and buzzing her way down to us.

"She'll light your way!" Blaze calls.

"Thank you!" we call back. "We'll bring her back to you, Blaze," Violet adds. "We promise."

Ember, when she reaches us, zips and flits here and there, throwing her warm electric light over a desolate scene of ruined boats and scattered life jackets. At one side of the cavernous space is a crack in the rocky floor, down which seawater pours. There is a pool on the other side, filled by spray and smaller falls. The wrecks here are modest, some little more than rowing boats.

I hear Violet's breath catch.

"Are you OK?" I ask.

Violet nods, but I can see that she's not. When your parents go missing in a rowing boat, the discovery of wrecks like these in such a desolate place is not exactly cheering. I want to point out that there aren't any skeletons though, but then it occurs to me that something must have happened to the bodies of those who fell with these boats, and so maybe the lack of skeletons is the most chilling thing of all.

Violet walks to the edge of the pool and sadly picks up an oar that floats there.

"There's a cave," I say, spotting it in Ember's crackling light. "Looks like the only way out."

Violet drops the oar, and together we pick our way over the seaweed and ruin towards the opening. But as we get closer, we see that the water extends into the cave as well.

"Please don't tell me we have to swim," I groan, the newer, braver Herbie starting to run out of me.

"Maybe one of these boats is still OK enough to use." Vi points to the wrecks. "This one, for example." And she approaches a nearby craft. Its mast is smashed off, as is part of the keel, but the hull seems sound.

"Let's get it in the water and see if it floats," I reply, and together we drag it towards the pool, Ember dodging about ahead. We thrust it into the water and are relieved to see it bobbing there.

"Oh!" Violet gasps.

"What?" I reply. It's nice that the boat's afloat, but it's not *that* exciting.

"Look!"

Violet points towards the prow of the boat. Ember, who must understand from the action that her light is needed there, hovers close, her glow illuminating the varnished wood of the dinghy. And we see a name, painted in chipped but readable letters.

SEAHORSE

Vi and I look at each other in stunned silence.

Godfrey Mollusc's trusty little sailing boat!

"*This* is where she ended up!" says Vi. "Do you see what that means, Herbie?"

"Ish," I admit, scratching my chin. "But, um, maybe you can tell me what *you* think it means, Vi, so we can compare notes."

"Godfrey lost his boat right next to Dismal Beacon," says Violet, "and the currents brought it all the way here. So, if the currents did that with *Seahorse*, then they must have done the same to Sabrina's rowing boat. She fell down here too."

"I'm not sure *must* is the word I would use," I reply, "but, yup, you might well be right."

"If I am right," Vi continues, "then we are still on Sabrina's trail. And if she survived the fall, then there's only one place she would go."

And we both look out across the pool to where the water vanishes into the cave.

"You go back and get that oar," I say, straightening my uniform front. "I'll wade in and secure the boat."

THE CRYSTAL CAVE

THERE'S NO SILENCE quite as profound as the silence of the subterranean deep. Once we have rowed beyond the crash of the waterfalls, each ripple we make as Violet digs into the still water with the oar, or drip as she raises it again afterwards, echoes horribly, and makes us cower to be creating such a din in this world of darkness. It's only with the light of Ember, flitting about our boat – the doughty *Seahorse*, from the childhood of Godfrey Mollusc – that we can see anything of our surroundings at all.

"The pool is getting narrower," I say in a whisper from the back of the boat, where I'm using a pole I found to steer. "The rock walls are closing in."

The sense of entering a crack in the Earth is growing stronger.

"All this water has to go somewhere," Vi replies, looking up at the dripstones and crystal blooms above us, "and there's no way back, anyway."

"Maybe if you didn't row so quickly," I say, "we would have a chance to see. Slow down!"

"I've stopped rowing," Vi protests, with a hint of alarm. "There's a current here. It's getting faster!"

Violet suddenly pulls the oar out of the water, and cries, "Look out!"

A low mass of rock looms at us from the darkness ahead, right across the channel. I throw myself down into the boat as we whoosh beneath it, *Seahorse*'s broken mast barely scraping through. Then, in a rush of water, we're on the other side.

But the other side of where?

Vi sits back up and digs the oar in, to get us out of a spin. I do the same with the pole. We come to a halt, only now the water is more like an inky-black mirror, reflecting nothing but the darkness all around and the tiny point of light that little Ember brings. The sprightning settles onto my Lost-and-Founder's cap, her brightness gleaming warmly from the brass "L" and "F" on the badge.

"Somehow," Violet whispers again, "I can tell we've just gone from somewhere very narrow, to somewhere very, *very* big."

"If only," I whisper back, feeling that this vast quiet could engulf us forever, "we had a little more light."

Ember takes off again, shooting a small spark at my nose, as if reminding me that light is precisely why she's here. As I rub the sting away, she flies up and up, and yet more up, till she's nothing but a tiny, *tiny* little speck of light far above.

"It's huge!" whispers Violet, amazed. "Ember's light's too small to—"

KA-BLAM!

The sprightning, without even waiting for Violet to finish, lets off a flash of lightning that fills this sunless world with a moment of brilliance. And we gasp as we see a glittering cavern of crystal, arching over us like the vaulted ceiling of a diamond cathedral, reflecting and refracting the electrical blaze in a dazzling optical display.

Then darkness returns to reclaim us.

Ember spirals back down, and lands once more on my cap, her light smaller and dimmer than before, but managing to radiate a sense of being pleased with herself.

"Did you see anything useful?" Vi asks me. "Like a way out of here, perhaps?"

"No," I admit. But – wait. Looking again, I think I *can* see something now: faint points of light, in pairs, like glowing eyes all around us in the darkness. "What's that?"

"What?" Vi replies.

I rub my eyes, and when I look again the lights are gone.

"I'm still dazzled," I say, blinking, "that's all."

"ECHO!" cries Violet then, without any warning, at the top of her lungs.

KO-ko-ko... rolls the sound all around us.

"Can you not do that!" I protest from where I'm suddenly crouching in surprise at the bottom of the boat.

"There's no one here, Herbie," Vi replies with a grin. "And echolocation is a thing, you know. Bats do it."

And yes, I suppose she's right.

"FISH AND CHIPS!" I yell, in my own biggest voice.

IPS-ips-ips... comes the reply.

And this is such a good release of tension after our recent terrors that I shout it again. But this time, as the echo fades, we hear a new sound: a *pitter-patter*, as if something damp and invisible is running along an unseen shore.

Then we hear a *ploosh!* that sounds for all the world like something entering the water.

"What was *that*?" says Violet, looking out into the blackness.

"You said there was no one here!" I gasp, clutching the wooden pole.

"Yeah, but I don't know that for sure, do I?" Violet replies fearfully.

Ember, sensing our need for light once more, takes off from my cap and swoops low above the water. I look over the side of the boat and see, all around us, just beneath the surface, dozens of pale, sightless eyes, turned up to the light. And the eyes are glowing.

"There are things," I say with a gulp. "Things in the water."

Then *plop!*

One of the pale creatures breaks the surface and snaps a soft, fishy mouth at Ember, who flits away just in time, back to the safety of my cap.

The pale thing raises its head out of the water again. It stares right through me with luminous, cave-blind eyes. Then another lifts its head, and another and another, till we are surrounded by bald, baby-like, pale-eyed faces, gazing at us, their mouths opening and closing.

Then we see their hands.

Small, waving hands that rise out of the water and grope for the boat.

"W-w-wh-a-a-t ..." gasps one of the horrors, breathing out something terrifyingly like an actual word.

"D-d-oooo ..." gurgles another.

"Y-o-U-oU ..." trills a third.

"S-S-S-s ..." hisses a group of them at once, "s-S-s-s-eeeek?"

"Herbie!" Violet says, a look of mingled fear and wonder on her face. But I hope she isn't expecting me to say anything, because utter terror has me by the throat.

"W-w-haat ..." come the fishy voices again, as the abominations that surround us take it in turn to speak.

"D-do ..."

"Y-you ..."

"Seeek ..."

Then they finish their question all together, in a nightmarish chorus.

"In the daaark?"

And now dozens of pairs of glowing eyes are staring, as if waiting for an answer.

"Herbie!" Violet whispers again as we huddle together. "I know what these are. They're …"

I clench my eyes tight shut and nod. I know what they are too.

"Fargazi!" I manage to get out.

"W-H-AT …"

"DO-O …"

"YOU …"

"SEEEK …" come the voices again, more insistent now, as the creatures begin to pull themselves up the sides of the boat.

"IN THE DA-A-ARK?"

"We have to answer," says Vi. "Or—"

"Don't say it," I whisper back.

I've heard the legend of the fargazi, I know what will happen if we don't answer their question.

"WHAT … DO … YOU … *SEEEK*?"

"It has to be a true answer," says Vi. "That's how this works."

This, too, I know. According to legend, the fargazi gather around shipwrecked sailors, adrift at sea, and ask them a single question. If they answer with the truth, whatever that truth is, the creatures will lead them to safety. But if the sailor can't answer, or lies – well, let's not think about how it must feel to be dragged underwater and slowly devoured by those gaping, gummy mouths.

"The secret," Violet says, as firmly as she can. "We seek

the Deepest Secret of Eerie-on-Sea."

There's a collective exhalation of fishy breath at this, and a hardening about the eyes of the creatures.

"WHAT … DO … *YOU* … SEEK … IN THE *DARK*?"

Apparently this is not the answer the fargazi are looking for!

"The malamander!" I gasp out as one fargazer leans far enough into the boat to grab Violet's oar. "We seek the malamander!"

"AARGH…" gasp the creatures now, snatching ever more hungrily, pulling themselves closer still. "AAAARGH!"

"What's the answer?" Violet looks as desperate as I feel. "Herbie, what do we do?"

"We seek the light!" I cry. "Or – or a way out! Or Sebastian Eels! *Fish and chips!*"

By now one fargazer has seized a handful of Violet's coat. Ember sends a spark of electricity zapping into it, and the hand retreats, but soon more hands are entwining in her hair and grasping my uniform, and Ember's light is growing weak now from all her efforts to help us.

"WHAT DO YOU SEEK IN THE DARK?"

The question comes again as we struggle against the grasping hands, and somehow I know it is the last time it will be asked.

And we still don't know the answer!

FARGAZI ROUND

"HERBIE!"

Violet looks at me urgently, as the grabbing hands begin to pull her down.

"We *must* know the answer!" she cries, wrapping Erwin protectively in her coat. "That's the point. It's not a trick question; it's not a riddle. Somehow, we *do* know the answer!"

And that's right enough, too. The fargazi never ask a question their victim can't answer, though it might be an answer they haven't yet realized they know. Either way, it still has to be the truth.

"Vi!" I cry as the soft, clammy hands try to tug the pole from my grasp. "The mermonkey!"

"What about him?" she replies, vainly fighting off the embrace of the creatures. "He didn't help."

"But he did!" I insist. "He typed the word..."

And I say it, as purposefully as I can, even as soft fingers start to scrabble around my mouth and eyes.

"Mermedusa! We seek the MERMEDUSA!"

"AAAH…" comes an answering chorus, in a light breeze of watery breath. "MER-MED-*US*-SAA."

Immediately the hands recede, and the hundredfold little grips on our clothing lessen as the creatures let go. One by one, each fargazer slips back into the water.

"SEEK – MER-MED-*US*-A…" says the last of the creatures, rolling over in the water, before turning its glowing eyes back onto us.

"*Is* that really what we seek?" Violet whispers. "It's news to me!"

"But it's not news to them," I reply. "So, it must be the truth. And look!"

Out in the great subterranean lake, we can still see the pale glow of the eyes of the fargazi. They are swimming away from us now, on their backs, their gazes still turned on us. But it's clear they are not swimming in some random pattern – they are taking up positions, lighting up a line that stretches away from our boat and off into the dark.

"They're showing us the way!" Violet exclaims. "Just like the legend says. They are showing us how to get out of here."

She lowers the oar into the water, and I do the same with the steering pole, and together we gently propel *Seahorse* along the line of eyes. And as we pass, each fargazer – looking up at us with its baby face and gulping mouth – closes its eyes and sinks back down to the deeps.

The last fargazer of all rises as we approach, and throws something white and gleaming into the boat.

"Clermit!" I cry when I see what it is. "There you are!"

I grab up my clockwork hermit crab and tip the water out of him.

And I slip him back beneath my cap.

"Thank you!"

The fargazer blinks at me, before it, too, sinks below the surface.

"They seem so lonely," says Violet as it vanishes from view. "Down here in the cold and dark. I wish we had something for them." Then she adds, "Do you think Sabrina met the fargazi too?"

I shudder. If she did, she might not have been as lucky as us. Maybe this is where Sabrina Eels met her end. But I don't want to say that out loud.

"I can see a cave," I say instead, swishing the pole to turn the prow of *Seahorse* to where, in Ember's faint light, a narrow opening can be dimly discerned in the rock. "Let's just get out of here."

We enter the opening – another narrow crack – and here we can propel the boat by pushing our hands against the rocky walls. But we are soon in the grip of another current.

"Hold on!" Vi calls back to me, pulling the oar onboard.

I sit down, clutching the sides of the battered *Seahorse* as once again we pick up speed. The water beneath us begins to churn, and I suddenly remember that just as water can settle into placid pools underground, it can also become a powerful waterfall in a moment.

"Ember!" I cry. "Show what's ahead. Please!"

The sprightning zips forward, zigzagging like a bee. But the cave is starting to twist too, making it impossible to see far ahead, and *Seahorse* is banging and scraping against the sides now, tipping alarmingly at every turn.

"We need to get off!" I call to Violet.

"I know!" she replies. "But how?"

The boat rushes out into another wide space. The current is ferocious now, but in the dim light we can see calmer waters nearby, which lap at a pale subterranean beach.

Violet digs the oar in desperately, to steer us to the beach, but the current snatches it from her hands. The oar is gone!

"Herbie!" she cries.

Suddenly I know that if we don't do something *right now*, we'll be gone too. So, I do the only thing I can.

I jump over the side of the boat!

Not, I should point out – as I gasp at the fearsome cold of the water – because I've suddenly gone loopy. Jumping into underground rivers is the last thing I want to do, believe me. But part of the deal with being newer and braver is that you just have to do bonkers stuff from time to time. Of course, not knowing whether or not my feet will reach the bottom *is* a teensy bit of a worry, I admit, but judging by the angle of the beach, it should be just about OK.

And it is!

So now I'm up to my belly button in icy water, digging my heels in as I try to drag *Seahorse* out of the current. But I can't.

"Vi!" I gasp. "Jump!"

Violet leaps in beside me, just as the boat escapes my grip. *Seahorse*, released back into the currents, is swept away to vanish into the dark. Then it's all we can do to fight the currents ourselves, till together we collapse on the shingle beach in exhaustion.

"There's no way –" Violet pants and sits up as Erwin emerges spluttering from her coat – "no way that Sabrina did all this on her own, is there, Herbie?"

I sit up beside her.

"I don't know any more, Vi. I just don't know."

"What is this place, anyway?" Violet adds as we clamber to our feet on the beach. Our footsteps crunch like a mouse in a box of breakfast cereal.

Vi crouches and scoops some of the shingle into her hands.

"Oh," I say, when I see, in Ember's light, what she's holding.

The beach isn't made of shingle at all.

It's made of bones.

Millions upon millions of bones from small creatures – rodents, birds, fish – mixed with crab claws, lobster plates and the calciferous remains of things we can't identify. We look up this bank of death to the rock wall far above. And there, just at the edge of Ember's light, we see someone sitting, as if waiting for us.

BEACH OF BONES

"HELLO!" VIOLET CALLS to the figure up above.

There is no reply.

But, since there is also nowhere else for us to go, we have little choice but to climb the beach of bones and approach this mysterious figure. We climb in the light of the sprightning, our feet slipping in the shift and clatter of the deathly beach.

"Are you lost?" Violet calls to the sitting figure, clearly as amazed as I am to find someone else down in this hope-forsaken place. "Can we help?"

Then she freezes. Beside us, part of the beach slides away to reveal the face of a skull.

A human skull.

And we see it isn't the only one.

Ember, darting from side to side, shows us other skeletons among the bones, staring up with empty socket eyes, some still dressed in the ragged clothes of many years ago. Sailors, smugglers, outlaws – whatever they were – who never saw the light of the sun again.

"Dead!" Violet gasps, grabbing my arm. "Herbie, they are all dead!"

"Not …" comes a faint reply, "not … all."

And above us, in the gloom, the seated figure we saw earlier raises one feeble arm. My heart almost explodes with terror. Oh, what wouldn't I give for one good, powerful torch right now!

"We're coming!" Violet cries, forging up the beach. "Hold on..."

Then she stops.

It's only as I reach her side that I see why.

Sitting against the rocky wall at the top of the bony shore, bloodied and half drowned, is someone we recognize.

"Sebastian Eels!" Violet whispers.

And it's true. The famous author of Eerie-on-Sea is pale and haggard, his jacket ripped, blood glistening on one shoulder.

"How did *you* get here?" I blurt out before I can think of anything better to say.

"Same way as you, Herbie," our arch-enemy replies with a faint grin. "I expect."

"What happened?" Violet asks, approaching warily. "Your shoulder..."

Eels winces as he opens his jacket to show a torn and bloodstained shirt.

"Malamander," Eels says, weakly. "Your old friend and mine, eh?"

"What do we do?" I whisper to Violet. Because what *do* we do? It's clear Eels is badly hurt. "Do we – do we just leave him here?"

"You'd like that, wouldn't you?" Eels says, bitterly. "What's one more skeleton in this forgotten graveyard? But..."

And he turns his pain-filled eyes onto Violet expectantly.

"We *can't* just leave him, Herbie," she says automatically, like something is speaking for her. It's probably the same something that makes her rescue injured animals without thinking if they could hurt her or not.

Eels rewards her with a broken smile.

"But," Violet continues, "we don't know how to get out ourselves. Maybe we'll all leave our bones for the crabs."

And that's when we hear a "Prrup!" from Erwin.

The bookshop cat, exploring despite his sickliness, has stopped and turned his whiskers into a particularly dark shadow. Even in the half-light we can see a faint breeze ruffle his fur.

"A way out!" Violet cries. "Oh, clever puss. Come on, Herbie. Let's go."

"Wait!" Eels says. "What about me? I thought..."

"You thought wrong then." Violet looks at him with hard eyes. Then they soften a bit. "But we'll send help, once we have found our way back to the town."

"No!" Sebastian Eels cries, lurching forward, sending the

bones skittering down the beach. "Take me with you!"

"Why should we?" asks Violet.

"I – I can't stay here. Alone. In the dark. I need to, to *do* something – tonight. It has to be tonight!"

"Everything you do," says Violet firmly, "is bad. So, whatever we stop you from doing by letting you fester down here a bit longer is *bound* to be good!"

"Bye," I add with a wave.

"But my sister!" Eels is pleading now, crawling towards us. "My poor Sabby. She has waited in the dark too. For so long. Don't do it for me; do it for her. Help me reach the – the—"

"Deepest Secret?" I suggest. "Of Eerie-on-Sea?"

Eels nods, grimacing with pain.

"I can show you where it is. I can, oh – oh, I can share it with you. Yes, *share* it! I'm not the only one to have lost someone, am I? Violet, your parents! Help me, and I can bring them back, too."

Violet strides back over to the stricken man.

"Where are my parents?" she shouts, her question echoing around the cavern. "Tell me!"

"I – I don't know," Eels confesses. "But," he adds, as Violet begins to turn away, "you don't need to know that, not if you have a way to wish them back again. A way to wish for your heart's desire."

"The malamander's egg!" I gasp. "That's the only thing that can give you what you wish for."

"Is that it?" Violet towers over Eels now. "After all this time, the Deepest Secret of Eerie-on-Sea is just the malamander's egg?"

"No," Eels says. "Well, yes, the egg is everything, it can give you *anything*. But you can't have it while the malamander lives. I've learned that the hard way, as you two, of all people, know. No, the Deepest Secret is – something else."

"Mermedusa," I whisper, the word popping out on its own.

"How—?" Eels looks stunned, his pain momentarily forgotten. "How do you know about that? Are you … remembering?"

"What?" I frown.

"Nothing," Eels says quickly. "I just mean, *no one* knows about that."

"You do, though," says Vi, folding her arms. "So, keep talking."

Sebastian Eels hangs his head, defeated.

"Mermedusa," he says, "is a name lost in time and shadow. She is the oldest of the legends of Eerie-on-Sea, forgotten by almost everyone. But she's the reason there are any legends at all. She unites everything that is eerie. She is the one creature in the world who can take the egg from the malamander, because she—"

"She's the malamander's mate." Violet nods, putting it all together. "The malamander's long-lost companion *is* the Deepest Secret. And you –" she glares at Eels – "you want to use her."

"I want to save her!" Eels cries, wincing as he tries to sit up. "Save the mermedusa! Bring her back to the malamander so that in exchange, in gratitude to me, she will use the magic of the malamander's egg to give me back Sabrina. And fix all the terrible things that I have done."

"*This* is your plan?" I'm amazed. "This is why you made the Eerie Hum? To attract the malamander for this?"

"Yes!" Eels gets to his knees and holds his hands together to beg. "Please, help me. Please! If the two creatures meet before we can get there, then it will be too late. They will leave this world, taking the magic with them, and Sabrina will be lost forever. And it will all be my fault!"

Silence falls then, as Eels finishes confessing his extraordinary plan. Violet tugs me away, out of earshot.

"Do you believe any of that?" she demands, her eyes wide.

"Er," I reply, "that is to say, um…" I straighten my cap. "What I believe, Vi, is that in Eerie-on-Sea just about anything is believable. And maybe the mermedusa is the reason why."

"Your parents!" Sebastian Eels calls weakly from where we have left him. "Herbie, your past! Help me now, and I promise you will both have your heart's desire."

Violet looks at me. I look back at her. We both look down at Erwin, who does a very human shrug.

"What did you say?" Violet demands of Eels then.

"What?" He looks confused.

"When you met the fargazi," Violet explains. "As you must have, if you come to be here. When the fargazi asked what you seek, what was your answer?"

Sebastian Eels looks desperate, like a terrified child.

"Forgiveness," he croaks. "I seek forgiveness. And to make everything right again. That's the truth. I swear it!"

Dammit! I can't help thinking. *That's a good answer.*

"Very well," says Violet, after a pause to consider. "We'll take you with us, and you can show us where this mermedusa is. But I warn you, Sebastian Eels, if you double-cross us, if you so much as think of tricking us, we'll leave you in the dark, and take our chances alone. Understand?"

In Ember's light, we see our enemy's pale face nodding eagerly.

"I'll be good," he says. "I promise."

THE HOWL
AND THE PUSSYCAT

IT TAKES VI and me a moment to get Sebastian Eels upright. We see that the wound to his shoulder is very bad. But, supporting him under his good arm, we are able to walk, like a strange kind of six-legged animal, towards the narrow gap that Erwin has found, Ember lighting our way.

That gap leads to a twisty rock passage that wends unevenly upwards, with several offshoots. But, always following the breeze, we finally emerge into a man-made tunnel.

"This is different," says Vi, looking at the brick arches above us. Set in the floor of the tunnel are iron rails like a tramway. "People built this."

"Smugglers," says Eels, between ragged breaths. "They used the rails – to move their barrels. It's a good sign."

"Is it?" I ask.

"We've reached the Netherways, Herbie!" Violet cries in

excitement. "But now which way should we go? The breeze has gone."

"That way." Sebastian Eels tips his head to the right.

And we – Vi and I – have little choice but to trust him. When we reach the next place where tunnels cross, with multiple forks in the path ahead, I realize that we're already so far into this labyrinth that I couldn't even find my way back to the beach where we lost *Seahorse*, let alone find Blaze and his uncle again.

"Now where?" I ask, as we prop Eels against the wall to get our breath back. Who knew authors could weigh so much?

"This way –" Eels lifts his hand feebly to point – "I think."

"You *think*?" Violet turns on him. "I thought you had the only map of the Netherways."

"I don't have it on me, do I!" Eels splutters. "And it's impossible to memorize it all. But we should keep going downwards."

"What do you think, puss?" I ask.

The sickly bookshop cat, who has to walk now that Vi and I are both propping up Eels, twitches his whiskers in a different direction entirely.

"Mu-wow," he explains, swishing his tail.

"You would rather trust that animal," demands Sebastian Eels, "than me?"

"Yes," says Violet simply, "but, since you've been down here before, I suppose we'll have to go your way."

And so, aiding our injured companion once more, we

shuffle on. Then we reach a complex junction with five ways to choose between, and now it's impossible to miss the hesitation in Eels' voice.

"You're too heavy," I gasp. "We need to rest."

"No!" Sebastian Eels snaps. "I mean – please, no. Not yet, Herbie. The mermedusa is just a little way from here."

And he points one way, just as Erwin goes "Prrp!" at another, his ears rotating like radar.

"Maybe we should follow Erwin," I say then. "His catnav has saved us before."

"Are you serious?" Eels looks incredulous. "Forget that mangy feline!"

"Wait," says Violet. "Can you hear something?"

And that's when, faint as imagining, a distant sound reaches us from the tunnel Erwin has chosen.

"The wind howling," says Eels. "Nothing more."

But Erwin, cocking his head like a (whisper it!) dog, sets off down his chosen tunnel, towards the howl.

"Come on!" I cry as Vi and I scrabble to get the protesting Eels to follow the cat. When we reach the next junction and we hear the sound again, it's louder than ever.

"What *is* that?" asks Vi.

"No time for this," Sebastian Eels protests, but he's in no state to resist now.

Erwin the cat, despite his own poor condition, is already little more than a faint white bottom, vanishing up a flight of stone steps far ahead. Nothing will stop Vi and me from following him now. It's as we reach the top of the steps ourselves that the howl finally becomes distinct.

"Voices!" Vi cries. "Not the wind. A howl, yes, but a *human* howl. Herbie, someone is calling!"

We strain our ears to listen, and hear one word being called into the dark, tinged with a despair of ever being answered: *"HELP!"*

And then, after a few more twists and turns in the maze of the Netherways, we find the source of the cry.

In a circular chamber, where multiple tunnels converge, we see a heavy metal grill over a hole in the ground. And down in the hole, by the light of little Ember, three terrified faces look up at us.

Anonymous Philanderers!

Or whatever they're called.

"Thank goodness!" gasps Angela Song, rattling the metal grill. "Herbie! Violet!"

"You!" bellows Professor Newtiss when he sees Eels with us. "You left us down here to die!"

Fluffy Mike, still amazingly wearing his aviator sunglasses, pokes his battered microphone between the bars, as if, even now, trying to record for the podcast. However, judging by the ruin of shattered machines and broken recording equipment that we can see in the corner of the chamber, his microphone will be connected to nothing now. And on top of the pile is the wreckage of the portable hum detector itself, smashed to bits.

Violet quickly props Sebastian Eels against the chamber

wall. I can't help noticing that in our haste he has started bleeding again.

"We're wasting time," he gasps. "We can let them out again afterwards. As I planned…"

"He destroyed everything!" Angela cries. "Our recordings – everything!"

"Where's my notebook?" The professor shakes the bars like a caged bear. "My research?"

"Gone." Eels gives a bloody leer. "To the bottom of the sea."

I ignore the cry of dismay this news brings and examine the iron grill, which is padlocked shut. I slip Clermit out from beneath my cap, and give him a gentle shake, sending seawater drips in all directions.

"Are you OK, little buddy?" I ask the shell in my hand.

Nothing.

"I know you've had a dunking," I continue, "and I'll give you the best clean you've ever had when this is all over, I promise, but we need to pick one more lock."

"He's – he's talking to a shell," says Professor Newtiss, in an incredulous whisper.

But then – rather judderingly – Clermit extends his scissor pincer to snip me a greeting. I place him on the ground.

Clermit unfolds his brass legs, wobbles a bit as he gets his balance, and then scuttles woozily over to the lock.

"I so wish you were getting this!" Angela says to the sound man. Fluffy Mike can do nothing but shake his head in frustration.

Clermit reaches into the lock and turns it with a *SLUNK*. The padlock pops open. The corroded hinges shriek as the podcasters push the grill up.

"You have ruined everything!" Angela cries, leaping out first and rushing at the stricken Eels, her fists clenched, her elegant black clothes all awry and spattered with mud.

"Help!" Eels calls feebly. "Violet! Herbie! Explain!"

"It would take too long," says Violet, putting her hand on Angela's arm. "But for now, please, we need Eels with us for a bit longer. The best thing you can do –" she turns to the podcasters – "is get back to the surface, to bring help. Find Dr Thalassi. He'll know what to do."

"It's all gone," says Professor Newtiss, frantically searching through the shattered equipment. "Everything! He's left us nothing. Not even a blurry photo!"

"You," Angela points accusingly at Sebastian Eels, "have not heard the last of *Anomalous Phenomena*."

"Do what you must," Sebastian Eels spits in reply, coughing up blood. "But no one – will believe you now."

And, probably at the sight of Eels so badly hurt, Angela Song finally lowers her fury and turns to Violet.

"There'll be nothing to believe at all," she says, "if we can't find our way out. Which way do we go?"

"I think," I tell her, "that I can help with that." And I point at one of the openings, beyond which a flight of steps is dimly visible. "That way will take you straight back up to Sebastian Eels' house."

"How do you know?" says Violet.

"Because," I reply, "of this."

And I stoop to lift a power cable, which snakes across the chamber floor before leading up the flight of steps.

"What is it?" Angela asks.

Well, isn't it obvious? If Sebastian Eels has been recording the cry of the mermedusa, then it stands to reason he'd have run a power cable down to wherever she is. One end will be plugged in at his house. But I don't say all this aloud.

"Trust me," I tell the podcasters instead. "I'm a Lost-and-Founder. Just follow that cable, and you'll be fine."

"Aren't you two coming?" Angela looks concerned. "It's dangerous down here. Especially with him."

And she glares at Eels.

"Soon," Vi replies. "We just have something to do, then we'll be right behind you. We promise."

Amazingly, Fluffy Mike manages to get the light on the front of his shattered video recorder working again. Then the sound man, Angela Song and a wild-eyed, defeated Professor Newtiss leave us to return to the surface and Eerie-on-Sea, to probably not make podcasting history after all.

"Prrp?" asks Erwin then, and we find that the cat is waiting beside the cable. While one end goes up, the other, of course, disappears down a different flight of steps, to the unknown.

"We'd better get going," I say. But when we prepare to lift Sebastian Eels, he waves us off feebly.

"Leave me here." Eels' voice is a whisper. "It's too late for me now. Go! Before it's too late – for us all."

"What?" says Violet as we crouch beside him.

"I'm finished." He coughs, clutching his jacket around him. He looks deathly pale. "You'll have to do it for me."

"Do what, exactly?" Vi and I look at each other in alarm.

"Tell the mermedusa…" says Eels. "Tell her to call. One more time. I have brought – the malamander. It is closer than ever. If she calls, it will come. Then – once she has the egg – she will reward you. But, please…"

"Yes?"

"Don't forget me."

"Don't forget Sabrina, you mean?" Violet says. "Your sister."

"That's what I meant." Eels closes his eyes, looking like he's close to passing out. "We are – the same thing."

And I suppose that's true. With twins, I mean. And as Eels slips into unconsciousness, Violet makes him as comfortable as she can. I pull the torch from my pocket and find that it has dried out and works again. I put it in our enemy's hand, just in case. I can't leave him in total darkness, despite everything.

"So much for Sebastian Eels," murmurs Violet as we look down on the ruin of the man who has tried so hard to ruin us all.

And then, alone once again, and with bright little Ember lighting the way, we follow the cable down.

THE CAVE OF
FORGOTTEN DREAMS

DOWN AND DOWN and *down* again we go, slipping and sliding as we follow the cable. Soon I feel sick with the sense of solid rock above, heavy as a mountain, between us and a surface world I almost can't believe in any more. But then, just as my growing despair of ever seeing the sun again threatens to overwhelm me, we find ourselves entering the creepiest place of all: a vast cavern where a giant, hideous being, seated on a throne, has been carved out of the living rock.

"Mermedusa," I whisper, looking up at the statue towering above us. The figure has the body of a spindly human but the head of something else. Something with a wide, abysmal mouth, a halo of tangled hair and two dark, vacant eyes.

And I stop, transfixed.

It's the face from my dreams – the terrible face that invades my mind whenever the Eerie Hum is sounded. And, in the shifting shadows of Ember's fizzing light, the giant statue seems to lean forward to look down, as if waiting for me to bow.

"Who carved this?" says Vi, incredulous. "Who comes all the way down here to spend months, years maybe, carving something like that? And *why*?"

I can only shrug. Was it Romans? Was it Celts? Was it someone even older whose name is forgotten?

"Whoever made it," I whisper, "left it to guard that."

And I point to a spot below the statue, to the opening of a cave. Into that cave runs the power cable.

"Do you realize what this is, Herbie?" Violet looks at me then. "Down that tunnel, at long last, is the Deepest Secret of Eerie-on-Sea. And maybe –" she pauses, amazed at the thought – "maybe, even, our heart's desire."

"Are you ready?" I ask her.

She blinks at me before answering.

"Are *you*?"

I nod. I guess I'll have to be!

Violet raises her finger so that Ember can land on it to act as a lantern, to light our way.

And so, we approach the mighty statue and step into the cave below.

The first thing we notice is that the walls of the cave have also been carved. Swirls and patterns and geometric shapes twist and spiral together, as if alive in the shifting shadows.

"Are these people?" says Violet, pointing to a cluster of human-like figures, also carved into the rock.

"Yes," I reply. "And look, here they're swimming! Under the sea. And those must be fish, and a whale, and even an octopus."

"Herbie!" Vi cries, looking up to the roof of the cave. "Boats! On the surface of the sea. People are sailing them; *fishing* from them. That must be what those wavy lines are. Fishing nets, filling the ocean."

As we walk along the decorated cave, it really does feel like we are taking a journey beneath the sea.

"Everything is getting caught, the nets are full of fish," I say as we reach a new set of carvings, "but there's something else in there too, something – strange..."

I trail off. I cannot describe what I can see in words, except to say that it has tendrils. And that it twists and twines within the nets. Whatever it is, it's fighting the boats – fighting to break away and reach the safety of the deep, tugging the fishers down, drowning some, while others, with vengeful spears and catching nets, pursue it.

"The mermedusa?" says Vi, holding Ember high and tracing her finger around the mysterious form. "Fighting to be free?"

I nod. I *know* that it is.

Then we see that one strong fisherman – carved in bold relief in the rock – dives deeper than all the others and ensnares the mysterious creature.

Next the carvings show the mermedusa trapped in an underground place.

Bound by a chain.

A rock, as vast as a whale, is pushed by the strong fisherman, to block her way out. It is a prison, and the mermedusa is trapped inside forever. All this we see in the carvings on the walls of the cave, as step by step we walk through a story told in pictures.

Then Violet grabs my arm.

Ahead of us, a huge rock blocks the way, as if it had crashed through the cave roof thousands of years ago. At the base of the rock is a pool of water, and the cable leads down into it.

But this isn't what made Violet grab my arm.

Someone is crouching before the pool, with one arm held out towards the water. It's a girl in an embroidered winter cloak, with braided blonde hair that gleams in Ember's light like spun gold.

"H-hello?" I call.

The girl doesn't move, so we edge closer, expecting at any moment for her to spin around and confront us. But she doesn't. Eventually, we draw up beside her and see that she is still as stone, her arm outstretched, one fingertip just touching the surface of the water.

"Pandora!" I whisper as I understand who this is. "Pandora Festergrimm!"

There is no response, not even a hint of movement. And

I see with a jolt that the girl's perfect face is made of porcelain, and her eyes of coloured glass, and behind one ear, where the braids are pulled back, is a gap that shows the dusty mechanical workings inside.

"So, she *was* made of clockwork, after all," Violet whispers. "And she has been down here, lost and alone, for two hundred years!"

"She was going down there," I say, following the direction of the girl's finger where it points underwater. In the dim light, it's just possible to see the dark opening of an underwater tunnel beneath the rock that blocks our way. "Or wanted to."

Vi and I exchange glances. We both know this is the end of the journey, that we've reached the deepest and most secret place at the heart of the Netherways, far, far below Eerie-on-Sea. The only way forward will be to climb into that still pool and swim along the tunnel, to whatever lies beyond.

"Sebastian Eels did it," Vi whispers, nodding at the cable. "So, Herbie, we can do it too."

I nod. Neither Herbie – not the newer, braver one, nor the one I used to be (and still am really) – can possibly disagree with that (even though we both really want to).

And so, together, Vi and I take off our coats. I remove my cap, place Clermit inside and set it down beside wound-down Pandora. I wonder for a moment if Clermit will react to the girl, but now he is wound down too.

"Prrp?" says Erwin, his eyes wide and blue, his ears low.

"You can't follow us, puss," says Violet, gently scrumpling

the sickly cat's head with her knuckles. "You and Ember will have to stay and guard over our things. We'll be back just as soon as we can. We – we promise."

Like Sabrina came back? I think. *Like Pandora? Or Violet's parents?*

Does anyone EVER come back from this place?

"How long will it be?" I ask. "The tunnel? How long will we have to hold our breath?"

But, of course, Violet has no more idea than I do. I've never seen her look so unsure about anything. She lifts her finger and blows Ember off with a gentle puff. The sprightning darts about the cave, as if distressed that she can't follow us either, but electrical sprites and water are not a good mix.

"I'll go first," I say quickly, before I can change my mind.

"I can go first, Herbie," Violet counters. "It's OK."

"No. I should do it," I insist. "If I don't go first, I think I might not be able to go at all. And, besides…"

"Yes?"

"I have a feeling, even though I still can't remember why, that – *somehow!* – I have been here before. And – and that might help us with what's going to happen next."

Violet nods like she isn't surprised.

"How will I know when to follow?" she says. "How will I know you're OK?"

I crouch down to where my trousers are shredded. There are any number of loose threads, and I tug a likely-looking one, pulling and pulling till the bottom of my uniform leg has been reduced to a rough ball of royal porpoise blue thread. I give one end to Violet.

"I'll pull on this," I tell her, "when it's safe to follow."

Violet gives a frightened nod.

I turn towards the pool and look down into the water. Then, with my heart pounding in my chest and my resolve already crinkling at the edges, I step into the pool. My legs are quickly submerged – the sides of the pool are steep – but this isn't what shocks me most.

"It's – it's warm!" I cry. "Vi, the water! It isn't cold."

I wade further out, the water quickly rising to my middle, then my chest. Soon I'm barely able to keep my head above water.

I take a deep breath, pinch my nose, and drop beneath the surface.

The pool is empty. By sprightning light I see that nothing lives here at all – no creatures, no plants. There is only bare stone, and the dark of the tunnel ahead, where the cable leads.

I let some air out of my lungs and sink to the bottom. But even then, with Ember flitting in agitation in the air above, I can see nothing but dark in the tunnel.

I kick forward and swim inside.

LUMINESCENCE

DON'T TRY THIS AT HOME!

Not that I imagine many people have access to a forgotten underwater tunnel under a giant boulder, deep down in a secret labyrinth beneath their house, but still – it's a bit bonkers what I'm doing. But, I am a professional, and so, here I go, holding my breath and doing it anyway.

As I swim into the tunnel, I feel the thread reeling out behind me from my torn uniform. I try to see something – *anything* – that might indicate the length of the tunnel, but there's nothing to see at all.

Oh, bladderwracks!

Keeping as flat as I can, I grab my way along, seizing the power cable and pulling myself through the darkening water, desperate to get myself to the other side.

My head fills with a dull throb as I continue to hold my breath.

Will the thread be long enough?

Will Violet feel the tug?

And, when I get there, what will I see…?

SEE!

Suddenly I realize I won't be able to *see* anything, even if I do reach the other end of the tunnel. We hadn't thought of that! How *can* there be light, all this way down here? What am I going to *do*?

And then, just as I feel panic take hold and threaten to force me back, I do see something. Actually see it! A faint glimmer ahead.

Am I imagining it? I stop and try to see clearly, my eyes stinging in the salt water.

But I can't see anything now.

And my lungs are starting to scream.

I need to breathe!

I grab the cable and pull and pull, banging my head and scraping my arms, but now I have to *get out*, I have to *escape*! And then, suddenly – *amazingly* – I do! I swim out into another pool of water, lit, miraculously, by a faint light that filters down from above the surface. I burst up into the air and heave in a breath.

Straightaway I see that I am on the other side of the giant rock, in a pool just like the first. The air here is breathable, and yes, there *is* light. From somewhere ahead – where the cave opens into a larger space – comes a haunting glimmer of shifting light whose source I cannot imagine.

I climb out of the pool and crouch dripping on the cave

floor. Beside me, in the gloom, I can make out the end of the power cable. And now, finally, I get to see what it's plugged into: a device, glaringly modern in these timeless surroundings, left here to record sound.

Only, the unit is smashed – completely destroyed.

Ahead of me, a wider cavern beckons – dim and mysterious and eerily lit by the unaccountable light. But then I remember Violet.

I give the thread from my trousers several sharp tugs. After a moment, I feel it tug back. Violet will soon join me, confident that there is actually somewhere to get to now that I, Herbert Lemon – Lost-and-Founder at the Grand Nautilus Hotel – have shown that it's safe.

I pull my soaking uniform front flat and flick some muck off a button.

People often ask me if the town I live in is *really* Eerie-on-Sea – a legend-haunted place that pretends to be a normal seaside resort in the summer. Or if it's actually *Cheerie-on-Sea* – a proper ice-cream-and-tourist town, which just happens to feel a bit spooky in the off-season. Well, those people will have to make up their own minds about that. But, as I stand here, deep underground, facing the mystical unknown after swimming through an underwater tunnel, I suddenly wonder if I've actually been that newer, braver Herbie all along.

Then, bursting through the surface, Violet arrives. She gasps for breath as I help her out of the water.

"Where's the light coming from?" she asks, once she's got her breath back.

"Don't know yet," I reply. "I was saving some adventure for you."

Then she notices the recording device.

"So, *that's* it, is it?" she says. "But did you have to smash it, Herbie? It might have been useful."

"I didn't smash it," I explain, and then we look at each other and both say "Oh" at the same time.

Because, if I didn't smash it, who – or what – did?

"Look at the floor." Violet nods to the layer of soft, clay-like deposit that covers the ground of the cave. "Footprints. So, you really haven't been into the cavern yet."

"How can you tell?"

"Because, Herbie," Vi replies, "judging by the footprints, no one has."

I look again and see that she's right – my footprints, and Vi's, are easy to see, while the big, booted feet of Sebastian Eels have left their own distinctive marks. But none of them go further than a pace or two from the water's edge. They certainly show no sign at all that Eels entered the cavern.

"If anything," says Vi, "it looks like he couldn't get out of here fast enough. Looks like he jumped back into the pool pretty sharpish."

"Like he was scared?" I say. "Like he wanted to avoid whatever it was that smashed the recording device?"

Vi nods. We turn and look towards the cavern.

"The malamander?" I say. "Or the mermedusa?"

"One monster is scary enough," Violet adds, "but, you know…"

"What?"

"Well, the sounds the two creatures make are so different, Herbie, that maybe the malamander's mate isn't just another malamander at all. Maybe it's something else entirely."

"What do you think a mermedusa is, then?"

"Oh, I don't know," Violet replies. "I just think we shouldn't expect the two to be the *same kind* of creature, that's all. I mean, the malamander lays a *crystal* egg, Herbie, that can grant *wishes*. These are magical creatures we're talking about. We should be ready for anything."

And with this alarming thought we walk forward.

I've never really known what the word *grotto* means, but as we gaze around this new cavern – at the stalactites hanging from the ceiling, over myriad rock pools of limpid water – I feel like maybe *grotto* is just the word to describe this place. A few of the stalactites from the ceiling and stalagmites from the ground have met to form columns of stone. And the light? Well, we see now that this comes from the pools themselves, which are filled with a bioluminescent seaweed I've never seen before. And over the rocks, spilling across the ground and up the walls, is a rich mossy growth, festooned with tiny flowers that wave on stalks as if from a gentle breeze. In the walls are the ends of chutes, down which seem to fall not just water, but other things too. Heaps of wreckage and bones have collected beneath them, over untold time.

In the centre of this eerie grotto, one pool of shimmering bioluminescence is much larger than the rest, almost a small lake. The waters of it move slightly. At least, if the shifting reflections of light on the dripstones above are anything to go by.

We come to a halt, huddled slightly together, dazzled by the weirdness and mystery of it all.

"Hello?" Violet ventures, her voice falling dull as it's absorbed by the moss.

Not a sound.

"Have you ever heard of glowing seaweed before?" I say, approaching the nearest rock pool.

We peer down into the waters at the long leaves and tendrils. The light, now that we look at it closely, pulses slightly.

Violet lowers her hand towards the water.

"Vi!" I say in warning, but Violet continues till her fingertips touch the surface.

"Warm! Like the water in the tunnel. And – Herbie, does it seem like there's something else in the water to you? Something under the seaweed?"

"Maybe." I crouch down to get a closer look. "It's hard to tell, not without lifting the— Oh."

My voice dies in my throat.

Violet has reached into the water and parted the seaweed.

And now there is no mistaking what it is that's hidden beneath the fronds.

It's a hand. A *human hand*!

SHIPWRECK BOY

VIOLET DRAWS BACK THE SEAWEED, and we see that the hand is attached to an arm, and the arm to a body – the body of a young man.

"Bladderwracks!" I gasp. "Who is that?"

The man is dressed in an old-fashioned sailor's uniform, like the ones you see in the Eerie Museum. He is wrapped in tendrils of seaweed, with a particularly bright one twisted around his head.

"Is he dead?" Violet asks.

Well, I don't know, do I? And yet, even as I look at him lying there, bathed in the eerie glow of the strange seaweed, I can somehow tell that he isn't exactly one thing or the other. He looks, for all the world, as if he's in the deepest of peaceful and enchanted sleeps. Apart from the fact that he's *underwater*!

Vi waves her hands in front of the sailor's face, but gets no response. His eyes are closed, anyway.

"What do we do?" She looks at me. "Do we get him out of there?"

"Yes," I reply simply. "Though something tells me it won't be that simple."

Violet reaches into the water anyway and tries to pull the man's arm out. But as she does this, the tendrils binding him tighten, and she can't lift it. Then some of the tendrils start to reach for her, so she snatches her hand away.

"He's been captured! How did he get here?"

Of course, I don't know that either. Looking around at the chutes, though, in the walls of the grotto, I wouldn't be surprised if many of the people who get lost in the Netherways end up falling down here eventually.

"If this man is in this pool –" Violet looks at me wonderingly – "don't you think we should see if anyone else is here? Trapped in the others?"

We look out across the grotto. The dozens of smaller pools, all glowing with the same strange light, suddenly take on a whole new possibility. Violet's face lights up, and I know exactly what she's thinking.

"No, wait!" I cry. "Violet!"

But Violet is already running to the next pool, where – without hesitation – she draws aside the seaweed.

"Herbie!" she cries. "Look, someone else!"

There, lying in the pool, is an elderly woman. I've never seen her before, but the way she is dressed tells me she must be one of the fisherfolk of Eerie. Like the sailor, she seems to be in a profound, peaceful, underwater sleep, held in place by the same glowing tendrils.

"They must be here, Herbie!" Vi shouts, running to yet another. "They *must* be!"

"Oh, bladderwracks!" I say again. I know I won't be able to stop Violet now.

I reach my own hand into the nearest pool, pull apart the foliage and reveal a face I feel I *do* know, even if I've never actually seen it before.

"Vi!" I shout. "Violet, come quickly!"

"What?" Violet runs towards me, to stare down into my pool. Under the water is a girl with black hair, about our age, wearing the remains of an orange life jacket. And beneath the bright and pulsing frond wrapped around her forehead are features that bear an uncanny resemblance to someone we know only too well.

"Sabrina!" Violet whispers in wonder. "Sebastian Eels' long-lost sister. We've found her!"

I look again at the chutes. Could Sabrina have fallen down one of those? Or swum through the tunnel like we did? No, not with that life jacket. But my thoughts are broken by Violet speaking again.

"Herbie!" she implores. "Herbie, my parents! They must be here – help me find them!"

"Vi, wait…" I start to say, but she's already running from rock pool to rock pool, digging her hands into the glowing seaweed.

And it's then that the seaweed strikes back.

A tendril, much bigger and brighter than most, bursts out of the lake at the heart of the grotto, and slaps itself tightly around Violet's head.

"Violet!"

But Violet has no time to cry out, no time to react. Her eyes roll up, her limbs fall limp and she slumps to the ground.

"No!" I jump towards her, but more tendrils, from a completely different pool, dart out and smack me off my feet. As I try to get up, another and yet another strike me down, and I barely have the chance to see Violet's body, entwined now by a mass of fronds, being dragged to one of the larger rock pools. Then my friend is pulled under the water.

"Violet!" I yell, struggling to my feet once more.

The water in the rock pool is swirling as the tendrils and fronds wrap themselves tightly around something beneath the surface. Something that can only be Violet.

And what do I do? Do I run over there and get snatched myself? Or do I flee back up the cave and try to escape? Even as I think this, I know I could never leave without Violet.

"Give her back!" I shout at whatever is there. "Let her *go*!"

We were so foolish. All the signs that we were in terrible danger were there, from the moment we set foot in the grotto. And yet we kept on poking around in the rock pools like summer tourists on a day out.

"Mermedusa!" I roar, screwing up my fists. "Mermedusa! Let Violet go!"

My shouts die to nothing in the soft moss of this sea-fairy grotto. I want to run to Violet's pool and hack at the tendrils, but something is happening. In the central lake that seems a hub to all the others, a greater brightness has begun to shine. The cavern, which was only dimly lit before, brightens as a small dome of light breaks the surface of the lake. But it isn't just a dome.

It's the top of a head!

Two black eyes open in a face that I know from my visions, surrounded by a halo of tendrils. The rest of the cavern goes dark as the bioluminescent head clears the water.

"Shipwreck Boy," says a murmuring, whispery voice that seems to come from all around me. "You have returned."

"I–I have?" I say.

"Shipwreck Boy," says the voice again, and suddenly I realize the sound is coming from the thousands of tiny, waving flowers in the moss. "You have failed me."

"Oh," is all I can say now.

"Like all the others," the whispers continue, "you have failed."

The head rises further, a glowing bulb above the water's surface.

"But –" I flap my arms – "but I–I don't know what you mean—"

Then the whole cavern explodes with light and a great

thrashing of water and sound as the creature in the pool screams at me in fury and despair.

"FREE ME!"

And she rises from the pool, sinuous and jellyfish-strange, like a thing of the very deepest sea, raising her arms, pulling something with them, something in which she is caught.

An ancient chain of silver.

"IT BURNS!" the mermedusa shrieks, straining against the metal that binds her. *"BURNS!"*

And then the creature sinks back down into the water with a whine of pain from the flower-mouths all around.

"Burns, Shipwreck Boy," the voice says then, falling back to a murmur. "I burn. Burn – to be free."

"I can free you!" I gasp, from where I'm cowering on the floor of the grotto. "I can break the chain. Just let me get Violet, and—"

The flowers hiss, and tendrils rise from the lake threateningly.

"Too weak," says the mermedusa. "All too weak. Crack the rock, break the chain! But too weak."

"Violet!" I cry, edging towards the pool where she's trapped. "Let her go. Together we can help you. We can break the chain!" Then I add, "Or call the malamander to set you free."

The waters crash, and the mermedusa rears once more.

"Malamander!" she shrieks. "For an age I have called! Yet I am *abandoned*! Lost!"

"But he's here!" I shout back. "The malamander's close! He's been searching for so long! Calling you for so long! But now he's closer than ever. One more call and he'll come!"

The mermedusa hisses, and a thick tendril bursts from the water beside her. Before I can dodge away, it slaps around my neck in a vice-like grip. I gasp, and scrabble at it, but I know I won't be able to escape. I'm dragged over to the pool where I last saw Violet.

"I am abandoned!" the creature moans. "I am lost! But I reclaim you, Shipwreck Boy. Your small dreams will be mine once more. I return you to my sleepers."

And then, right in front of me, the leaves and tendrils of Violet's pool roll back like curtains, and I see her there in the water, sleeping peacefully.

But she is not alone.

On either side of her are two other people: a bookish-looking Black man with a pointy beard, his glasses in the water beside him, and a small, pale, mousy-haired woman I can only describe as "sciency". Both have pulsing tendrils of seaweed around their heads. Both are as lost in enchanted sleep as the others we have seen.

Violet Parma's parents!

"Rejoin them, Shipwreck Boy. Rejoin my sleepers forever…"

Then the tendril at my neck slips round my temple, and everything goes dark as I'm pulled headfirst into the water.

MERMEDUSA

EVERYTHING IS BLANK NOW – blank as the darkness inside my own skull.

I stand in the blank as if standing on the surface of an infinite ocean, still as glass, and I wonder how I'm to make sense of it all. Have I been captured, or not? And either way, where am I?

"This is your dream," says the voice of the mermedusa. "This is where you are now."

"But where are *you*?" I reply, turning this way and that in the darkness, causing ripples with my feet. "I can't see you."

"In this place," comes the reply, "I am everywhere. But if it helps to see me…"

And then something happens in the blankness: another head appears – a human head this time – rising out of the ocean atop a slender figure clad in a gown that shimmers like the water. Now a wild-haired woman is standing before me, with bare arms and eyes as bright as stars.

I look down to find that I am dressed in an immaculate Lost-and-Founder's uniform, with a snappy new cap on my head and everything. I look up again at the woman.

"You are the mermedusa? You look – different."

The woman ripples with bioluminescent light, and for a moment, I sense rather than see a vast halo of tendrils around her.

"In your dream, I can take any form," the mermedusa replies, moving her lips and speaking now with a human voice. "This is how I appeared when we first met."

"But I don't remember meeting you. I mean, I think I would!"

The mermedusa raises one hand to point at me accusingly.

"Shipwreck Boy! You were my chosen one, my last hope. Yet, you return to me with nothing!"

"I don't know what you're talking about." I grab my cap in desperation. "I honestly don't! Is this real? Or is this really just a dream? Or...?"

"Truly?" The mermedusa lowers her hand, uncertain for a moment. "Truly, you cannot remember?"

Then she raises her hand again, and I feel my mind being ransacked. It's like my head is suddenly full of invisible tendrils, turning the furniture of my personality upside down, and searching the drawers and cupboards of my memories. Then the tendrils withdraw.

"You cannot remember!" the mermedusa declares, finally understanding. "You tell the truth!"

"The truth?" I shout as I try to shake my twanging mind clear. "I don't *know* what the truth is. I don't even know who I really am! I can't remember *anything* of who I was before. *Nothing!*"

"You came to me, Shipwreck Boy," the mermedusa says, looking upon me almost fondly now. "I saved you. You came to me, from the sea, just like the others, and I saved you."

"From what?" I cry. "From what did you save me?"

"You may have lost your memories," says the mermedusa, "but I have them still."

She places her hand on my head, and now my mind fills with images, with sounds, with – memories!

Memories of a fabulous ship at sea. And as I remember it, around me in my dream materializes the opulent ballroom of an ocean liner, with gleaming crystal chandeliers, men in dark suits and women in glittering gowns, music, dancing and laughter, and drinks being served.

And I'm there! In a different uniform, standing beside a sparkling buffet table laden with delicacies. The music ends and the dancers change partners, and I remember it all! I look at a large silver bowl of cherries, and see my face reflected in the side – my much younger face! Too young, surely, to be working? And yet...

"Lemon," says a gentleman with immaculate shoes and a snowy-white collar almost to his chin. He doesn't so much as look at me as he holds out his glass.

Now I see that in my hands is a silver platter of lemon

slices and a pair of tongs. I pick up a slice and drop it into the gentleman's drink, knowing that this is something I've done countless times before. The man glides away, without even a thank you.

"These are your memories," says the mermedusa, standing beside me now, "the memories you had when you came to me. This is who you really are."

"W-what about...?" I stammer. "What about my—?"

But before I can finish, there is a roaring sound, and a shriek – first of metal being rent, then of people crying out in fear. The ballroom tips wildly and the buffet slides from the table with a crash. My tray of lemon slices flies away as I topple over, and the screaming fills my ears.

Then the scene is gone – the ballroom, the chaos, everything – and time slips by till now I am out at sea, under a stormy sky, alone, clinging to a crate full of lemons that must have fallen from the ship. In the icy water, frozen to my bones, shuddering with shock, weak and despairing, I am tossed by waves towards a dark and jagged shore. A dark and jagged shore that I recognize now, but would not have then, as the cliffs of Eerie Rock and the town of Eerie-on-Sea.

The water splashing my face is the only thing keeping me awake. I want to cry for help, but I'm too weak. Then I'm caught in a torrent, washed down a channel and flung into a cave.

The crate spins uncontrollably as I fall down a waterfall to the bowels of the earth. It could even be the same vertical cave into which the *Jornty Spark* fell, but I have no time to recognize anything, and no light to see by, as I am swept, in my crate, down a chute to find myself spilled into the soft moss and eerie nimbus of the mermedusa's lair.

"Not my lair!" screeches the mermedusa into my ears, the illusion of a human appearance slipping away. "My prison!"

"You mean," I say, "that before I washed up on the beach in Eerie-on-Sea, I came here? To you?"

"Like so many." The mermedusa nods. "Now my sleepers are all I have to sustain me. All I have – to feed on."

"Feed?" I gasp, suddenly imagining a fat bluebottle fly on a dead carcass. "What do you mean, *feed*?"

"I-ma-gi-na-tion!" The mermedusa breathes out the word with a satisfied sigh, relishing each syllable. She beckons towards me, and I feel a tug at my head. And that fat fly I was just imagining? Well, it's there now, right in front of me, buzzing about like it's real! Even though I only dreamed it! And I watch, agog, as the mermedusa draws the fly towards her, opens her mouth and gulps it down without even a crunch.

"Feeeed!" she breathes into my face, her mouth filled now with vicious pointed teeth.

I feel sick at the sudden, monstrous look on the woman's face. The human shape collapses completely, and I see once again the tendrilled, luminescent jellyfish being who caught Violet.

Violet!

"Listen," I say, "I'm sorry you're trapped, and I would help you if I could, but *you* have trapped my friend." I remember the sight of Violet under the water in the pool, beside her long-lost parents. Her parents! "*You* have made a prisoner of her. Please let her go! Let them all go!"

"I… " gasps the mermedusa. "I … cannot."

Then a new image appears in my dream, as the mermedusa's tendrils become visible. They snake away from her body in a rippling network, and at the end of each a human figure is curled like a foetus, sleeping, as pulses of light travel along the tendrils back to the creature at the centre of it all. It's like a vast tree unfolding before my eyes. And among the hundreds of lost souls on the branches of that tree, I see Violet, and her parents, and Sabrina, and the young sailor, and – I realize, with a jolt – myself, curled up in endless sleep. All of us prisoners of the creature called mermedusa.

"Feeed!" screeches that creature again.

"Why?" I shout. "Why do you keep us here, asleep forever?"

But I know it's a stupid question. Because, finally, I understand. The mermedusa feeds on dreams. On imagination. These people she has snared are all she has to sustain her in this endless imprisonment. And a starving person will do whatever it takes to survive.

The images collapse back to blankness as the mermedusa regains her human form. Now, once again, I am standing before the woman with the starry eyes.

"In the beginning," she says, "when I was first ensnared,

I had power still. I conjured up creatures against those who had entombed me. But even the greatest of them all, the mighty storm fish Gargantis, couldn't break my chain or shatter the rock – now her sleeping holds it up!"

"*You* made Gargantis?" I gasp, amazed.

"From the imagination of my sleepers," comes the reply. "And from the distant dreams of those who live above, I conjured the storm fish into this world, and more besides. I put Blue Men and sea hags in the waves, and tritons on the ocean floor; I gathered treasures for pirates, and fargazi to torment the lost, mermaids to beguile, and sprightnings to bring light. I wove from nightmares a shadow demon, to drive the people underground in fear, to find me. But they trapped it in a lantern! I conjured a daughter for a clockwork-toy-maker – the man's heart's desire – to bring him to the Netherways. But he lost her and so lost himself!"

"You did all that?"

"Yes!" the mermedusa cries, visibly shrinking. "But still my powers faded. With only mortal minds to sustain me, so my conjurings became smaller. I seeded the dreams of a man of science, but all he did with the curiosity was build a museum. I blessed a beachcomber with treasures from the sea, but she was too dazzled by the shore to seek the truth beneath it. I gave a lonely bookseller a talking cat – her particular dream! – but she lost herself in the books, and the cat had a mind of its own. And so, at last, my power withered to almost nothing."

The mermedusa, still in the form of a human woman, lowers her head, hiding her face in strands of sodden hair. She raises one arm, straining against the silver chain, but lets it fall.

"And still, I burn."

"But what about me?" I ask, because I don't know what else to say. "Where do I fit in?"

The mermedusa says nothing.

"You said I was your last hope?" I continue, going to the woman's side and, after a hesitation, taking her hand. "What does that mean?"

"No more conjurings," she says. "Only my sleepers and a slow death for us all. You were my final try. I chose you, Shipwreck Boy, of all my sleepers. A boy with an open heart, like the heart of my lost malamander, to be returned to the surface, to bring help. With the last of my force, I filled your mind with all you needed to know, all my memories of loneliness and despair—"

"I don't remember!" I protest. "I can't remember any of it."

"Weak," says the mermedusa. "Human minds are so weak. I tried to give you my memories, but all I did was destroy your own."

"But you still sent me back up?"

"In your crate of lemons, exactly as you came to me. I sent you to wash ashore, to be found, to bring me help. To set me free."

"They found me on the beach," I whisper. "They took me in. They gave me a name, since I couldn't remember my own. They gave me a job even. I became Herbert Lemon. And finding lost things became my new life."

"Yet you did not find me." The mermedusa bares her teeth. "You did not return."

"I didn't know I had to!" I protest. "But, I *did* become a Lost-and-Founder. And I *am* an expert when it comes to finding lost things. And I *have* returned! Now I can set you free."

The mermedusa tips her head back sharply. Her lank hair parts, and one gimlet eye blazes down at me in challenge.

She raises her shackled wrists and hisses impatiently.

I grab the silver chains. I heave at them, and pull and *pull*, but how can I break them with bare hands? I need tools! I need—

"I need to wake up," I say, suddenly remembering that all this is some kind of weird dream, and that right now I'm a prisoner myself, in a rock pool, underwater. "Let me wake up, mermedusa, and I promise, I will break those chains. I will set you free."

The woman looks at me with an expression of desperate hope. I want more than anything to help her. But then her features fall away, dissolving as she drops her human disguise and confronts me once more with her true and terrible self.

"No-o-o," she moans, her wide mouth turned down and her teeth bared. "No! You will rejoin my sleeperss, S-S-Shipwreck Boy. You will s-stay at my s-side forever!"

And she opens her mouth to devour me.

THE END OF THE DREAM

"WAIT!" I GASP, shrinking back from the jaws of the mermedusa, from being crunched up and swallowed like that bluebottle fly. "We brought the malamander here! Me, and my friend Violet, we brought it! At midwinter! The night it lays its egg!"

The mermedusa pauses. She snaps her mouth shut and sends a shiver shuddering along her tendrils, with an impatient pulse of bioluminescent light.

"My malamander is here?" The mermedusa stares at me now. "The *egg* is here?"

"We brought it," I say, desperately trying to do an impression of someone who lures malamanders all the time. "It's close, looking for you. It's always looking for you. If you let me wake up, I can help you call it."

"I am too weak," the creature wails. "My call is too weak. Too secret, too lost. I call every year, but my malamander never comes."

Why can't the malamander hear her? The two creatures' calls are meant for each other. But then again, deep in the Netherways, behind the water in the tunnel, and beneath that great rock – not to mention the clamour of the waterfalls and the raging sea beyond – maybe not. If only I could *amplify* the sound...

"Fluffy Mike!" I cry as an idea hits me.

"AAAAH!" breathes the mermedusa again, her teeth grinding, her patience with desperate Lost-and-Founders clearly running out.

"No, wait!" I cry. "Can I – can *you* conjure something? Just a little something? With whatever is left of your powers? You can –" *gulp!* – "feed on my imagination. If you like."

The creature leers at me, in fury but also curiosity. I clench my eyes shut, but instead of giving in to my terror, I *dream* the thing I need – conjuring it into my mind's eye with all the imagination I can muster.

And it's not Fluffy Mike himself, of course – he'd be pretty useless right now, I reckon – but the portable hum detector that he and Angela put together. The unit that can not only detect the mermedusa's call but also *play it back*! I concentrate hard on remembering the device. Of course, the original is broken, smashed by Sebastian Eels, but, well magic *is* magic, isn't it? And so, I summon the machine into my mind as vividly as I can, trying to make it as real as that fat bluebottle fly, and...

The mermedusa shrieks as if in physical pain, as I push

the imagining onto her, along her own tendril, as forcefully as I can.

She reacts violently, lashing out, snatching back the tendril that is wrapped tightly around my head.

And I wake up.

I gasp and gulp in a mouthful of warm, salty water. I burst upwards, desperate for air – coughing, covered in seaweed.

Now I'm sitting, back in the waking world, dressed in my actual, ruined uniform, in a rock pool, surrounded by weakly glowing tendrils and leaves. I roll myself out of the pool, and lie retching on the soft mossy ground of the grotto.

"Shipwreck Boy!" wail the myriad voices of the little flowers around me. "What have you done?"

"I'm trying to help!" I plead as the mermedusa rears up in her lake. The tendrils that held me are rearing too, and I doubt they just want to send me to sleep this time.

"My power!" the mermedusa cries. "The last of it. Gone! You have destroyed me!"

"You mean...?" I say, still coughing as I get shakily to my feet. "You mean, it worked?"

And there, sitting by the rock pool, looking as cobbled together as ever, is the green screen device that the podcasters built – the portable hum detector!

Is it the actual, very same one? Have the broken parts just vanished from the cave floor above to appear here with me now, mended? Or is this a copy, conjured by the imagination of a boy and the dying enchantment of a long-lost mermedusa?

I have no idea.

Doesn't matter, I say to myself, *as long as it works!*

I heave the unit onto my shoulder and switch it on. The green screen crackles to life, the electric light clashing strangely with the luminescence of the mermedusa's grotto. I grab the radar mic on the coily flex, and thrust it out towards the mermedusa.

"Sing!" I cry. "Sing to the malamander!"

The mermedusa, her face twisted with fury, towers over me.

"You said I was your last hope!" I cry. "I am. This is it – the last hope actually happening, *right now*! Sing! Sing like you have never sung before!"

The creature quivers, her tendrils paused mid-strike.

Then, perhaps remembering why she chose me once before, she opens her arms, tips back her head and begins to call. Except, of course, I can hear nothing. The lines on the green screen go crazy, but all I sense in the subterranean grotto is the strange and eerie hum.

Then, the song ends abruptly – the mermedusa hunches forward as if in exhaustion, and subsides back into her pool, losing her brightness. Even the tendrils and fronds in the rock pools relax and begin to turn brown as the light in the grotto starts to flicker and fade.

"What's happening?" I ask.

"Weak," sighs the mermedusa. "My strength – is gone."

And she slips back under the water.

"I – I'm sure the malamander will come," I insist, as I run to the nearest chute and clamber up the wreckage and detritus that has piled beneath it. "Hold on!"

I switch the portable hum detector from Record to Broadcast, dial the volume up to Bonkers Level 10 and then shove it up into the hole in the grotto wall.

Oh, and I press Play, of course.

The mermedusa's infrasound song vibrates up the chute, making my teeth chatter. The hum detector feels like it will be shaken from my hands, when from up in the chute there comes an answering rumble, as the rock itself starts to tremble. Stones begin falling, clattering around me, until suddenly a large rock – dislodged from somewhere far above – crashes down the chute and smashes the machine in my hands.

"No!" I cry, falling back. The hum is cut off to silence, and the green screen goes blank.

"No, no…" I cry again, flicking the switch on and off.

Nothing happens – the machine is broken!

Did I do it? Did the recording play long enough for the malamander to hear?

Meanwhile, the rocks falling down the chute are becoming a cascade. It almost sounds like something is coming down it, and coming fast.

Something *big*!

"Oh, bladderwracks!" I cry. "That was quick!"

I barely have time to scrabble out of the way before there is a thunderous crash of tumbling stones from the chute. I shuffle desperately backwards, and see something enormous hunching like a giant mantis in the dispersing cloud of dust.

Glistening with scales and bedecked with spines, the invincible malamander emits its mightiest roar.

REUNION

THE MALAMANDER TOWERS terrifyingly in the grotto, quivering with fury. The monster's entire focus seems to drill down onto me, lying on the floor, surrounded by the broken machine I used to summon it.

Oops.

But then I hear a faint splash in the water behind me. I turn to see the mermedusa's head break the surface of the pool, her eyes black with astonishment at the sight of the malamander. And the malamander, its eyes finally resting upon the creature it has sought for lifetimes, lurches towards her. There is only one thing that stands in its way now.

Me!

Well, I'm not actually standing. But I am, I think it's fair to say, in *completely* the wrong place at *exactly* the wrong time, and about to be squashed like a gooseberry if I don't get clear pronto.

I remember a lesson Dr Thalassi once gave me about the

birds and the bees. It was a biology lesson, of course, though he didn't actually have any birds or bees, just a diagram showing where baby octopuses come from. It was all a bit, well, *embarrassing*, as I recall, though I suspect more for the doc than for me. Nevertheless, I know enough about the "icky business" to guess I do *not* want to be around for what's likely to happen next!

However, even as I roll myself out of the danger zone, I remember what Violet said, about how, with magical creatures like these, maybe biology as we know it doesn't apply. But, if that's the case, what *will* happen when the nightmarish fish-man of Eerie-on-Sea meets the dream-stealing mermedusa? And will I even survive the encounter to explain it all to Dr Thalassi?

I crawl to the pool where Violet is captive, and reach in. The tendrils holding her are looser than before. I tear off the one around her head, grab her by the arms and heave her out of the pool.

She opens her eyes, and soon she is coughing and spluttering like I was just a moment or two ago.

"Herbie?"

"It's OK, Vi," I say, hoping I'm right about that. "No time to explain, but – but *look*!"

The malamander has crashed into the lake. It reaches the mermedusa and crouches low before her, as if in a bow. The mermedusa pulsates with deep bioluminescent light, her tendrils arching around to envelop the other creature.

"Heavens!" Violet gasps, dragging her soaking hair from her eyes. "What's happening?"

Well, I don't know, do I? All we can do is watch in awe as the malamander raises its hands to its chest to pull horribly at a gap in its scaly armour. Inside we see a pulsing light, and we can almost hear the sound of the creature's beating heart.

Then the malamander cups its mighty clawed hands before its chest as if holding something. Beams of red light dart from its heart, and suddenly, somehow, the creature *is* holding something – a sphere of brilliant red crystal that wasn't there before.

But no, not a sphere exactly.

An egg!

"Herbie, it's happening," says Violet, her eyes full of wonder as the malamander offers the fiery crystal egg to the mermedusa.

The mermedusa's most delicate tendrils cluster around the egg, gently lifting it. The air in the grotto chimes with a ringing sense of wonderful anticipation, as a vortex of energy begins to gather about the two magical beings. Already, in the eye of the vortex above them, something like a hole is opening.

A hole from this world to another.

But even as I goggle at this miracle unfolding before our eyes, I hear a sound from the grotto entrance. I turn to see someone standing there, dripping.

Sebastian Eels!

With insanity in his eyes.

Despite his terrible injuries, Eels begins a desperate run.

The hole in the vortex opens wider and wider. Below it, the creatures don't register the new arrival, caught up as they are in their enchanted reunion. Eels runs right past Vi and me and then leaps desperately at the gap between the malamander and mermedusa, where the fiery red egg is held up between them. The mermedusa's head snaps around, just in time to see Sebastian Eels sail through the air and snatch the egg.

Eels lands with a splash and stumbles, but rights himself. There's a look of terror and disbelief on his face at what he's done.

But what *is* he trying to do? Surely Eels knows there is no escape. The mermedusa has thousands more tendrils, and the malamander is already rising to its great armoured feet, howling in deadly outrage.

Does Sebastian Eels *want* to die?

The mermedusa sends a tendril whipping straight for the man's head.

But there's a flash of silver, and we see that Eels is wearing the metal band that we saw him with earlier. At the touch of the silver, the tendril recoils.

And now Sebastian Eels is holding the malamander's egg high, his eyes closed, his face set in urgent concentration as he starts to evoke the fabled wishing power of the glowing red crystal. The vortex of power shrieks as the portal opens wider still. With a roar of fury that makes me clamp my hands to my ears, the malamander lunges at him.

"No!" yells Eels, throwing one hand out in defence as the monster leaps.

There is a roar of wind.

The malamander, already in the air, is sucked suddenly upwards into the portal above.

With a bellow of surprise, it disappears into it.

And is gone!

The mermedusa hurls tendril after tendril at Eels, but the wind grows stronger still, sucking everything in the grotto into the magical hole out of our world. Vi and I start sliding towards it, and Sebastian Eels has to throw one desperate arm around a huge stalagmite to stop himself being dragged along, clutching the egg for all he's worth. The mermedusa, caught by surprise, shrieks as she, too, flies up into the gaping portal.

For a moment the silver chain remains taut, still tethering the creature to the grotto, and to our world. But, at a nod from Eels, the chain shatters into a hundred glittering links.

And now the mermedusa is gone.

Eels makes a frantic gesture with his hand. The portal closes with a clap of thunder and the sudden onset of roaring silence.

Vi and I slump to the ground as the wind dies down and the vortex of power collapses to nothing. Sebastian Eels sags to the base of his stalagmite, pale as chalk, a look of shock on his face.

Then he lifts the malamander's egg in his hands. We see its fierce red light reflected in his eyes.

He starts to laugh.

"What happened?" Vi gets to her feet, looking as dazed as I feel. "What have you done?"

"Done?" the man cries, grinning insanely. "Why, only sent those two horrors back where they came from, that's all. Minus, of course, one magic egg!"

"What do you mean 'back where they came from'?"

"You don't think creatures like that belong in our world, do you?" Eels replies, tossing the egg from one hand to the other like a toy. "Besides, they were going back there anyway. That's what they both wanted, after all. I just – helped them on their way. And now, the malamander's egg is mine!"

"*This* is what you wanted?" Violet cries. "All along?"

"Of course it is." Eels smiles, jumping up. I see now that he has also magicked away his injuries. "After my last attempt to get the egg went … *awry* –" he glares at us – "I realized finding the mermedusa would be the only way to distract the monster that lays it. Once I could protect myself from her tendrils, that is."

And he taps the metal band on his head.

"Silver has always been their weakness. But even I didn't expect it would be this easy. Only a huge pulse of magical energy could bring those two creatures back into our world now, and they won't be getting that from *me*, that's for sure. Ha!"

"But," says Vi, "what about your sister?"

"Oh, I can sort that," Eels says dismissively. "If I like. Now that I have this…"

And he strokes the red crystal in his hands.

"If you *like*?" cries Violet. "But, you said…"

"I would have said anything, Violet –" Eels looks suddenly solemn – "to get my hands on the malamander egg. Surely you know that by now. But yes, I'll bring Sabrina back from the dead. Then, together, we can see about making a few – ah – *changes* to the world. Starting –" he grins at us darkly – "with you two."

UNDOINGS

"**BUT YOUR SISTER IS HERE!**" I cry, feeling it's high time I took charge of the lost-and-foundering that still needs to be done. "She isn't dead at all! She's been here all along. Look!"

And I point to the rock pool where we saw the girl who can only be Sabrina Eels, lying in her torn life jacket. Vi and I part the tendrils – severed now, and growing faint – and sit the girl up.

"What?" Sebastian Eels almost drops the egg. *"WHAT?!"*

"You think you know everything," Violet says. "But you didn't know that your own sister was sleeping here all along. All you had to do was free the mermedusa, and—"

"Actually," I say, interrupting Violet now as I remember that there is another reunion waiting to happen. "Speaking of being here all along, I think you should take a look at this other pool, Vi, just over here…"

And I try to show her where her own parents are lying, waiting to be awakened. But Violet is too busy helping

Sabrina Eels to awaken to pay much attention to me.

"Easy," she whispers, stroking stray black hair from Sabrina's face as her eyes flutter. "Take it easy. You're safe now."

"Wh...?" says the girl, making what must be the first sounds that she has uttered for decades. "W-where...?"

"It's OK," says Violet. "We're friends. We've found you."

"Sabrina!" Eels bellows his sister's name as he darts forward, his eyes bulging from his head. "How? *Here?* All along? *Alive?*"

"Quiet!" Violet says. "You think you're in shock, imagine how it must be for her."

"But the mermedusa!" Eels is staring at Violet now. "It *kills* its victims. Feeds off them. Like a vampire."

"It does no such thing!" Violet hisses back. "If you'd spent more time trying to understand, and less time stealing and trying to control everything, maybe..."

Eels, though, is in no mood to be lectured. He shoves Violet away, and cradles his sister in his arms.

"Sabrina!"

"Who...?" the girl croaks, looking up at the tousled, bloodied, middle-aged man who is holding her. "Dad?"

"No, no!" Eels shakes his head, his eyes glistening. "It's just the family resemblance. It's me, Sabby. Me! Your Sebastian. Your brother! I've found you – found you at long last!"

But the girl just looks confused, and now a bit scared.

"I'll show you!" Eels pulls his sister out of the water and props her up beside the rock pool. "Watch. You haven't aged at all, but I have. Thirty years! I can fix it, though."

He steps away from her, and holds the malamander egg over his head.

Eels closes his eyes, and as he concentrates the vortex of power reappears, swirling around him, so that for a moment he's hidden from view. Then the power dissipates away, as quickly as it came, and we see that the Sebastian Eels we know is gone.

In his place stands a black-haired boy, about the same age as Vi and me.

"Is that better?" says the boy. "Is this how you remember me?"

"Seb!" cries Sabrina with joy. "Seb, it's you!"

"Bladderwracks!" is all I can say now.

"Oh, Sabby!" the boy Sebastian cries, leaping around in joy. "It *is* me! We are together again, at last! And I have the house! Our family home! Mum and Dad are – well, we can talk about that later, but the important thing is, you are found again! And the world is at our feet."

"Who are they?" asks Sabrina, looking at us.

"Oh, just a couple of nobodies." Eels waves the question away. "Herbert Lemon and Violet Parma. They're like Godfrey used to be."

"Godders!" Sabrina gives a weak smile. "Is he here too?"

"No." Eels' face darkens, and he looks again at the egg in his hands. "No, he won't trouble us any more…"

"You can't have it!" Violet shouts, stepping forward. "The

egg. It isn't yours. You can't just use it. It's too dangerous."

"Who is going to stop me?" says the boy called Sebastian Eels, looking down his nose at Vi. "Not you, that's for sure. And what exactly is my crime here? What have I done wrong? I released two magical creatures from endless suffering, and I recovered my sister when she had seemed lost forever. I should be applauded. I should *make* you applaud me…"

And he hefts the egg threateningly in one hand.

"What about everything else you've done?" I say, coming to stand by Violet's side. "All the things you did before? All the crimes, and violence, and – and the *murder*?"

"Murder?" says Sabrina, recovered enough to look horrified at this.

Eels turns a look of fury on to us. He holds up the egg again and whispers to it. I try to move, but feel myself gripped by some unseen force.

"Don't – you – *dare*!" cries Violet, but we are lifted into the air, and I think in panic that we are about to be sent out of this world too, to join the malamander and mermedusa. Then I feel a clinch of pain all over, and suddenly I find that I'm fixed.

Set in stone!

Vi and I aren't being sent anywhere – with horror, I see that I have been entombed in one of the large stalagmite columns of rock – into the very cold heart of it – with just my face protruding. I cannot move at all!

"Vi!" I cry, but Violet is the same – fixed hopelessly beside me.

"Herbie!" she cries in terror.

"You two can hang around here for a while," says Eels with a smirk. "And, in about a thousand years, when some archaeologist stumbles over your skeletons, you will make a fine mystery."

"Sebastian!" says Sabrina, struggling to her feet. "Seb, what is this? What are you doing? What have you *done*?"

"It's just," he says, "a few little nuisances that need tidying up. And it's true, I have done some, shall we say, *naughty* things over the years. But don't you see? With this power, I can *fix* them, Sabby. I can start again, with you." Then he strokes the egg thoughtfully. "In fact, why don't I start now? All the bad things I've had to do over the decades to find you again – I will make it all go away right now. You should stand back..."

He motions to his sister to give him space.

And there's nothing we can do, Vi and I, but watch in horrified fascination as once again Sebastian Eels raises the egg above his head, closes his eyes and begins to whisper.

Can he really undo all the bad things he's done? Can magic really fix all the misery the man has caused over the years? I have no way of knowing. But one thing's for sure, he won't do anything nice for us. With a terrible realization, I understand that Sebastian Eels really has won this time, finally, and Vi and I can do nothing now but face our horrible end.

The vortex of power is back once more, fiercer than ever, swirling around the egg and the boy holding it.

"Seb!" Sabrina cries, shrinking back in fear. "Seb, *stop*!"

A look of pain comes over Eels' face, but he masters it, and the swirling gets stronger. Then he cries out, clutching his temple.

"What's happening?" I shout, above the roar.

"Don't know!" Vi yells back. "But he has done *a lot* of bad things."

The storm of enchantment is becoming a tornado. Eels is struggling to stay on his feet. It looks like he is trying to calm it, to dampen the magic down, but the vortex gets fiercer than ever, and Eels cries out again. In the maelstrom of power we see images now, fleeting pictures that must be memories of Eels' past crimes, showing hints of wrongdoing we can scarcely even imagine. The misdeeds of Sebastian Eels, gathered together in a single moment by the power of the malamander egg, are not something that can just be tidied away and forgotten by the world, it seems, nor something that Eels can control.

"I can't stop it!" he cries in panic above the roar, angry red light streaming from the egg in his hands. "I can't— I *can't stop it*!"

And Sebastian Eels is lost in the vortex of energies he has released. The grotto starts to quake, stone to shatter, and the water to dance in the rock pools, as the magic builds and the moment culminates and the maelstrom of sound and light and guilt and despair takes on the mass and character of a miniature sun ... and explodes.

ALL WASHED UP

THE NEXT THING I KNOW, I'm washed up on a beach.

It's the beach at Eerie-on-Sea, and I wonder vaguely if there should be a crate of lemons with me, like last time. The water laps at my face, and I cough as I sit up.

"Shipwreck Boy," says a voice.

I lift my head and the mermedusa is there, crouching over me. Then she changes, her beautiful, terrible form vanishing beneath a veil of enchantment, so that, once again, she appears as the bare-armed woman in the waterfall gown – the woman with wild hair and eyes like the stars. She gives me her hand and pulls me to my feet.

"You came back?" I say.

I look around me at the beach, lit by the austere light of midwinter morning, and see that I am not the only one emerging from the sea. Violet is close by, and there are other bodies in the surf, the waves crashing and the snow falling around them.

"Are they...?" I ask, suddenly panicked.

"All is well," says the mermedusa, smiling now a smile of such warmth that the cold of the beach melts away. "They will awaken soon. But I wanted time alone with you first, my Shipwreck Boy."

She raises her hand and I see what she holds.

The malamander egg!

She breathes over it and everything stops: the snow fixes in the air where it falls, and the waves become still where they roll. I get to my feet. My uniform is dry and repaired, I am amazed to see, and my cap is back on my head, the reassuring weight of Clermit beneath it. The mossy grotto, the entombing stalagmites, all of it is gone.

"Eels?" I ask. "What happened to Sebastian Eels?"

The woman holds out her other hand and lets something drop into mine.

It's a diamond.

A bright uncut diamond of intense purity.

"This is all that remains of Sebastian Eels," the mermedusa says. "Crushed by the weight of his own misdeeds."

"The magic," I reply, turning the crystal in my hands in wonder, "it wasn't meant for him."

"It is not for anyone in your world. But I used the power that destroyed him to return here, one final time."

"What happens now?" I ask.

"You were my last hope," the mermedusa replies. "I chose well. And so, as I leave your world forever, I offer you a reward. What is it, Shipwreck Boy, that your heart desires?"

I look up at the woman standing before me.

"The way you look now," I say, "this disguise that you put on for me – you said she was a form I would find acceptable. What did you mean?"

"This is a woman from your memory." The mermedusa smiles again and brushes a few strands of hair from my forehead. "The person dearest to you. She was your mother."

For a moment I can't reply.

"Is this," says the mermedusa, "your heart's desire?"

"How long?" I whisper. "The shipwreck – where I came from. How long ago did it happen?"

When Violet looked into this question, with Jenny Hanniver's help, she told me she'd drawn a blank. With no ship called the SS *Fabulous* for more than a century, it seemed there were no answers there. Now that I've seen Sabrina, though, unchanged after decades of enchanted sleep...

"One hundred years," the mermedusa replies matter-of-factly. "Shipwreck Boy, you were one of my sleepers for more than a century."

I look down.

"So, my mother...?"

"Long dead." The mermedusa lifts my chin and looks sadly into my eyes. "But, if you wish it, I can return you to her time."

I look up at the face above me. My mother's face. But not my mother's face, not really, not with something unnatural in the wildness of her hair and the brightness of her starry eyes. I am in the presence of an illusion – a magic from another world. And this magic is offering me the chance to return.

But to what?

"Who am I?" I ask. "What is my real name?"

The mermedusa passes her hand over the malamander's egg.

"Look in your pocket."

I reach down, suddenly noticing a weight in my coat. I pull something out.

It's a book.

"*The Cold, Dark Bottom of the Sea*." I read the title aloud. "By Sebastian Eels. This looks like the actual copy I got from the book dispensary!"

"Sebastian Eels stole your story," says the mermedusa. "He changed the names, made the tale his own. But he recognized you when you washed up, recognized you for a survivor of a long-ago shipwreck. That is what set him on his search for the Deepest Secret of Eerie-on-Sea, and his quest to recover his sister. Read the book, Shipwreck Boy. I have restored the true names. Including your own."

And the book opens, and the pages flick by until they stop. I read the top line of the page, and see a passage about a young boy who works in the dining room of a luxury liner, serving slices of lemon. I read the boy's name.

I close the book.

Now, at last, I know who I am.

And my memories come flooding back.

But it's another life I'm remembering, isn't it? Separated from my life now by a hundred years, and a gulf of time and death. Could I really go back to it? Is the magic of the mermedusa really powerful enough?

And if I do go back, what happens to everything I have become since?

I look down at Violet, still frozen by enchantment, along with all the world around me. Then up at the pier, and the crooked, battered town of Eerie-on-Sea beyond, with its warm firelit houses and huddled folk.

"When a lost thing," I say then, "has been in my Lost-and-Foundery, unclaimed, for more than a hundred years, it becomes mine. That's the rule. And I reckon the same goes for me, too."

I straighten my cap and flick an imaginary speck of dust from a brass button.

"I'm Herbert Lemon, Lost-and-Founder at the Grand Nautilus Hotel. And I think that's exactly who I'm supposed to be."

I slip the book back into my pocket.

The mermedusa nods and kisses me on the forehead with my mother's lips.

"Then you want nothing, Shipwreck Boy?"

"Well now," I reply, after a pause, "I wouldn't exactly say *that*. Violet still needs to be reunited with her parents..."

The mermedusa passes her hand over the egg once more,

and the snow starts swirling again. Violet gets to her feet and looks around. It's clear she can't see me or the mermedusa. But she does see someone else struggling up the beach, some way off. It's a bookish-looking man with glasses and a short beard, helping a mousy-haired woman out of the sea – a woman who manages to look "sciency" despite being completely soaked through.

"Dad?" Violet gasps. "*Dad!* And … and, *Mum*?"

The two people stop and look at Violet in astonishment and confusion.

"Er," I say to the mermedusa, "could you please maybe tweak things so that Vi's parents don't find it odd their daughter is no longer a baby, but now a twelvish-year-old girl, with crazy hair, a too-big, borrowed coat, and a flair for adventure? Otherwise, it'd take loads of explaining and that will spoil the moment."

A further wave of the mermedusa's hand, and now the man and the woman are running madly through the water, as Violet runs at them, and then they meet, all three, in a giant hug that makes the man's glasses fall off, but he doesn't care, as the two adults grab their daughter in a moment I will never forget for as long as I live.

"Is that all, Shipwreck Boy?"

"Where's Sabrina?" I ask, looking around. "We should do something to help her, too. And Pandora! Pandora Festergrimm! What's going to happen to *her*? Maybe –" I dare to say – "maybe Pandora can be a real girl, after all? Please?

Better that, I think, than a lost clockwork one. And it'll make things easier when she's adopted by the town, as I'm sure she will be, just like I was. Can you do that?"

"It is already done," says the mermedusa.

And now I see them both, a black-haired girl in a torn life jacket clinging to a golden-haired girl in an old-fashioned winter coat, helping each other out of the surf and onto the beach.

"I have sent all my other sleepers back to their own times," says the mermedusa then, "to be found by their loved ones."

"What about the *Spark*?" I ask. "Blaze and his uncle and little Ember? Could you put them safely back in the harbour? With the kettle singing and a fine breakfast sizzling in the pan? And could you please fix the cameraluna? And the mermonkey? And maybe do something for Mr Mollusc, too, to make him a bit less unhappy. And..."

"Shipwreck Boy." The mermedusa raises a slender hand to stop me. "All this I can do. But what do *you* want?"

"I think," I say, looking up at the face I know I am seeing now for the very last time, "I think, if you wouldn't mind, that I would just like to be found again. Please. For good, this time. Like when I first washed up here. Only this time, with Sabrina and Pandora, and Vi and her parents, too. I think, now, that all anyone in Eerie-on-Sea has ever wanted is just to come home."

The mermedusa passes her hand over the egg a final time, and I hear a cry of "Halloooo!" from up the beach, and now everyone is there: Mrs Fossil, hurrying down to us with her bucket swinging, three hats tied on her head with a piece of string; Jenny Hanniver in her shawl, with Erwin in her arms, hurrying beside her; Dr Thalassi, sliding down the shingle, his bow tie and smart shoes looking completely out of place on the beach. And above them, at the end of the pier, round Mr Seegol, his stubbly head pink in the cold winter air, waving enthusiastically, causing the seagull beside him – Bagfoot! – to squawk. Lady Kraken is on the pier too, tucked under an embroidered blanket, in her bronze-and-wicker wheelchair. She gives us a stiff little wave, while behind her, holding an umbrella to keep off the snow, Mr Mollusc nods his head to me in a way that is, for him, *almost* friendly.

And there's amazement on the beach as we are discovered with the tide. And wonder at the sight of Violet's parents, lost these twelve years! And welcome for the blonde girl, Pandora, who cannot possibly be recognized, and for black-haired Sabrina with her, who will no doubt cause a sensation when she reveals her identity, and then everyone is looking at me, beckoning and waving, and calling, "Come on, Herbie!" and I turn to the mermedusa to say goodbye and she is already gone.

FAREWELL AND ADIEU

THE BEST WAY TO END a seaside adventure is with fish and chips, and I think we can all agree that the best way to eat fish and chips is as part of a slap-up celebration (with cake, too, if you can get it) in the company of all your family and friends. And so, while it *is* very early in the morning, and yes, there's a lot of gasping in astonishment still to do as everyone gets to grips with what's just happened, I don't see why the end of *this* adventure should be any different, do you?

We must look a strange, mismatched bunch, though, as we head up the seaweedy steps to the pier and Seegol's Diner. Violet's parents are so overwhelmed they can hardly speak, while Jenny seems like she can't say enough, what with her "I can't believe it's you, Peter!" to Vi's dad, and "Violet *always* said you were out there, somewhere, waiting to be found!" to her mum.

"I feel like I've woken from a dream," says Peter Parma

eventually, hugging his daughter for the millionth time, "to find that the impossible has happened."

"If it happened, Peter," says, Bronwyn, Violet's mum, "then it wasn't impossible at all, was it?"

And she hugs her daughter too.

"I really must insist on giving everyone a thorough medical examination," says Dr Thalassi then, completely missing the mood of the moment, and getting a groan from everyone there. "But," he adds, catching my eye, "if there's one thing this last year has taught me, it's that, sometimes, fish and chips come first."

I give him my grin of approval, full beam.

Oh, and I'm pleased to say no one has overreacted to the sudden appearance of a girl called Sabrina Eels. Not yet, anyway. And as for little Pandora Festergrimm – who seems to have no memory of anything at all – everyone just gathers her in with the rest, while Mrs Fossil puts one of her coats over the girl's shoulders.

"What is that?" asks Pandora, pointing into Mrs F's bucket.

"Oh," the beachcomber replies. "It's sea glass, my dear." And she takes out the very same glass pebble that I found the other day and hands it to the girl. "I hunt for it on the beach. It's what I do."

"It's beautiful!" Pandora rolls the sea glass around in her hand. "Can I find some too?"

"We can go out later," Mrs F replies, "if – if you like."

"I would like," says Pandora. "Will you teach me how?"

Mrs Fossil nods. And blinks something from her eye.

"Chips, Herbie?" says Jenny Hanniver as we reach the diner. "First thing in the morning?"

"If Mr Seegol doesn't mind making them," I reply.

"My fryers are always ready, Herbie," says Mr Seegol with a bow. "You know that."

"Chips it is, then, Mr Seegol!" declares Lady Kraken, clapping her twiggy hands with girlish glee. "Come along, Godfrey," she adds, as Mr Mollusc struggles to get her wheelchair through the front door. "Do stop messing about. Breakfast all round. My treat! I haven't been to Seegol's for years."

And then we set to it, moving tables and chairs so we can all sit together. Her Ladyship is parked in a prime position – from where she can direct proceedings – as Mr Seegol heads to his island kitchen to turn everything golden.

It's only then, as I see Mr Mollusc come face-to-face with Sabrina Eels, that I suddenly realize there's one thing I forgot to ask the mermedusa to fix. As the grumpy middle-aged man with a horrible moustache meets the shell-shocked twelve-year-old girl who hasn't aged a bit in the last thirty years, I brace myself for a particularly awkward reunion.

Oh, why didn't I see it? I should have asked the mermedusa to magic Sabrina *forward* in age, to make her the age she'd be now if she'd never disappeared at all. Then she and Godfrey could have found each other again as *equals*, both as wrinkly and old as each other. And with a little extra twist of enchantment, I could even have made them *fall in love* – as perhaps they would have done if their friendship had never been interrupted – and then, maybe, they could get *married*. Maybe *that's* how Mr Mollusc could have found the happiness he so badly needs. I'm such a dunderbrain to have missed—

But then I slap myself – a big fat metaphorical slap, right across the noggin, because *What am I thinking?* Who am I to wish away thirty years of Sabrina's life, just like that? And who am I to make two people who were only ever childhood friends fall into actual grown-up *love?* What gives me the right to interfere in the lives of other people?

It's the kind of thing Sebastian Eels would do.

So now, finally, I understand how dangerous magic can be, and how even in the short time I was making wishes of my own – at the end, with the mermedusa promising me anything – how close I came to disaster. But even as I realize this, I also can't help wondering what *will* happen now between "Godders" and "Sabby"?

"Hello," says the girl, shaking the hotel manager's offered hand. I can't help noticing he is still wearing the watch I returned to him. "I'm Sabrina," she adds, a look of vague confusion on her face. "Sabrina Eels. It's – Godfrey, is it?"

The man pauses and blinks at the girl.

"Funny," he says. "For a moment you seemed strangely familiar. But, no matter – nice to meet you, Sabrina, and yes, my name is Godfrey Mollusc. Although it's *Mr* Mollusc, if you don't mind. I do have a position of some importance in this town, after all. Now, if you would *kindly* help me with these chairs…"

And just like that, the problem fades from existence. This must be the mermedusa's doing too. I did ask for Mr Mollusc to be happy, after all, and maybe forgetting the past is the best way for him to find a brighter future. But it chills me to the core to think that a great childhood friendship has just been magicked away to nothing like that, with a wave of the mermedusa's hand. I find myself staring at Violet, and she notices.

"What?" she says.

"Nothing," I reply. "Just glad that pesky egg is gone, that's all."

"Shh!" She grins, glancing at the others. "Probably best not to mention it right now."

"Personally," I reply, "I'd be happy if I never have to mention it ever again."

It's a little while later, and Vi and I have gone out onto the deck, to toss chips in the air for Bagfoot and his pals. At the very end of the pier, of course, where Mr Seegol can't see us.

Beyond the handrail, the high tide of Eerie Bay is pounding the shore relentlessly, making everything tremble.

"Your parents, Vi!" I blurt out. "You found them! When no

one thought it would be possible."

Violet closes her eyes and raises her fists in a sudden, beaming display of acute joy. Then she turns to me.

"*We* found them, Herbie," she says. "Together. And you always believed it, didn't you?"

"I always believed in *you*," I reply. "I'm not sure that's quite the same thing."

"And it's so *weird*!" says Violet, as we look to the far horizon, where fresh snow clouds are beginning to build. "To think I may never have come to Eerie-on-Sea at all. Right now, I could still be living far, far away, with my Great-Aunt Winniegar, and none of this would have happened."

"You wouldn't have been you if you hadn't come, Vi." I shrug. "Thank you, by the way."

"For what?"

"Just thank you."

"Is this the end of our adventures, Herbie?" Violet looks suddenly sad. "Is it all done? Is the magic of Eerie-on-Sea over now that the mermedusa has gone?"

"The only thing more mysterious than magic," says a feline voice we have terribly missed, "is what tomorrow will bring."

And with that the bookshop cat jumps onto the handrail, brighter than we've seen him for ages, and purrs his rumbliest purr.

"Erwin!" cries Violet, grabbing him into her arms. "You're better!"

"A town that has a talking cat in it," I say, "has surprises still in store, I reckon."

"True." Violet grins, still stroking the cat. Then she adds, "I wish everyone could visit Eerie-on-Sea at least once, Herbie. Don't you? They just have to find it, that's all."

I shrug. "Whenever someone visits a battered old seaside town in the off-season, when most things are shut, and the wind rattles the beach huts and drives rain up your nose, and only the locals are bonkers enough to go down on the beach, where treasures wash up with the tide, and legends abound, then I reckon they've been to Eerie-on-Sea already, Vi. Maybe without ever knowing it."

And I stroke Erwin too.

"Oh," I add, fishing around in my coat pocket, "I almost forgot. This is for you."

And I hand Violet the large, uncut diamond that the mermedusa gave me.

She looks at me in confusion.

"It's Sebastian Eels," I say. "Well, what's left of him." And I explain how the famous writer of Eerie was magically crushed by the colossal weight of his own accumulated crimes. "I think," I add, as my astonished friend holds up the crystal to catch the morning light, "that this time Sebastian Eels is gone for good."

"It's beautiful!" Violet whispers, the diamond sparkling in her hand. "But – but how can something so clear and pure be made out of such villainy?"

Well, I *definitely* don't know the answer to that, do I?

"And what do I do with it?" Violet asks then. "It must be worth a fortune, Herbie. Why give it to me?"

"Maybe I've just had enough of big crystals," I reply, and Violet laughs.

"Perhaps I should pass it to Sabrina," she says. "It is her brother, after all."

"You could. But Sabrina Eels will surely inherit her brother's house and money now. I'm not sure she needs an enormous diamond, too."

"What then? I don't want to keep it, surely you can see that."

"You could sell it," I reply. "To help start your new life with your mum and dad. Or donate it to some good cause, maybe. Or – or just pass it on to someone who really needs it. But whatever you decide, Violet, I think the choice should be yours."

Vi holds up the fabulous stone once more, brilliant in the frosty air.

"Someone who really needs it," she repeats thoughtfully, as if to herself. "In that case," she adds, "I'll give it to ..."

"Yes?"

"... the future!"

And pulling back her arm, Violet Parma throws the diamond from the end of the pier, as hard and as far as she possibly can.

The crystal glints in the cold light of winter, catching a

320

thousand reflections of our strange little town as it tumbles into the waves and the endless tides of the vast and unknowable sea.

THE END

ACKNOWLEDGEMENTS

AS I REACH THE END of Herbie and Violet's adventures, I have many, many people to thank. But when it comes to listing all the booksellers, teaching staff, reviewers and readers who have undoubtedly helped with the success of this series, I feel as queasy as Herbie at the thought of leaving anyone out. So, it's safer if I don't mention names at all. But if you have ever read my books to your class – especially if you did all the voices – thank you! If you have recommended my books to a customer in your bookshop (and maybe turned *Malamander* face out), thank you! If you have taken the time to leave a review online, when it would have been so easy not to, thank you! And thank you, especially, to the children themselves, for responding to Herbie and Violet's stories with such wonderful words and pictures of their own, and for sometimes sharing them with me. This author is never happier than when he sees his books in a classroom or a school library or in front of a young person's nose. So, a huge Eerie-on-Sea THANK YOU to all my readers, of whatever age. There will always be a table for you at Seegol's Diner, and a room at the Grand Nautilus Hotel.

Thank you to my family: to Celia, for her positivity, patience and putting-up-with-things-ness; to my boys, Max and Benjamin, for inspiring Herbie in the first place (thanks, Benjy!); and to my faithful hound, Alpha – constant companion and lead researcher on the beach. Oh, and thank you, too, Lupin, for all the cat scratches. And mice...

Thank you to my parents: Tim, for step-parental constancy and technical support (thanks, big T!), and Penny Graham-Jones – my wonderful mother – for everything else, not least all the Eerie-on-Sea props she has made (especially the much-worn and well-travelled Lost-and-Founder's cap).

Thank you to my agent, Kirsty McLachlan, for loving Herbie and Violet's adventures first, and for being so brilliant about them ever since.

Thank you to all at Walker Books – on both sides of the Atlantic – for taking on Eerie-on-Sea, and for publishing the books so handsomely. Very special thanks to my editors, Emma Lidbury and Susan Van Metre, for holding me to a high standard throughout, and for pushing me at every step – I can't thank you enough. I only hope I wasn't too grumpy! Thanks to Denise Johnstone-Burt for her expert guidance and editorial input; Ben Norland for being such a joy to work with on the design side; Rosi Crawley and Kirsten Cozens, for their stellar promotional work on the series; Josh Alliston and the team, for the superb cinematic trailers for each book; the sales teams in the UK and Australia; Karen Coeman and Lara Armstrong for their tireless work internationally; and also to Clare Baalham, Anna Robinette and Rebecca J Hall.

On the US side, at Walker US and Candlewick Press, huge thanks to Maria Middleton, Lindsay Warren, Larsson McSwain, Maggie Deslaurier, Johanna Schutter, Mary McCagg, Karen Lotz and Tracy Miracle – you made the books so beautiful for American readers. And thanks, especially, for flying me out to meet them!

Thank you to the fabulous illustrator Tom Booth for bringing Eerie-on-Sea to life on his side of the ocean, and to George Ermos for doing the same with the cover art on mine.

Thank you to all the international publishers who have brought Herbie and Violet's adventures to readers in their countries. In particular, special mention to Tolga Yozcu, Merve Okçu and everyone at Genç Timaş for publishing such stunning editions and for flying me to Turkey to meet my wonderful Turkish readers – *Çok teşekkür ederim!*

Special thanks also to the many translators of my books, many of whom I have enjoyed corresponding with. They have dealt with my quirky, seat-of-the-pants English with patience and good grace. If the books are popular in Turkey, Ukraine and the Netherlands (to name just a few), it's thanks to the brilliance of Barış Purut, Marta Sakhno and Aleid van Eekelen (to name just a few!).

Thank you to the readers of the audiobooks – Alfie Allen, Russell Tovey and Matthew Horne. With special thanks to the incomparable Will M. Matt for so brilliantly reading them all in the US editions.

Thank you to all the podcasters who have supported my books (even *Anomalous Phenomena*).

Thank you to authors M. G. Leonard, Catherine Doyle and Jennifer Bell, who helped launch *Malamander* back in 2019 with such kind words.

Thank you to the "wannabe Jenny Hanniver" at the World's Smallest Library, for her tireless championing of Eerie-on-Sea.

Thank you to Hob, for folkloric support and magical biscuits.

Thank you to Julian Sedgwick, for being an inspiration.

And finally, for chapter 18 of this particular book ("What Molluscs Like Best"), apologies to A. A. Milne.

THE
EERIE-on-SEA
GUIDEBOOK

Welcome to *The Eerie-on-Sea Guidebook*.
The following pages cover the principal
sights of our strange little seaside town.
For those of a nervous disposition,
we recommend *The Cheerie-on-Sea
Guidebook*, available in all good souvenir
shops during the summer months.

You, however, have chosen to visit us in
winter, when sea mist creeps up the beach
like vast ghostly tentacles, and saltwater
spray rattles the windows of the Grand
Nautilus Hotel. The letters "C" and "H"
have blown off the pier, dear reader,
and there's no turning back now...

Sights of Eerie-on-Sea ---
The Grand Nautilus Hotel

There's nowhere quite like the Grand Nautilus Hotel of
Eerie-on-Sea. But if you get lost in its dimly lit corridors –
as the floorboards creak, and all the doors look the same
– just make your way down to the Lost-and-Foundery,
and Herbie Lemon will help you find your way.

THE WRECK OF THE *LEVIATHAN*

If you're on Eerie beach at low tide, trapped by
quicksand, confused by sea mist and cut off from safety
by the rising sea, on no account approach the wreck of
the battleship *Leviathan*. Especially at midwinter, when
the wind howls about Maw Rocks, and some swear
they have seen the unctuous malamander creep.

SIGHTS OF EERIE-ON-SEA
THE EERIE BOOK DISPENSARY

At Eerie-on-Sea's famous Book Dispensary,
you don't choose the books – the books
choose you. The ghastly mechanical
mermonkey is waiting, hairy and strange
at its typewriter, to see who will dare
put a penny or three in its hat…

— SIGHTS OF EERIE-ON-SEA —
The Whelk & Walrus Pub

The Whelk & Walrus is the haunt of the fisherfolk of
Eerie-on-Sea, and you should probably never go there.
Some of the deepest and fishiest plots ever hatched in Eerie
were hatched "down the Walrus" over whispered secrets
and pints of Clammy Dodger. You have been warned!

SIGHTS OF EERIE-ON-SEA

THE HOUSE OF
SEBASTIAN EELS

The imposing home of
Sebastian Eels – author of
horror stories and local
celebrity – is not an official
tourist attraction but can be
viewed from a safe distance.
Someone once knocked on the
door to ask for an autograph.
They were never seen again…

—— Sights of Eerie-on-Sea ——
The Theatre at the End of the Pier

The theatre is a cheery sight at the end of Eerie pier.
Up close, however, it looks more like the tumbledown
haunt of bats and seagulls. If there is a show on,
make sure you don't fall through the rotten
floorboards to the sea below.

SIGHTS OF EERIE-ON-SEA
FESTERGRIMM'S EERIE WAXWORKS

The waxwork gallery at Eerie-on-Sea has been
boarded up for decades, due to a terrifying incident
no one likes to talk about. There are rumours it will
reopen again sometime soon, but don't hold your
breath. If you get a chance to peek inside, whatever
you do, don't turn your back on the waxwork figures!

— Sights of Eerie-on-Sea —
Mrs Fossil's Flotsamporium

No trip to Eerie-on-Sea would be complete without
a visit to Mrs Fossil's famous Flotsamporium. As the
town's one and only professional beachcomber, Mrs
Fossil can help you with all your seashell, glass-pebble
and driftwood requirements, however strange.

THOMAS TAYLOR has always lived near the sea – though that's not difficult in the British Isles. He comes from a long line of seafarers but chose a career as an illustrator because it involves less getting wet and better biscuits.

His first professional illustration commission, straight out of art school, was the cover art for *Harry Potter and the Philosopher's Stone* by J. K. Rowling. This led to a lot more drawing until he finally plucked up the courage to try writing for himself. It turns out that turning biscuits into books is even more fun when you get to create the story, too.

Thomas currently lives on the south coast of England, where he has never yet heard an eerie hum, though he has smelled a few. The quicksand is real too, and he did once try to help someone who had sunk in the gunk to his knees, only to get stuck himself. This is the story of his life.